The ruined temple glittered in the moonlight

"This is a holy place, an ancient place," Brett mused. "The spirits are quiet here. You've sensed that, haven't you? You've spent enough time in Southeast Asia to know what I'm talking about. This place should be left to sleep in peace."

Rachel lifted her eyes to the midnight darkness of his face. "You really mean that, don't you?"

Brett touched her hair very lightly. "Do you have plans to come south?"

The question surprised her. "No . . . I mean, I haven't made plans."

He straightened to his full height. "I want you to come to Bangkok."

He'd thrown her off balance again. "I . . . I don't know."

"I want to spend time with you," he said, moving back, setting her free, she thought with relief until he spoke again. "Alon—"

ABOUT THE AUTHOR

"It's hard to say goodbye to characters as compelling and realistic as those in the Saigon Legacy series," says Marisa Carroll. But after almost two years, the McKendrick family story is complete, and the two-sister writing team is moving on to their next book. The sisters are hard at work on *One to One*, part of a Harlequin special project involving the Big Sisters program, due out this summer.

Books by Marisa Carroll

HARLEQUIN SUPERROMANCE
268–REMEMBERED MAGIC
318–GATHERING PLACE
418–RESCUE FROM YESTERDAY
426–REFUGE FROM TODAY

HARLEQUIN AMERICAN ROMANCE
127–NATURAL ATTRACTION
160–JENNA'S CHOICE
190–TOMORROW'S VINTAGE
256–COME HOME TO ME
286–TIES THAT BIND

Return to Tomorrow

MARISA CARROLL

Harlequin Books

TORONTO • NEW YORK • LONDON
AMSTERDAM • PARIS • SYDNEY • HAMBURG
STOCKHOLM • ATHENS • TOKYO • MILAN

For Nancy Roher,
editor and friend...
because you knew Rachel deserved
a love of her own before we did

Published January 1991

ISBN 0-373-70437-2

RETURN TO TOMORROW

PROLOGUE

"I DON'T THINK IT'S a good idea for Rachel to be going back to Thailand." Micah McKendrick swirled the ice in his glass of lemonade, special lemonade, laced with smooth, aged whiskey. He watched his brother from hooded blue-gray eyes.

"You aren't going to get an argument from me." Simon McKendrick settled back against the cushions of the couch, his gaze wandering around the firelit room. It was a shambles; cushions and pillows scattered everywhere, paper plates and cups sitting on tables and cluttering the mantelpiece. It was exactly what a room that had just housed a combination rained-out Fourth of July picnic/high-school graduation celebration was supposed to look like. Leave it to his Annie not to let an unseasonably cold and wet Chicago holiday spoil her fun . . . or the celebration of Doug's triumph. A year ago he wouldn't have believed the boy would achieve that goal. He had Micah and his bride to thank for setting his stepson on the right path.

The twins, and the dog, raced through the room, stirring debris as they went. "Slow down," he yelled automatically.

Domestic chaos, he was learning, was something you got used to, living in a house where there were two teenagers, two almost-teenagers, and one just-about-on-his-own college junior and a geriatric dog underfoot and under the same roof—his roof and Annie's. He could hardly believe they'd been married a year and a half.

"Didn't you try to talk her out of it when she came down here last month?" Micah asked, returning to the subject uppermost in both their minds.

Simon didn't answer for a moment. Instead, he glanced at Micah over the rim of his glass. There was a little more silver in his thick, dark hair but, all in all, he looked better than Simon could remember seeing him in a long time. Domesticity, hard as it was to believe, seemed to suit his brother almost as well as it did himself.

"Of course, I did." Simon looked down at the floor. Half a hotdog bun had rolled off a plate and lay by his foot. He picked it up and put it on another abandoned plate on the coffee table. "I talked a blue streak." And he'd gotten exactly nowhere. Rachel, the eldest of the three siblings, was every bit as stubborn as he and Micah.

"How about Annie?" Micah asked.

Simon looked at his brother, hazel eyes locking with Micah's guarded blue-gray gaze.

"Annie thinks she should go." He didn't often quarrel with his wife. But on this subject they'd had a major difference of opinion. "She thinks it will do her good."

"Carrie thinks so too." Micah shook his head in bewilderment. "How can going back to the place that stole half your life do you any good? Women. Their reasoning is beyond me."

Simon knew living with and loving his taciturn and reclusive brother was a challenge that many women wouldn't have accepted. But Carrie Granger McKendrick, like his Annie, wasn't just any woman. She was one in a million. They'd both been luckier than any man deserved to be to have found them.

"Carrie knew Rachel had been in touch with this Dolph character three weeks before I did," Micah continued.

"I checked out Father Dolph," Simon revealed, taking a healthy swallow of his lemonade. It went down smooth and mellow. He gave Micah a small salute in appreciation of the added whiskey. "He's legit. He's in charge of one of the smaller, Church-affiliated refugee camps along the Thai-Laotian border. I didn't visit that one when I was there last fall, but they're all pretty much alike." His voice was grim. "Adequate food and housing but a pretty bleak way to live."

"Unless you consider the alternative—being marched off to Saigon or Hanoi or Phnom Penh as forced labor—or worse."

"We don't know for certain that would happen."

"The hell we don't. Tiger..." Micah broke off, leaving the sentence unfinished.

"I should have known you were still in contact with the guy."

"Don't change the subject." Micah took a big swallow of his drink.

"Be careful how far you trust the man." Simon obliged his brother by returning to the original topic of conversation, but his thoughts remained troubled by the reference to Tiger Jackson, Micah's expatriate air force buddy. At best, the man was a mercenary, at worst, a criminal in league with one of the most notorious and ruthless drug lords operating out of the Golden Triangle—that remote area of Southeast Asia where Thailand, Laos, and Burma meet. "At least she's agreed not to leave until after the rainy season. Maybe Mom can talk her into staying in the States until Christmas."

Micah snorted. "How safe will she be at this camp? Most of them aren't more than a grenade throw away from the border."

"This one's practically rear echelon. Twenty klicks or so from Laos." Simon tried to smile but gave up the attempt. He leaned forward, his hands between his knees, twirling his glass as he talked. "We're working on getting these people someplace permanent to stay." He'd been traveling openly for the government in the past six months, inspecting refugee facilities around the world, reporting back to his superiors, testifying before various congressional committees and doing his damnedest to get innocent victims of half a dozen warring nations a place to live, to belong, to call home. It was a far cry from the undercover work he'd been involved in for many years, less exciting and somewhat less dangerous, but more rewarding.

"You don't think we can change her mind, do you?"

Simon shook his head. Just then Leah, Annie's adopted half-Vietnamese daughter, glided into the room with Carrie's baby son. She deposited the teething infant in Micah's lap.

"Carrie wants you to please give him his bottle. With any luck he'll fall asleep." Leah cocked her head, straight, night-black hair falling over her shoulder, and examined the bright-eyed baby. "I don't think that's going to happen," she observed with all the knowledge and experience four years of baby-sitting had given her. "He looks like he's ready to party."

Micah took the little boy who would soon be legally his son, accepted the bottle Leah held out to him and settled the infant in the crook of his arm. "Tell his mother I'll do my best." Micah grinned at the pretty teenager, then looked down at the baby with great contentment.

"Don't forget to burp him when he's done. They always spit up on you if you don't, and that is so gross."

"Don't I know it." Micah held the bottle to his son's mouth, and the baby sucked contentedly. "Don't look at me like that," he growled, catching Simon's amused eye on him.

"I think it's sweet," Leah said dreamily. "Men holding babies are so sexy." She drifted out of the room on a wave of perfume.

"Beware," Simon said dryly. "They grow up and turn into teenagers."

"Now you're the expert, huh?"

"Ain't life funny." Simon grinned.

"Yeah." Micah was suddenly serious once again. The old haunted look came back into his eyes. "I still don't think Rachel should be going back. Nam screwed us all up pretty good but Rachel most of all. And regardless of what your buddies at State tell you, we don't know for sure that this Father Dolph is on the up and up."

"His full name is Dolph Hauer," Simon said very quietly. "He's Father Pieter's nephew. I don't think there's anything in the world we could do to stop our sister from going to Thailand if she's doing it to honor the old man's memory."

"No, you're probably right there." Micah looked as strong and unbending as the mighty oaks of his north country home, but his big, scarred hands were gentle as he resettled his son in his arms. "But there's one man over there I can trust to keep an eye on her."

CHAPTER ONE

"WHAT MADE YOU WANT TO return to Southeast Asia, Mrs. Phillips?"

That was a very good question. Rachel McKendrick Phillips lifted her eyes from her soup and studied the face of the man across the table. Was there something more to this young State Department official than her first impression had led her to believe? Or was he merely curious about her past, as so many others were, and had chosen this particular way of opening up the subject?

"I've come to Thailand," she said with just a hint of the smile that more than one reporter had described as elusive and hauntingly sad, "as a favor to an old, dear friend."

"Ah, yes, that would be the Dutch priest, Father Pieter Hauer, I believe his name was, who was with you in that hill village in Laos."

Rachel stiffened, betraying her surprise at the extent of his knowledge. A small, stinging dart of anger pricked her. The slight annoyance she'd felt all morning at being in Harrison Bartley's company escalated.

"Yes." She hoped her curt answer would stop his flow of questions.

"The old man is dead now, isn't he?" The junior-grade diplomat was nothing if not tenacious.

Rachel stared at his round, unformed face for a long moment before answering. "Yes, he's dead. He's been dead for seven years."

"But there's a nephew, isn't there, also a priest?" He paused, his fork suspended over a bite of his duck salad. "Working with hill tribe refugees somewhere up in the Golden Triangle, isn't he?"

"North of Chiang Rai." Rachel returned her attention to her meal.

"Downright primitive up that way." Harrison Bartley shook his head as if in sympathy.

Not a hair shifted out of place. *It wouldn't dare,* Rachel decided, looking up once more from her excellent soup, flavored with an herb known as lemongrass, for which the restaurant was named, and fiery with tiny red and green chilies.

"I think I can adjust," she said quietly.

Harrison Bartley had the grace to look sheepish. "Yes, Mrs. Phillips, I expect you can."

"Look, you might as well call me Rachel. We're going to be spending a lot of time together over the next few days." Taking advantage of the fifteen years' difference in their ages to impose her will, Rachel changed the subject.

"Thank you, Rachel." He smiled and Rachel revised her estimate of his charm upward slightly. He did have a very nice smile. His teeth were white against his skin. His hair was a dark mahogany brown, fashionably cut and styled. His white linen suit had certainly been made to order, probably in Hong Kong. He would be a valuable addition to any hostess's insurance list of single men available to fill a vacant seat at a dinner party on very short notice.

Rachel realized as she watched Bartley toy with his food that he wasn't ready to drop the subject of her past. She waited. How would he phrase it? The question he was dying to ask? *What was it like, Rachel, being a prisoner of the Vietnamese all those years?* Or would he be more subtle, in keeping with his chosen calling? *It must be difficult, Rachel, returning to a part of the world where you've known such hardship and...degradation....*

"It must be diff—"

Rachel cut him short. "I spent five years in a Vietnamese work camp somewhere in Laos after the fall of Saigon," she said, her voice even and emotionless. It was still the only way she could get the words past the automatic tightening in her throat, the familiar clutch of fear that squeezed her heart and made it hard to breathe. "Father Pieter and I escaped and made our way through the mountains until we were found and taken in by the Hlông. It was almost ten years later that my brothers learned I was alive and came to Laos to find me. Surely all that must be in my official records, Mr. Bartley."

"Yes, it is. Sorry for the third degree. Part of my job is asking questions, you know. Look, why don't you call me Bart? I feel uncomfortable calling you Rachel and you're still addressing me as Mr. Bartley."

"All right," she agreed reluctantly.

"When Alf Singleton, my boss, was called back to Washington to brief the President on Khen Sa, he asked me to look after you." The charming smile was in place again. "He said that you were a very special lady and to get you to Chiang Rai safely or my...

butt . . . would be in a sling. Alf's got a very colorful way of expressing himself but he meant what he said. I made it a point to learn what I could.''

"I do appreciate your help." Rachel relaxed a little. Her brother, Simon, couldn't have known that his trusted friend, Assistant Ambassador Alfred Singleton, would be unable to escort her north. She'd have to make do with D. Harrison Bartley as a guide.

Bart leaned toward her. "And I promise, no more questions."

"Mai pen rai," Rachel said, and picked up her glass of bottled water, giving a small salute.

"Never mind," Bart translated loosely from the Thai. "I should have known you'd throw their favorite saying at me sooner or later this afternoon." He picked up his own glass. "Cheers."

BILLY TODD PUSHED ASIDE the curtain of wooden beads that covered the archway leading into the bar of the Lemongrass with an impatient gesture. The damn things were a real nuisance, but the tourists expected them and so there they hung. The room itself was dark and cool and nearly empty, but beyond the screened windows the terrace tables were filled with the late lunch crowd, mostly Japanese, some Americans with a few Australian sailors and retired British schoolteachers thrown in. A waiter entered the service door from the terrace and Billy beckoned him over. They carried on a low conversation in Thai for a few minutes. Then Billy made his way to the private area at the back of the restaurant.

"What are you doing back here so soon?" The speaker, a tall man, outlined by the bright January

sunlight shining through the arched window, didn't
bother to turn around at Billy's approach. He continued to stare out at the thatch-roofed dining area with
its view of high rises and gilded temple roofs beyond
the low, flower-bordered wall. Billy walked up beside
him and observed his friend from behind the tinted
lenses of his sunglasses. They were both tall men,
broad-shouldered and narrow-hipped, in their early-to
mid-forties. Americans. One white, one black, so in
tune with each other's thoughts and habits that their
speech sometimes resembled a kind of verbal short-
hand.

"Take it easy, Tiger. I've got everything under control." A former combat infantryman, Billy Todd had
spent his last tour of duty with a secret search-and-
destroy team in Laos. Tiger Jackson had been his
commanding officer, only a captain then, but tough
and disciplined, an ex-air force Raven who had logged
too many hours in the air war. Billy pushed his hands
into the back pockets of his worn and faded jeans and
rocked back on the heels of his crocodile-skin cow-
boy boots.

"Who's watching the hotel?" Brett "Tiger" Jackson turned his head to meet his oldest friend and
business partner's gaze.

"Lonnie's there."

"Lonnie? He's so strung out he can't even watch
over himself." Thick, blond eyebrows met in a frown
above eyes the same dark blue as a midnight sky.

Billy shook his head but his expression was grave.
"He's tight. Someone scored for him last night. He'll
be okay until tomorrow."

"Dammit, Billy, I thought you were going to keep your eye on him. I don't want him buying hits off the street. The stuff out there these days is too unstable. There're too many amateurs and get-rich-quick thugs getting into the game. You swore you could keep him in line until I could arrange another buy."

"I did my best, man. He's a big boy now."

"Yeah." Brett's tone was ironic. "He's a big boy, all right." He patted the pocket of his shirt, looking for the cigarettes he'd given up two years ago. Lonnie Smalley had been his company corpsman his last tour in Nam. A fresh-faced Ohio farm boy, with a smile a mile wide and everything in the world to go home for. Only he never had gone home. He'd become a casualty of war, as much as the young boys he'd tried to save and couldn't. The burden of that failure had driven him to try to forget in the euphoria of first morphine, then heroin. He'd cut himself off from family and friends, never leaving Southeast Asia, living on the fringes, on the shady side of the law to support his habit. One day, a few years after the war ended, he'd appeared on Brett's doorstep, a burned-out shell of a man, and he'd found a home. What had happened to Lonnie in Vietnam may not have been ex-lieutenant colonel Brett Jackson's fault, but from that day on Brett considered his former corpsman his personal responsibility.

"I tried. Sorry it happened, Tiger."

"It wasn't your fault, man. He's been slipping away from us more and more often lately. He's just too damn good at disappearing these days."

The two men stood in silence for a long moment, each lost in his own thoughts. The war was long ago, if not so far away, but some days it seemed much closer than others.

"I found out when the lady's leaving for Father Dolph's camp," Billy said quietly, the soft drawl of his native Georgia still evident in his voice, even though he hadn't set foot in the States in more years than he cared to remember.

"When?" Brett's voice was clipped. They spoke in English but in an undertone. Even here in the Lemongrass it wasn't safe to assume the walls didn't have ears. Caution was second nature to them now. Caution learned in the jungles of Laos and Vietnam in their youths and honed to a sixth sense by the life they'd led for nearly twenty years.

"Day after tomorrow."

"Be ready."

"I always am, Colonel." Billy gave his friend a sidelong glance. Brett paid no attention to the use of his old military title.

"Who is this woman I'm keepin' track of, anyway?" Billy asked.

Brett grinned and relaxed a little. "She's Micah McKendrick's sister, the one we should have helped get back to the States two years ago. I don't want anything to go wrong this time."

"It won't." Billy chuckled. "Everything's going great."

Brett wasn't so sure of that. The last thing he needed in his life now was another complication, another responsibility. Sometimes he just wanted to dump it all, turn his back and head for the beach. He was forty-four years old. He deserved a little peace and quiet. This deal was definitely beginning to get to him.

Until an hour ago he'd have said nothing or no one could have diverted him from the business at hand. Now he wasn't so certain. That was before the woman at table sixteen had shown up at the Lemongrass.

Sad, beautiful, no longer young, her face held all the character of her years, and something more. Something that reached out to him at a level below conscious thought, a part of him that was primitive and male, the hunter, the provider. Bangkok was a city of beautiful and desirable women. Brett Jackson had known many of them, he'd even loved one or two, but few of them had intrigued him so from the moment of first encounter. It wasn't the way he operated; spontaneity was grounds for early and permanent retirement in his line of work. One-night stands were damned near as dangerous. Anyway, this lady had class. He'd bet a bundle one-night stands weren't her style, any more than they were his.

"Did you get a good look at her?" Brett asked, his own dark blue gaze still fixed on the woman at table sixteen. He was talking about Rachel Phillips but his attention was focused on the flesh and blood woman before him. Definitely not just another bored socialite on the make. Her clothes were too ordinary, although the red silk blouse and white full skirt fit her slender frame admirably. Her silver-threaded black hair was styled too simply and her makeup—she wasn't wearing any—was a dead giveaway in his book.

"I got a real good look at Mrs. Phillips." Just a hint of wry amusement in Billy's tone alerted Brett that something was up. He turned to face his old comrade-at-arms.

"What's up, man? You're too damn laid-back about this whole business." It wasn't like Billy to have gone off and left Lonnie alone to watch for Rachel Phillips—especially someplace as busy as the Royal Orchid Sheraton, where it would be very easy, indeed, for a lone woman to slip past him.

"I already sent Ponchoo back to pick up Lonnie," Billy said, reading his mind. "We'll have him tucked away in his own hooch by two."

"And what about Mrs. Phillips?" Brett didn't try to soften the low growl of impatience in his words.

"She's right where I can keep an eye on her."

"What the hell does that mean?"

Billy nodded toward the terrace. "That's her. The black-haired woman in the red blouse. That's Rachel Phillips. She's a damn fine-lookin' white woman."

"Damn fine." Brett gave a snort of mirthless laughter as he shoved his hand through his thick blond hair, amused that his quarry had found her own way into his lair. "Who's the gigolo she's with?"

"Some turkey from the U.S. embassy. One D. Harrison Bartley, by name. One of Alf Singleton's flunkies. He's harmless."

"That's her escort? He's going to be responsible for her safety up in the hills?" It also explained why she'd turned up at the restaurant. It was a favorite of the embassy crowd.

"That's the drill." Billy looked a little uncertain, himself, as he sized up Harrison Bartley with shrewd brown eyes and found him wanting. "There shouldn't be any problems. The border's quiet, no shelling for over a week, and they won't get that far north, anyway. Khen Sa's been stayin' close to home. Her Thai's pretty good, by the way, at least according to what Buon just told me. She shouldn't have too much trouble with the up-country dialect.''

Brett cut short his recitation. "I don't care how you do it," he said gruffly. "Just make sure you don't let her out of your sight." He'd given Micah McKendrick his word that he'd see his sister arrived at her destination safely and was handed over to Father Dolph without any untoward incident. It was the least he could do for his old friend. Especially since he hadn't been able to help him two years before. He didn't intend for anything to go wrong this time around.

THEY LEFT THE CROWDED business district of Chiang Mai with its busy shops and noisy street vendors behind, early on the second day of their journey. Bartley's Land Rover climbed out of the valley at the foot of Mount Doi Sutep, heading north into the hills. Below them the gilded spires of the city's two hundred temples reflected the fire of the morning sun.

Tucked away in a cardboard cylinder in the back seat with Rachel's other things was one of the brightly colored, beautifully painted paper parasols for which Chiang Mai was famous. It was a small token of welcome to northern Thailand, Bart had said with his charming smile. Rachel had accepted it readily in the spirit of goodwill in which it was given. But that had been five hours ago and her store of goodwill was very nearly used up.

After stopping for lunch at a roadside park, they left the highway somewhere south of Chiang Rai, the last town of any size they were to pass through on their way to the border camp. The paved road ended an hour later, soon after they'd started climbing steeply into the mountainous jungle, heading toward an ancient *wat*, a Buddhist temple, that Bart insisted probably dated from the thirteenth century and was well worth the extra time it would take to find it. The sun had long since passed its zenith, the short January day was drawing to a close, and they were lost. At least in Rachel's opinion. Harrison Bartley, so far, hadn't admitted he no longer had any idea where they were.

Above them the jungle canopy met across the narrow road, a green, mysterious archway, shutting out the sun, confusing the senses. Closer to the ground, pressing almost to the sides of the Land Rover, the understory of the forest made a living barrier, a claustrophobic tunnel-like path, the stuff of nightmares. Rachel's nightmares. For years she'd wandered such a dream path, looking for a way home, trying to find her brothers and her parents, searching for the baby she'd lost....

"How much farther is it to the temple?" she asked in what she hoped was a perfectly ordinary voice. She looked down at her hands clenched into fists on her thighs and made herself relax, stretching her fingers. She'd been planning this trip for nearly a year. A few more hours, one way or another, would make no difference. Taking a deep, steadying breath, she tried not to look at the living wall of bamboo and vines, orchids and nettles that made up much of the nearby growth.

"We should be there within the next few minutes." Bart wasn't very good at hiding his emotions. His voice was edgy with uncertainty. Rachel picked up on it immediately.

"Do you have any idea at all where we are?" She half turned on the seat to face him, realizing all at once just how young and very inexperienced he probably was. He didn't look directly at her but kept his eyes on the trail—it could hardly be termed a road any longer.

"Not since we made that last turn after crossing the river," he admitted. "I haven't recognized anything from the map for the last half hour."

"You have a map?"

"Of sorts." He shrugged. "A friend from the embassy gave it to me, but there is no telling how accurate it is."

Rachel felt her hands curl back into fists. Her nails bit into her flesh and the small pain made her angry. Anger, she'd learned long ago, was much easier to deal with than fear. Fear made you weak and prey to defeat. Anger made you strong, gave you the strength to keep on fighting. It was much better to be angry than afraid. And she was afraid, afraid of being lost once again in the uncharted jungles of Southeast Asia, the alien, hostile land where she'd spent nearly a third of her life against her will.

"Turn around," she said, and heard the harsh rasp of panic in her voice.

Bart took his eyes off the road long enough to shoot her a questioning look. "Are you okay?"

"I'm fine," she said, but more quietly, with more control. "Just turn around."

"I'm sure we're going in the right direction." To Rachel's way of thinking, he didn't sound certain at all.

"I still think we should turn back. If we don't waste any time we can make Chiang Rai by dark."

"Chiang Rai?" Bart sounded annoyed. "We don't want to backtrack all the way to Chiang Rai. We should be twelve, fifteen kilometers east of there by now. According to the map, this road eventually leads back to the main route."

"But you can't be sure of that. I don't want to spend the night in this truck. Please turn around."

"I can't," Bart pointed out. "The road's too narrow. Look, the next clearing we come to we'll check our direction with the sun."

"You mean you don't have a compass?" Rachel didn't try to keep the disbelief out of her voice.

"Sorry, they're hardly standard issue at the embassy."

"I have one in my duffel." It was beginning to look like a good thing she'd also packed some bottled water and dried fruit. They'd probably need it before they found their way out of the jungle. "Stop and I'll get it out."

"No need." Bart pointed ahead of them a few dozen yards. "We're coming to a clearing." The "clearing" was merely an elongated opening in the seemingly endless stretch of jungle. A narrow stream ran through it. The trail crossed it on a bridge of half-sunken, flattopped teak logs. The sun was disappearing behind the topmost branches of the trees. When Rachel saw it, the fear inside her grew stronger than ever. The sun was almost directly in front of them, not behind them and to their left, as it should have been if they were still traveling in a northeasterly direction.

"We're going the wrong way." Panic beat inside her with dark, strong wings. How often had she heard herself say that to Father Pieter during the long weeks they'd struggled through just such undergrowth in their flight from their Vietnamese captors?

Harrison Bartley stuck his head out of the window of the Land Rover and squinted up at the fast-dropping winter sun. "Damn, I think you're right."

"Turn around," Rachel said. "Now."

To his credit, Bart didn't argue. He drove a short way onto the primitive bridge and began to back around onto the low bank of flat stones and red mud bordering the stream. The roadway was so narrow he simply couldn't make the turn any other way. Rachel sat stiffly on the leather seat. She could smell the living jungle in the moist, hot breeze stirring the leaves along the stream edge. It was an earthy, damp smell, composed as much of the dead and dying as of the new and emerging. It was at once familiar and strange, exciting and terrifying.

They had almost completed the turn when the back wheel of the Land Rover slipped off a stone and sank into the mud. Bart gunned the motor. It stalled and they sank deeper. With an oath Bart ground the starter. The engine caught, held, then sputtered into silence.

"Flooded," he said, making the word a curse.

All the sounds of the jungle the motor had drowned out rushed in to fill the silence. Birds chattered and squawked. Somewhere not too far away something small and frightened squealed in terror. Tigers still roamed these mountain jungles, as did panthers and wild boars. Rachel had not forgotten that fact.

Death—and ruthless men who could make life worse than death—stalked the pathways beyond the trail.

She was going to be stranded here for the night with a man she hardly knew. Alone with him in the cramped confines of the Land Rover. That scared her almost as badly as the lengthening shadows creeping closer and closer, even as she willed them away. She had been alone with no man except her father and brothers since Father Pieter had passed away.

Bart got out of the truck and walked around to the back, the thick mud of the stream bank sucking at his shoes. Rachel heard him muttering under his breath. He slammed his fist against the back window. Any last hope she had of getting out of their predicament in a hurry died away.

"Is there any way we can drive it out?" she asked, defying her own personal demons in leaving the co-cooning safety of the Rover's cab. "Is there a come-along in the toolbox, an ordinary rope, anything like that?"

"Nothing heavy enough to get us free. She's in up to the axle," Bart reported in a clipped tone. He scrambled up the bank, trying to shake the red clinging mud from his shoes, scowling down at the streaks of dirt on the leg of his fashionable khaki slacks. "There's no way in the world we're going to get it out of here without help. I'd be grateful for any suggestions you have on the best way to accomplish that."

Rachel wanted to cry. Instead, she racked her brain for some means of getting them rescued, even if it meant walking out of the jungle on her own. One fact she did face with characteristic forthrightness: she was going to be spending the night in the jungle with Harrison Bartley whether she wanted to or not.

"Listen," Bart said, tilting his head. Rachel heard it, too. The sound of an engine, moving closer from the direction in which they'd just come. "Someone's coming. We couldn't ask for better timing. With any luck we'll get a tow out of this swamp."

"With any luck," Rachel said grimly, then added, "Do you have a gun?"

"TIGER'S GOING TO HAVE US strung up by the thumbs if we don't catch up with Rachel Phillips and her Ivy League embassy flunky pretty quick."

"I don't know how the hell they got off the main road without us seeing them," Lonnie said. He'd been dozing off and on for the past hour and didn't even know it.

"We must be slippin', buddy."

"Yeah."

"They can't be too far ahead now. I just wonder how they found the road leading to the *wat* in the first place." He didn't know if it was by luck or design, but he was damned sure going to find out.

"Maybe they have a map."

Billy downshifted the jeep and shot Lonnie a questioning glance. "What makes you say that?"

"No reason."

"You might have somethin' there, buddy. If they do have a map that shows the temple's location, it's gotta disappear. Damn fast."

"Got you, Sarge."

From then on they drove in silence. Lonnie Smalley sat grim-faced and white-lipped. Billy had told him to stay in Chiang Mai but Lonnie didn't listen to him. He didn't listen to anybody anymore, except Tiger. The voices in his head, the dream people he encountered in drug-induced sleep appealed to him far more than anything in the real world.

Billy hoped that once he got word back to Tiger that Micah McKendrick's sister was safe and sound they could get on with the job they were supposed to be doing. If they could carry off the deal with Khen Sa, the Opium King, they could write their own ticket, shape the world to their own mold. If, that is, he caught up with Rachel Phillips and her companion soon enough to keep them from falling into the Thai warlord's hands and ruining everything they'd worked so hard to bring about.

RACHEL TRIED TO FIGURE her chances of making it across the stream and through the tangle of dusty scrub along the side of the road to the dubious safety of a hiding place in the jungle beyond. Her heart beat high and fast in her throat. Her palms were sweaty and she wiped them along the sides of her dark green cotton skirt. She should have worn slacks, and heavier shoes. She glanced ruefully down at her thin canvas loafers. She wasn't any better equipped for being out in the bush than Bart was. It would be suicide to run. Instead, Rachel squared her shoulders and lifted her chin to face the tall black man advancing from the battered American army jeep that blocked the narrow road. His face was impassive, his eyes unreadable behind the mirrored sunglasses he wore. He looked very strong and very dangerous.

The red-haired man beside him, shorter, thin to the point of emaciation, was almost as frightening, except for his eyes. Green as new leaves on a maple tree, they held so much sadness in their depths that Rachel was almost shaken out of her fear. Until she looked again and saw his pupils were narrowed to pinpoints. That was enough. She didn't need to see the needle tracks on his arms or his throat to know, with another sickening lurch of fear, that the man was a heroin addict. They stopped a few feet short of the mired Land Rover.

"We're stuck," Harrison Bartley explained unnecessarily. "Could you give us a tow?" He spoke in English, not Thai.

"We can probably manage it." The accent was American, southern, the words oddly soft-spoken, coming from such a large, aggressive-looking man. "In the morning."

Harrison Bartley thrust out his hand with a grin to introduce himself. The black man's last words caused him to falter and drop his arm. "In the morning?"

"Be dark in fifteen minutes at this altitude. You're stuck real good. Take what you need and come with me."

"Now see here," Bart said with all the authority he could muster, "we're expected at Border Camp Six by seven o'clock."

"You ain't gonna make it."

"My name is Harrison Bartley. I'm an aide to assistant U.S. ambassador Alfred Singleton. You sound like an American. I insist you help this lady and myself to get back on the main road immediately."

"Buddy, you can insist all you want," the black man said, not even trying to hide his contempt. "That Land Rover ain't goin' nowhere. Now you and the lady can hitch a ride with my friend and me, or you can sit tight and hope the only thing you have to worry about prowlin' around here tonight is a tiger or two."

"Where are we going?" Rachel was surprised and pleased to hear her voice was steady. She was shaking so hard she was afraid the trembling would communicate itself to her words.

"There's a Buddhist temple about three klicks that way," the red-haired man spoke for the first time. "The monks don't much cotton to women but they'll let you spend the night." He smiled and it transformed his ruined face. Rachel managed a tiny smile in return.

"I don't think you understand," Bart attempted once more to talk the two men into trying to move the mired Land Rover.

"You don't understand, buddy," the black man said menacingly. "Get whatever you need and let's get going." He was wearing an olive-green T-shirt that strained across heavily muscled shoulders and fatigues of the same color. The hilt of a knife protruded above the top of his boot. He spread his legs and folded his arms across his chest. "Move," he barked, and Bart did just that.

"Is there anything you need for the night that I can help you with, ma'am?" the younger man asked politely. Rachel shook her head.

"I have everything I need right here." She indicated a roomy woven tote, a *yaam,* that did double duty as purse and overnight bag. "It is important that

I get word to Father Dolph Hauer at Border Camp Six. He's expecting me."

The black man removed his mirrored sunglasses for the first time. His eyes were dark brown, hard as agates, hard as the line of his jaw. "Father Dolph's been at Camp Six for two years. He's learned by now not to expect anyone or anything until they show up on his doorstep. This way." He gestured toward the jeep with his thumb.

Rachel took a step forward, then another. Her legs were shaking but not so badly as she'd feared they might. She stopped directly in front of the tall black man. She held out her hand. "My name is Rachel Phillips." If he was a bandit, as she still half suspected he might be, and he intended her harm further down the road, then she was determined he know her name. She refused to become a nameless victim, not ever again.

For a long moment he did nothing. Then he took her hand in his. He gave it a quick, powerful shake. "Billy Todd. I'm a teak buyer. I'm meeting . . . a business associate . . . at the *wat* I told you about."

A teak buyer. Teak smuggler, more likely. Rachel didn't voice the thought aloud but she relaxed a little inside. Something in Billy Todd's handshake had reassured her, however ridiculous it seemed. He might be operating outside the law, he most likely was, but she no longer suspected him of being a highway robber and murderer.

The younger man also held out his hand. It trembled noticeably. "Lonnie Smalley," he said. "I'm from Ohio."

"I was born and raised in Pennsylvania, Mr. Smalley," Rachel said, attempting a smile.

"That practically makes us neighbors, this far from home. Call me Lonnie." He shivered, although the air was still hot and close. His skin was dry and rough, his color an unhealthy gray beneath the red of sunburn.

"Let's get goin'." It was an order, not a request, from Billy Todd. Lonnie Smalley jumped to do his bidding. Rachel also moved forward without a protest. Harrison Bartley made one more attempt to assert his nonexistent authority and found his arm caught in a vise-like grip. "Get in the jeep or start walkin'."

This time he did as he was told.

Rachel climbed into the jeep reluctantly, for when Billy Todd turned away from her, she saw the bulge of a gun tucked into his waistband beneath the thin cotton of his shirt. Perhaps she was foolish to trust him at all. As if sensing her thoughts, he turned and looked her straight in the eye. He didn't flinch or look away, as Rachel studied his hard-cut features for a long moment. Satisfied, she dropped her gaze.

She had no choice but to accompany him. Perhaps it was because she was back in the hills, where the *phi* spirits ruled everything, that she could do nothing to save herself. Or, perhaps, her instincts were right and she was going into the unknown to meet her future.

CHAPTER TWO

THE JUNGLE WAS QUIET. The night air at this altitude, just over three thousand feet, cooled quickly after sundown in the winter. The birds were silent. Only a faint breeze rustled the palms growing at the base of the ruined temple wall.

Brett Jackson propped one foot on the parapet and stared out at the five stone Buddha statues sitting in a row in the moonlight. Their hands were folded across their round bellies, their lips curved in smiles of great serenity.

"This place looks like it belongs in another world at night," Billy said, coming up behind him, soft-footed in the darkness.

"It does." Brett flipped open his lighter and touched the flame to his pipe. He'd given up smoking cigarettes but he still allowed himself one pipe a day.

"Yeah, I guess you're right. This might as well be another world compared to Columbus, Georgia."

"Or a ranch outside Butte." Brett had been born and raised in the Big Sky country of Montana, a land of wide open spaces, high skies and bone-chilling cold that now seemed alien to him. He hadn't been home in five years, not since his father died. The pipe and silver lighter had belonged to the old man. It was one of his last ties with the past.

"A long ways and a lot of years." They were quiet for a while, listening to the jungle settle into silence.

"How's the Acharya handling our visitors?" The old holy man and his half dozen young followers had recently moved into the *wat* and claimed it as their own. Brett had used the ruined temple as his base camp for several years, but now its days of usefulness were numbered. Not only because of the aged monk and his followers, but because Harrison Bartley had a map of its location, however crudely drawn, and that meant its existence was becoming known in Bangkok and Chiang Mai.

"About as well as can be expected." Billy grinned. "Our Ivy League diplomat complained long and loud about his supper. Seems cold rice and thin soup don't cut it with the embassy set. Mrs. Phillips, she handled it real good. She thanked the old man for giving shelter to a lowly *farang* woman and passed out some dried fruit to the monks for tomorrow's meal. They appreciated it, even if the Acharya didn't."

"Good for her." Brett had heard Rachel's voice echoing through the empty high-ceilinged rooms of the temple, but he hadn't shown himself. "Are they all settled for the night?"

"Everyone's tucked in, safe and sound. I'm going to make one last patrol and turn in myself."

"I'll be right behind you." His sleeping quarters were in the main section of the temple, the only area where the roof hadn't fallen in. The monks weren't pleased to house him there but the powerful radio transmitter and other electronic devices he needed to keep in touch with Bangkok couldn't be left to the mercy of the sudden drenching thunderstorms that came up unexpectedly, even during the dry season.

Billy melted into the darkness. A few minutes later Brett saw him, a darker shadow against the mammoth stone shapes of the Buddha statues, and then he was gone. Brett lingered on the parapet. Something held him there, perhaps the spirits of the temple or the memory of Rachel's voice. Or maybe it was only his own restlessness that kept him awake.

He couldn't stop thinking about the deal with Khen Sa.

No one, so far as he knew, had ever persuaded the wily warlord to allow them to take consignment of his entire supply of refined opium. Brett intended to do just that. The shipment would be worth almost one hundred million dollars when it reached the streets in the States and Europe. The man Brett Jackson was working for wanted that opium badly. Badly enough to offer Brett what he wanted most in the world—anonymity and enough money to buy the peace and quiet he longed for—in exchange for making certain the narcotics never made it to their destination.

If he lived to deliver the goods.

At the moment it was a toss-up whether he'd succeed in his delicate negotiations or not. He certainly didn't need the presence of D. Harrison Bartley on the scene.

Or the very feminine distraction of Rachel Phillips.

RACHEL COULDN'T SLEEP. She lay staring into the darkness, watching the moving patterns of moonlight through the intricate thatch roof over her head. It needed mending before the rainy season, she decided, or whoever slept in this cell next would certainly wake up wet. She sat up and pulled her knees to her chin, wrapping her arms around her legs to ward off the slight chill of the damp night air. Something had awakened her. She wasn't sure what, but sleep seemed, suddenly, very far away.

Rachel got up, smoothed the wrinkles from her skirt and stepped into her shoes, after shaking them out to make sure no unwanted visitor had crept inside. She would go out onto the crumbling parapet of the ancient temple and look at the Buddha figures in the moonlight. Perhaps their serenity and peace would communicate itself to her restless soul and she would be able to come back to her small room and sleep.

The temple had at one time, in ages past, been very large, covering several acres. Now, only the main section stood with roof intact. She paused at the foot of a wide staircase guarded by two winged lions. Her night vision wasn't good but tonight the moon rode high and bright, lighting her way. A *chedi*, or temple spire, rose above the treetops. The temple must once have been very grand. The outer skin of the walls had been stripped away by time and weather, leaving thick slabs of some unknown brick-red stone exposed to further erosion. The inhabited buildings were thatched in such a manner that they resembled nothing so much as large, untidy bird nests. The rest of the temple complex was now no more than huge slabs of rock hurled to the ground, as though scattered in some giant's fit of temper.

Rachel climbed the steps to the wide stone parapet. Level with the treetops, she walked along, aided by fitful moonlight as she picked her way among the broken stones. Above her, the sky was inky black, the stars achingly bright points of light. The night and the temple, with the jungle beyond the walls, seemed a place of enchantment from another time.

Then she smelled the pipe smoke and knew she was no longer alone with the spirits. A shadow moved, detaching itself from the larger shadow thrown by a griffin statue guarding a corner of the wall. Rachel took a step backward, prepared to run. The figure coming toward her was not a boy monk in flowing saffron robes. He was a man; tall, broad-shouldered, Caucasian.

He was also a complete stranger. She'd never seen him before in her life.

"I wouldn't run if I were you," he said, as she made up her mind to do just that. "You might fall and break a leg. I don't think the Acharya will feel enough *namjai*—enough milk of human kindness—to house a *farang* female for six weeks while you heal."

"No, I suppose you're right." In the Buddhist way of things monks topped the social order with ordinary men next, then Buddhist nuns. Ordinary women were at the bottom of the heap. Rachel held her ground despite the heavy, frightened beating of her heart. The man moved two steps closer. He knocked the bowl of his pipe against the stone and ground the smoldering tobacco beneath the toe of his boot. "Who are you?" she demanded.

"I might ask you the same question."

Rachel didn't answer. She watched him, instead. He was tall, as she'd already noticed, with a full head of dark blond hair that caught and trapped the moonlight in its depths. There was a shading of silver at the temples. His eyes were dark and glittered in the moonlight. He wasn't a young man. There were lines from nose to chin that could only have been etched into his skin with the passage of time. His jaw was hard as granite, shadowed, more by a day's growth of beard than by the night. She guessed his age to be very close to her own. He looked strong and dangerous.

"Are you a friend of the men who brought us here?"

"Yes, I am." He took another step forward and blotted out the moonlight. He was very close. Rachel could smell the smoke from his pipe that still clung to his skin and the faint, musky odor of his sweat. He was as tall and broad through the shoulders as her brothers, but his presence gave her no brotherly sense of security. Rachel took a hasty step back, tripped on an upthrust stone and almost fell. The man reached out, grabbed her arm, steadied her, then let her go in the blink of an eye when she flinched from his touch.

"Thank you," she said automatically.

"You're welcome, Mrs. Phillips," he responded with equal courtesy and, Rachel thought, just a hint of amusement.

"How do you know my name? Who are you?" she asked a second time.

"I thought by now you might have guessed who I am." She could not be certain in the play of light and shadow that partially obscured his face, but she thought he was smiling more broadly now.

"Why should I recognize you?"

"I assumed Micah would have described me to you. My name is Jackson."

"You're Tiger Jackson?" Micah hadn't told her for a long time how badly things had gone wrong in Laos two years earlier. Her attack of malaria had caused them to miss their rendezvous with this man who could have led them safely out of the country. Instead, they'd been picked up by a Vietnamese army patrol and held for ransom by a corrupt army colonel.

"I'm afraid so." He lifted one leg to rest his booted foot on the parapet. He leaned one arm on his knee, his pipe held easily in his large, strong hands. Rachel knew instinctively he could hold a gun just as easily—and use it, too. The knowledge left her feeling cold and frightened again.

"Did Micah ask you to keep an eye on me? Is that what you're doing here in the middle of the jungle?"

"Would you believe me if I told you that was my only reason for being here?" He tilted his head and watched her, his face a mask of light and shadow that hid all expression. His tone warned her she'd get no other explanation.

"No. I'd say you're here on some business of your own. My coming here is a coincidence. But you don't have to feel it's necessary to watch over me. I'm perfectly capable of taking care of myself." Rachel regretted the petulant tone of her words the moment they left her mouth. It wasn't this man's fault that her brothers still treated her as if she were some fragile and helpless woman-child.

"This part of Thailand is no place for a woman traveling alone." Tiger Jackson's voice was as hard as the stone beneath her feet.

"I'm not alone," she pointed out.

"Damn near as good as alone."

Irrationally, Rachel felt herself compelled to defend Harrison Bartley. "How was Bart to know the map was inaccurate?"

"He should have had enough sense to stay on the main road. Even someone with as low a security clearance level as Bartley's must know that Khen Sa is active in the region."

"Khen Sa. The warlord?" *And Opium King, if what Simon told her was correct.* Somehow she didn't want to bring up the subject of opium smuggling with Tiger Jackson. That was probably his real reason for being here, far from any civilization, far from any authority. It was hardly the prudent thing to do; still, somehow it didn't seem out of place at all to be carrying on a conversation about warlords, with a mercenary, in a setting such as this one. "Simon briefed me on Khen Sa before I left the States," she said carefully.

"Simon is your brother who works for the Census Bureau?"

"Yes." Rachel looked at him sharply in the moonlight. He was looking out at the jungle, his rough-angled profile hidden in shadow, his voice neutral, giving nothing of his thoughts, of himself, away.

"He's very well-informed. The Census Bureau usually doesn't have a lot of interest in Southeast Asian politics."

"Khen Sa is very well-known in Washington. He controls nearly all of the opium trade in the Golden Triangle. Am I correct?"

Tiger Jackson swiveled his head to face her directly. His voice was cold. "So I've been told."

"I think that's sufficient cause to make his movements of interest even to an employee of the Census Bureau, if his only sister is traveling in the region."

"It would be reason enough for my sister to stay at home."

"What are you doing here, Mr. Jackson?" she asked, not bothering to point out that she wasn't his sister. She didn't seem able to bring herself to call him Tiger, although standing in the moonlight, it was easy enough to imagine him as some large, predatory jungle cat.

"I'm here on business, as you already guessed." He answered easily, but his expression was still guarded. It probably always would be.

"What kind of business?" Rachel wondered if she were losing her mind or if the moonlight were playing tricks on her reason. She shouldn't be playing cat-and-mouse word games with him. "Are you also a buyer of teak?"

"Yes, I am." He still stood with one leg raised on the stone ledge. He looked relaxed; his hands and arms below the rolled-back cuffs of his khaki shirt were still. The image of calm was deceptive. Below the surface Rachel sensed a coiled tenseness, danger and aggression, power, held in tight restraint. "Billy Todd is my partner. He's been in Bangkok the last few days. He saw you in a restaurant."

"The Lemongrass?"

He hesitated, then nodded. "A friend pointed you out to Billy."

"Then it is only a coincidence that Billy Todd followed us down that road?"

"A very unfortunate one." He straightened to his full height and Rachel stepped back warily, unable to control the reaction as she assimilated the faint tinge of menace lacing his words.

"I don't understand," she managed, although her voice was husky with renewed apprehension.

"It's unfortunate that you were on the *wat* road to begin with. If *farangs* the likes of Harrison Bartley have heard about this place, it won't be long before it's overrun with tourists. I don't want to see that happen."

Rachel lifted her eyes, drawn to the midnight darkness of his, even though she didn't want to be. His face was still a mask, guarding his thoughts and feelings, but he did nothing to avoid her searching gaze. "You really mean that, don't you?"

"The Acharya is a good man. This is a holy place, an ancient place. The spirits are quiet here. You've sensed that, haven't you? You've spent enough time in Southeast Asia to know what I'm talking about. This place should be left to sleep in peace."

"I understand." Her words were no more than a whisper on the night wind. "I don't think you have to worry about Bart ever finding his way back here."

"No." He brushed his hand through his hair. "Not Harrison Bartley, but I think you could, Rachel McKendrick Phillips." Again, the ghost of a smile tugged at the edge of his mouth.

"Possibly." Rachel smiled, too. She didn't want to go but she knew she must. "It's getting late. I should go back to my room."

He nodded. "You've got a long day ahead of you. Good night." He inclined his head in a gesture of dismissal.

Rachel didn't go, surprising herself as much as him. Instead, she held out her hand. "I want to thank you for what you tried to do for me. Micah told me that you were waiting to guide us out two years ago. I was too ill to make the rendezvous."

He took her hand, equally formal. "I regret that very much."

"So do I." She owed this stranger a great deal, Rachel realized. It was through his contacts, his risks, that word of her living with the Hlông had finally come to Micah's ears. "Good night...." She hesitated as she slipped her hand free of the hard, warm strength of his grip. She didn't want to call him Mr. Jackson again. She was equally reluctant to address him as Tiger. *She wanted to know his given name.* The urgency of the thought surprised her as much as the little rush of pleasure along her nerve endings when he answered her unspoken request.

"My name is Brett," he said simply, "and pleasant dreams, Rachel Phillips."

"SHE'S SOME LADY, THAT ONE." Billy Todd materialized out of the shadows at the top of the griffin staircase twenty minutes after Rachel left the parapet. Brett didn't answer his friend right away. He didn't need to. Billy already knew Rachel Phillips interested him more than was good for him. Standing in the light of the gibbous moon, watching the breeze play with her hair, feeling the ghosts of the ages whispering around her, he'd found her more alluring than ever. Small, indomitable, courageous, she was just the kind of woman a man dreams of finding all his life long.

"I came back to tell you I've made arrangements to leave the jeep at the Akha village north of Chiang Rai. The ponies will be ready by day after tomorrow. We should have word if Khen Sa will see us by the morning after that."

"I'm getting very anxious to speak with our warlord friend." Brett's voice was hard.

"It's not going to be our silver-tongued arguments that'll sway the bastard. It's goin' to be the gold you've got stashed away down there." Billy cocked his head in the general direction of Brett's sleeping cell. "Do you think it's enough to persuade the general to our way of thinking?"

"It's going to have to be." Brett shoved his hands into the pockets of his pants. "I doubt if I can persuade our backers to come up with any more."

Billy chuckled but the sound held no mirth. "A million dollars in gold. This is going to be one hell of a coup if we bring it off. We'll be real, live, goddamn heroes." He slapped his palm against the stone. It rang like a pistol shot, startling a few red and green parrots from their roost in the trees alongside the temple wall.

Brett watched the birds wheel off into the deeper cover at the edge of the clearing. His voice was grim. "If we live long enough to be around for the end."

THE SUN WAS UP but still couldn't be seen above the tops of the hills surrounding the temple. Rachel wished she had a sweater to block out the early morning chill. A parrot flew across the path ahead of them. Harrison Bartley jumped in alarm and stumbled over a tree root. He swore long and loudly, not bothering to apologize to Rachel or anyone else for his bad temper. The three young monks the Acharya had designated to help them free the stuck Land Rover paid no attention to his words, walking sedately ahead along the steep trail. Neither did Rachel, for she had too many other things on her mind.

Or to be accurate, she had only one other thing on her mind. Brett Jackson. She wondered if Harrison Bartley had any idea they'd spent the night in the notorious gunrunner's stronghold? Perhaps he did but there was nothing he could do about it until he returned to Bangkok. He was an ambitious man. Locating Tiger Jackson's base of operations would be a real feather in his cap. Unfortunately for Bartley, he didn't have the skills to lead the authorities back to this place. It never occurred to the pompous young man that she might be able to do so. She said nothing to enlighten him. However much she deplored Brett Jackson's occupation, she was disinclined to see him caged and cowed.

There was a great deal more to the man than met the eye. She had no doubt he was as dangerous as Simon's contacts had led him to believe. But he also must have retained at least some of the qualities that had made him Micah's friend. Her mind told her he was ruthless and beyond the pale. Her heart told her he was also loyal, responsible and caring. She had realized that when he talked with such reverence of the past and the holiness of the temple lost once more in the encircling jungle.

He fascinated her. She was honest enough to admit that. The feeling was strong enough to overcome her usual reluctance even to be alone with a man. The first faint stirrings of interest had escalated during the remainder of the long, sleepless night. For a time she'd stared upward at the darkness, trying to put a name to the restlessness she felt inside. When she had, it surprised her even more, banishing any thought of sleep.

The fluttering ache deep within her body and her brain wasn't only curiosity about a man who was intelligent, compelling and completely sure of himself. It was something primitive and feminine and long missing from her life.

It was desire.

CHAPTER THREE

AN OLD-FASHIONED, ELECTRIC fan on Dr. Reynard's desk stirred the warm, muggy air in slow, eddying swirls. Rachel plucked at the thin, white cotton of her shirt, pulling it away from her body, telling herself she should be grateful to be working in an area of the camp that had electricity at all, instead of wishing for air conditioning.

Dr. Reynard went on talking. He was young, dedicated and idealistic. The seventeen pregnant Hlông women, sitting on the floor, listened politely as Rachel translated his lecture on hygiene. None of them spoke English. They had never heard of prenatal multiple vitamin tablets or the benefits of a regimen of light aerobic exercises in strengthening the muscles used in childbirth. They came to the lectures because she asked them to.

Dr. Reynard paused for her to catch up. He walked past the screen set up at the front of the room. His shadow cut through a still photograph of a smiling young mother holding her newborn son. There was a gasp of fear from one or two of the mothers-to-be.

"Doctor, please don't do that," Rachel pleaded, breaking into English.

"I'm sorry," he said contritely. "I forgot. Don't walk in front of the projector. Cutting off the light to the woman's image might do her actual physical harm. It's so hard to remember all the taboos."

"We can only do our best. For these women, every living thing is ruled by its *phi* spirit. And most inanimate objects have a spirit, as well." She raised her hands and soothed the women as best she could in a language that had no words for slide projector, multiple vitamins or aerobics. She reminded them in the sharp-edged, singsong intonation of their own tongue that Dr. Reynard was only a man, a foreign man at that, an unbeliever. The spirits, she assured them, would take that into consideration and would not be offended by his ignorance.

The women, dressed in baggy black skirts and blouses, their hair piled high on their heads but lacking the intricate threading of silver and gold they would have used to adorn themselves in their mountain villages, tittered and smiled behind their hands. Dr. Reynard looked offended, then smiled sheepishly.

"You've been here only a few days longer than I, yet you know so much." He made a temple of his fingers, bowed to the static figure on the screen, bowed slightly to the women sitting on the floor and walked over to his desk.

Rachel knew she should explain her past...some of it, at least...to the young man, but now wasn't the best time.

She wondered if any time would ever be the best time.

She finished translating the doctor's lecture in a few quick sentences. Most of the women sitting silent on the floor would choose to deliver their babies in their huts, with the attendance of a wise woman from their old village, if at all possible. They would bring the babies, later, to be examined. They would allow them to be immunized because they knew how powerful the foreign unbelievers' magic was. They might even send for her, and Dr. Reynard if there were complications for mother or child, but they wouldn't come to the infirmary to labor and give birth for any other reason. Jean-Luc Reynard had been in Camp Six for only a little over three weeks. He didn't understand the Hlông or the other hill people in the camp. But he would learn.

Now that the lecture was over, the women came forward shyly to bid farewell. They knew she had lived among them, in a village in Laos. She had been one of them, yet not one of them. She knew the customs and duties of a Hlông woman, yet she moved among the foreign males, her own kind, with assurance. They trusted her, yet they were in awe of her. In return, Rachel envied them their sense of belonging, their certainty of their place in their own world. She also knew how fragile that sense of place was, how completely disrupted it would be when they left the border camp for new homes in the west.

"Mail call." Father Dolph's tall, gangly frame filled the doorway, blocking out the sunlight. "Letters from the States," he called, brandishing a batch of various size envelopes above his head. The Hlông women bowed slightly as they filed by; none of them, even with their elaborate and upswept hairdos, came above his shoulder. "Valentines, if I don't miss my guess."

Sometimes, if Rachel closed her eyes, she could hear Father Pieter's voice transposed over his nephew's. He had been a few years older than Father Dolph was now, perhaps fifty-five, when she first met him, but the two men looked very much alike. And their personalities were similar, jolly, good-natured, fearless, devoted to their church and their flocks. Only Father Pieter's flock had been an orphanage in Saigon and Father Dolph's consisted of ten thousand refugees crowded into a tiny valley in the hills of northern Thailand.

"Valentines? And only a week late." Rachel held out her hands for the inch-thick stack of envelopes.

"Here are two for you, Reynard." Father Dolph handed over two white envelopes. Jean-Luc tried not to appear too eager to read his, a letter from his fiancée in Paris, Rachel surmised from a quick glimpse of the feminine handwriting on the envelope.

"Enjoy your letters," Father Dolph said, preparing to leave the building as quickly as he'd entered. He was always on the move, always between one task and another. "Rachel, could I see you in my office in about an hour?"

She looked up from a comic Valentine note from the twins and smiled. "Of course. I believe Dr. Reynard won't be needing me anymore this afternoon." She glanced in his direction to make sure of his reply. He nodded absently, too engrossed in his letter to pay much attention to anything else.

"Yes. Yes. Thank you for your help with the lecture."

Father Dolph shrugged and crossed his hands over his heart. "Love," he sighed, and laughed. Rachel laughed, too, but she didn't think it was funny. Love. Once, long ago, so long ago it seemed like a dream, she'd been in love with a young naval aviator. She'd met Kyle Phillips in Saigon while on leave from the field hospital where she'd been stationed twenty-five miles northeast of the city. He had swept her off her feet. They were married when Rachel finished her second tour of duty. The marriage lasted only a month before Kyle died in the wreckage of his jet fighter when it crash-landed on a carrier in heavy seas. Eight months later she'd returned to Vietnam, as a civilian nurse. When Saigon fell . . . the life she'd planned for herself after the war altered beyond imagining.

"One hour, Rachel, don't forget." Father Dolph's tone was emphatic.

"I'll be there." Rachel surfaced through layers of old memories to answer the priest's request. "I promise." She tilted her head, narrowed her eyes against the sunlight behind his back. "Unless you want me to come with you now."

Father Dolph grinned. "I don't want to take you away from your letters."

Rachel laughed and even Dr. Reynard looked up at the sound, lilting, sweet, with a hint of lingering sadness that would never go away. "Yes, you do. Come on, what's up?"

"Come with me, I'll show you. Jean-Luc, I'll be back." He waved one long hand in the doctor's general direction. The doctor nodded absently and went back to his letter.

"Young love." Father Dolph shook his head.

"What do you want to see me about, Father?" Rachel asked, changing the subject. She knew she'd never find love again. She'd known that for a long time, yet at night she sometimes dreamed, now, of a tall, blond man silhouetted against a jungle moon.

"I have someone I want you to meet." Father dodged a flock of chickens being chased across the path by three young boys, one of them hardly more than a baby and naked as the day he was born.

"I hope it's someone who types better than I," Rachel answered, making herself think of the stack of paperwork on her desk and not of the man in her dreams.

"I'm afraid not." Father Dolph looked momentarily taken aback. "I'm sorry. I forgot you asked for someone to help you who could type."

Rachel bowed courteously to an old woman working among the vegetable plants in front of her hut. The camp was crowded, more a small city in size and population than a temporary home for war-weary refugees. The woven mat-walled and thatch-roofed huts had an air of permanence about them. That was because many of the residents had been there for years, caught between the twin pincers of Western governments with too-small immigration quotas and the unstable and dangerous political situation in their homeland.

"It doesn't matter." Rachel brushed aside his apology. "Does she speak Thai?" Try as she might, Rachel couldn't keep a note of entreaty out of her voice. She was so busy, with so many women and children to care for that the thought of another well-meaning but unprepared volunteer to deal with was more than she could accept at the moment.

"She speaks Thai. And better yet, she speaks Hlông." Father Dolph looked down from his eight-inch advantage in height and smiled crookedly, almost like a boy. "The problem..."

"I knew there would be one," Rachel grinned, overcoming her momentary loss of optimism. Father Dolph was notorious for trying to find comfortable niches for square pegs. The miracle was, with the ten thousand souls under his care, he managed to make so many of the square pegs fit.

"She doesn't speak English."

"Oh, dear." Rachel knew her Thai was adequate but not fluent by any stretch of the imagination. The Hlông dialect, like those of other hill tribes, was simply not structured for dealing with technology... or bureaucracy.

"Ahnle is a lovely child."

"She is Hlông?" Rachel asked.

Father Dolph nodded, pausing in his long strides to sign a requisition form shoved under his nose by one of the staff members who had hailed him as they passed the camp offices. "She's a niece to the village headman. Her brother is a trader. He taught her Thai."

So the girl came from one of the less isolated villages. That was good. She would be less apt to jump at every shadow, be mistrustful of every instrument and procedure she didn't understand.

"Here we are," Father Dolph announced unnecessarily as they turned a corner and mounted the three rickety wooden steps to the sheet-metal building that housed the administrative offices of the camp. "I told Ahnle to wait. I thought I might be able to talk you into coming with me."

A straggling hibiscus tree stood sentinel in the dusty, fenced-off courtyard. Aside from a few stunted willows bordering the stream that ran along the compound's northern perimeter, the hibiscus was the only tree in camp. The rest had long ago been cut down to provide wood for cook fires and to warm the chilly winter nights.

A young girl, dressed in a white blouse and black sarong-style skirt, was seated in a straight-backed chair in front of Father Dolph's desk. Her hands were folded in her lap, her head bowed in a polite attempt not to stare openly at a stranger. She stood and made the traditional *wai*, a gesture of greeting, fingers steepled in front of her as she bent her head. Father Dolph and Rachel returned the greeting.

"Ahnle," Father Dolph said in his Dutch-accented Thai. "This is Rachel. You will help her with her work."

Ahnle nodded and bowed more deeply still.

"May you always dwell within the spirit gate," Rachel said in Hlông. It was a formal greeting. Living within the protection of the wooden archway that guarded each Hlông village was of great importance to the tribal people.

"May your grandchildren walk beneath it as your ancestors did," Ahnle replied, equally formal.

"Welcome." Rachel decided she might as well start Ahnle's English lessons, then and there. She smiled and the girl smiled also.

"I've already had Ahnle put her things in the spare room in your hut. I hope that's okay with you." Father Dolph spoke in English, also. Ahnle waited politely, her dark, almond-shaped eyes downcast.

"Yes, of course. I feel guilty with a cottage all to myself when everyone else is so crowded." Rachel smiled and accepted the slim folder of papers Father Dolph handed her from the top of a pile on his desk.

"Here are Ahnle's papers. She's been in the camp about a year so she knows her way around."

"Do you have family in the camp, Ahnle?" Rachel asked in Thai so that Father Dolph could understand.

"No." The answer was soft-spoken, polite, but wary. Ahnle looked at Father Dolph from the corner of her eye, then back down at the wooden floor.

"She is estranged from her relatives. Her brother has gone back into the mountains," he said.

"Into Laos?" Rachel felt a small ripple of fear crawl across her skin. Less than two years ago she had made that journey with her brother, Micah, in reverse, a nightmare trek of pain and illness that had ended in her recapture by the Vietnamese.

"He wanted to return to their village before the rainy season begins."

"Or more likely, to bring out the opium harvest."

"We don't know that." Father Dolph's voice was stern.

The Hlông village where Rachel had spent so many years had had its poppy fields, also, but the soil was too poor, the village too isolated to make the opium salable on the open market. It was the only medication the villagers had. It had made Father Pieter's last pain-filled weeks more comfortable. She had thanked God and the *phi* spirits for its availability. Yet, in the wrong hands, it became a weapon of great evil and destruction. A fleeting image of Lonnie Smalley's drug-ravaged face crossed her mind's eye.

"It's the most likely explanation." Rachel switched back to Thai. "Ahnle, why did your brother leave you behind?" It was unusual for a Hlông maiden to be left without benefit of a male family member to protect her. Ahnle looked to be about sixteen or seventeen, of marriageable age, which made it odder, still, that she should be unchaperoned.

Ahnle did not answer. She bowed her head but not before Rachel saw the gleam of tears in her dark eyes. She felt a jolt of sudden sympathy and the beginnings of understanding. She looked at Father Dolph with a question in her eyes.

He nodded, spoke softly in English. "Ahnle has a child."

"Is the baby ill, deformed?" The Hlông loved children but their life was harsh and demanding. Frail, sickly babies did not long survive the rigors of that life, as she knew only too well, and to her everlasting sorrow.

Father Dolph shook his head. "The father is unacceptable. His family has been at odds with Ahnle's for generations. They would never have met if they hadn't come to the camp. He has since left for Germany. He did not claim the child."

Rachel's heart went out to the young girl, still only a child herself. Ahnle remained standing quietly but she'd raised her head to stare at a point just past Rachel's left shoulder. Her hair was a glorious shade of ebony, so black it seemed to take light into itself and hold it in its depths. Her eyes were almost as dark as her hair. She was small and slim, just an inch or so shorter than Rachel, about five feet, tall for a Hlông woman.

"So she is unprotected and her child has no ancestors to revere." A dire fate for one of her people. Rachel squared her shoulders. Ahnle wouldn't suffer any more fear and disappointment if she could help her. "I imagine we can work her schedule around the baby." She spoke in Thai again so that Ahnle could understand. She smiled and held out her hand, half expecting the girl to do the same. Ahnle didn't smile. She bit her lip and shook her head, blinking back tears once again.

"No baby," she said holding out her empty hands before curling her fingers into her palms.

"The child was a boy," Father Dolph said quietly.

"A boy child." Rachel let the words sift from between stiff lips. Boy babies were very precious in Hlông society. Any irregularity in his birth would be overlooked in Ahnle's village if he grew tall and strong. She longed to take Ahnle into her arms and comfort her, but resisted. One did not touch a stranger in Ahnle's world.

"Ahnle's brother has no male children. He has taken the baby back to the village, and will raise him as his own."

"He will have ancestors," Ahnle said miserably. "I cannot care for him here. It is best." She started to cry.

"Don't cry, Ahnle." Rachel touched the rough cotton sleeve of her blouse. "The pain will pass."

"No. I will always grieve."

Rachel shook her head, denying Ahnle's words but understanding only too well the agony behind them. "Someday you will not grieve."

"How do you know?"

"I lost a son," Rachel said, leading the girl out of the cool, dark room. Then she spoke a deliberate, comforting lie. "You will not forget but someday you will remember without pain."

CHAPTER FOUR

"ISTAR BOONY?" AHNLE SAID, repeating Rachel's words as best she could.

Rachel laughed at the fractured pronunciation. "No, Ahnle. It's Ea-ster Bun-ny," she repeated, enunciating each syllable with exaggerated care.

"Eei-star Bun-y." Ahnle made a second attempt.

"Close enough." Rachel went back to her task of stirring hard-boiled eggs in the cups of food coloring dyes that she'd received in a package of Easter goodies from her mother. She'd been hoarding her ration of hen's eggs, one per day, for a week. She'd also traded some of the gaily wrapped Easter candies in the package to a woman from Ahnle's village who kept chickens in bamboo cages outside her hut for five more. Now she had an even dozen, two for each color of dye, the smallest amount you could decently color—at least according to Rachel's mother.

"Do bun-nies lay eggs in America?" Ahnle asked in her careful English. Her tone said she wouldn't be a bit surprised if they did.

"No." Rachel racked her brain for a simple explanation for the tradition of coloring chicken eggs and having them delivered by way of basket-carrying rabbits. "It's a custom of the ancestors to please the small ones." It was the best she could do.

Ahnle nodded, accepting the words, pondering their meaning. She learned so quickly. Rachel couldn't believe how much progress she had made in the past six weeks.

"It is good to make children happy." The familiar look of loss and longing came into her eyes as she thought of her son. Rachel bit her lip. Nothing she could say would help ease the pain. Only time would heal that wound.

"There." Rachel lifted the last egg out of the dye. She kept her tone brisk, deliberately light. "Now we'll put them in the baskets." She suited action to words, lining up four small woven baskets she'd traded more candies for along the street of makeshift huts where much of the camp's trading went on. She lined them with the improbably colored styrene Easter grass her mother had used as packing.

"This is very strange," Ahnle observed, poking some of the grass, a particularly lurid shade of lavender, with the tip of her finger. "Is it from a bun-ny nest?"

"If Easter Bunnies made nests, it would probably be with this," Rachel admitted. She had not attempted to explain the religious significance of the holiday to Ahnle. That was Father Dolph's department.

"America is strange."

"In many ways." Rachel smiled. "But it is also beautiful and full of wonderful things."

"I will see it someday. Maybe." Ahnle watched as Rachel piled three colored eggs in each basket, then sprinkled them with brightly colored, foil-wrapped chocolates in animal shapes.

"Perhaps." What if she took Ahnle back to the States with her? She had promised Father Dolph eighteen months of her life. But after that . . .

She didn't like to think too far into the future. For so many years she'd had to survive day by day, sometimes hour by hour. She couldn't look that far ahead without being afraid of what might come. She liked Ahnle. They worked well together. They were growing closer each day, despite the difference in their ages. She was old enough to be the girl's mother, it was true. In Ahnle's world she was old enough to be her grandmother. But here, in the hand-to-mouth existence of a camp almost within shelling distance of a hostile border, none of those distinctions mattered. They were two women bound together by the loss of a child. It was a bond they would always share.

"It is time for Mass," Ahnle said, hearing the recording of a church bell playing from the loudspeaker above the chapel. "Will you go? I will take the baskets."

"Yes, I'll go." Rachel picked up two of the small baskets. "This one is for Father Dolph. This one for Brother Gabriel—" the Belgian monk who was Father Dolph's assistant "—and this one for Dr. Reynard."

"That is three," Ahnle said counting. "Who belongs to the four?"

"You do," Rachel said, ignoring the fractured grammar in the last sentence. "Happy Easter, Ahnle."

"Thank you, Rachel." Ahnle smiled and bowed ceremoniously, then reached out and touched Rachel's hand, lightly, fleetingly. Among Ahnle's people touching was reserved for family members only. "Happy Eea-star."

"I'd better hurry or I'll be late for mass." Rachel turned away to hide the rush of feeling that surged into her heart.

"I will walk with you." Ahnle picked up the basket destined for Dr. Reynard. "I will give this to the doctor so you will not anger Father Dolph's God by being late."

AN HOUR LATER, RACHEL walked along the dusty main street of the camp, her heart and soul comforted by the timeless peace of the Mass. The heat of the day was beginning to fade. Storm clouds massed on the horizon, reminding her that the rainy season was almost on them. She shuddered to think of what the unpaved streets and pathways of the camp would be like after three or four months of steady, heavy rain.

Ahead of her, near the main gates, a UN Border Relief Organization truck was off-loading sacks of rice to be distributed among the camp residents the next day. They also supplied sugar and salt, canned meat and fish. The food was nourishing but dull. Drinking water, too, had to be trucked in. Water for washing and laundry was supplied from cisterns located in various places around the camp, or from the stream running along the north border of the compound.

Everything the camp used, everything they needed to exist here, had to be trucked in. It was an ongoing process that never stopped, regardless of the weather or occasional random shelling from Vietnamese-backed Laotian insurgents who occasionally infiltrated the next valley. If she walked this way again tomorrow, the trucks would still be there, or others just like them. Perhaps tomorrow the medical supply truck with the antibiotics and surgical supplies that Dr. Reynard had ordered two weeks earlier would arrive.

As she watched, another vehicle drove through the camp gates. It was a jeep, a U.S. army jeep, old, battered and disturbingly familiar. Rachel stopped in her tracks, watched as it drew to a halt before the camp guards' security hut. Two men got out, both tall and lean, hard-muscled, one black, one white.

"Rachel." Ahnle's touch on her sleeve was feather light, her voice soft, but Rachel jumped as if she'd been poked with a stick.

"Ahnle! You scared me out of a year's growth."

The girl looked puzzled and disturbed. "I did not mean to," she said contritely.

Rachel laughed. "It's just a saying. It means you startled me because my attention was on something else."

"What?" Ahnle asked with all the curiosity of a child.

"Nothing. Let's go back to the cottage. It is time to eat."

"I am hungry, too."

Rachel stood a moment longer at the edge of the wide, dusty main street that began at the camp gates and ended at the front steps of the administration building where Father Dolph had his office. The two men were still inside the guards' office. What would Brett Jackson and Billy Todd be doing here? The sun was going down, hiding its light behind the sharp edges of the western ridge of the valley. The shadows were long, making bright, confusing patterns as they played hide and seek with the setting sun. The two men's actions were no concern of hers anyway. She turned away.

"Mrs. Phillips."

Rachel stopped, turned slowly to face the man whose voice she couldn't forget. "Brett." His name slipped out before she could stop herself from saying it.

"Hello, Rachel."

"Hello."

He didn't return her smile. He stood before her, tall, stern, as unyielding as the mountains at his back.

"Afternoon, ma'am." Billy Todd touched his fingertip to his temple in a casual half salute.

"Hello, Billy." Rachel let her smile grow brighter, more assured. "I never expected to see you here."

"We stop to check up on Father Dolph every now an' again, when we're in the neighborhood."

Rachel looked away, into the hills, remembering. "I suppose we aren't very far... from the place we first met. As the crow flies."

"No, ma'am," Billy answered with a laugh.

"You didn't tell anyone here about the temple, did you?" Brett asked, his deep voice grating on every word.

"Of course not." Rachel's eyes flashed. Billy grinned harder at her spirited response. "I saw no reason to discuss our meeting with anyone here."

"Who's this?" Billy asked. Rachel tore her eyes away from Brett's hard blue gaze. Billy was looking at Ahnle.

"This is my helper, Ahnle." Rachel made the introduction in English. Her smile returned, soft and loving. "She is also my new friend."

Ahnle looked up, smiled shyly, wonderingly, at Billy but remained silent. Rachel realized it was probably the first time the girl had ever seen a black man, but she didn't seem afraid. She had come a long way from the timid, childish creature Rachel had met in Father Dolph's office that day. She was proud of Ahnle's newfound poise and air of composure.

"Father Dolph is hearing confession," she told the men when the silence threatened to grow too long. "He'll probably be busy for quite a while. It's Holy Week," she added, in case they didn't know. A fair number of the camp's residents were Khmer, relocated from the huge camps along the Thai-Kampuchean border. Many of them were devout Catholics.

"I imagine Brother Gabriel can find some use for this, if the padre's tied up." Billy pulled a wad of bills from the back pocket of his faded jeans. Rachel glimpsed American dollars, Thai *baht*, Indian rupees. It was a considerable sum in any currency.

Where had all that money come from? she found herself wondering. The sale of teak logs? It didn't seem likely. Simon's warnings about Tiger Jackson's line of work came back to her in a cold rush of disappointment and renewed suspicion. Her lips thinned into a straight line. She looked up to find Brett Jackson watching her with a scowl on his bronzed face. She looked away, confused and upset.

"I know where Brother Gabriel is," Ahnle said softly.

Rachel glanced at the girl in surprise. She had never spoken out that way in front of a man, any man, before. "I show you." She gestured toward the administration building.

"Go ahead, man. But hurry. We have to get back on the road." Brett's voice was rough-edged, impatient. Rachel looked down at her hands. Already she regretted her suspicious thoughts. It was no business of hers where the money came from. It was destined for a good cause; that was all that should matter.

"Won't you stay and eat with us?" She panicked for a moment, wondering how she'd stretch the canned chicken and rice that was to have been their dinner. Then she remembered the vegetables she'd bought from one of the refugees' small garden plots that morning. She could stir-fry those to add to the rice and chicken.

"No," Brett said abruptly.

"Some other time." Billy glanced curiously at his friend. "Thanks for the invite, though."

"Get that money over to Brother Gabriel," Brett said.

"Check. Lead the way, little missy." Billy grinned down at Ahnle, his teeth very white in his dark face. He motioned her forward, matching his stride to hers. She looked small and fragile alongside him, barely reaching his shoulder. Rachel felt a curious mixture of pride and worry as she watched Ahnle walk away so trustingly.

"The girl means a lot to you, doesn't she?"

Rachel swung her head back quickly to find Brett watching her with a predator's intensity.

"We...have a lot in common, despite the fact that I'm old enough to be her mother."

"You don't look old enough to be her mother. Her older sister, maybe." The corner of his mouth quirked upward in the hint of a smile.

"Don't be ridiculous." Rachel couldn't help smiling a little herself. "This gray in my hair isn't some kind of new fashion craze. It's the real thing."

"It's not gray, more like silver and it suits you."

Rachel could only shake her head. If she said anything else it would be dangerously close to flirting. She was alone with Tiger Jackson. There was no moon riding high above, no ruined temple in the jungle to lend a fantasy air to the conversation. It was a perfectly ordinary day, a perfectly ordinary, if unexpected, meeting. She was responsible for whatever she said to this man, whatever she did. She knew that. What she couldn't understand, wouldn't understand, was why suddenly her pulse was racing at breakneck speed and her breathing was so shallow and uneven she felt dizzy and light-headed.

"How are you settling in?" he asked, pushing his hands into the back pockets of his khaki fatigues. The movement stretched the soft cotton of his shirt tight across his chest. A pulse beat slow and steady in the hollow of his throat. He looked away, his dark blue gaze following Billy Todd down the street. Suddenly Rachel found it much easier to take a deep breath.

"I'm settled." Rachel sidestepped a bicycle carrying two boys and a basket of live, squawking chickens that careened past. "The work's hard, harder than anything I've done for a while, but I like it."

He turned to face her. "The facilities are pretty primitive."

"We do the best we can with what we've got."

"There are ten thousand people in this camp, Rachel. The best you can do is still only subsistence."

"I try. We all try. As hard as we can."

He looked past her, out across the camp, as though seeing it through her eyes. She felt free to watch him for a moment. Deep lines fanned out from the blue, blue eyes. Even deeper lines bracketed the corners of his mouth. His chin was strong and shadowed by a day's growth of beard. He looked tough, determined and dangerous, every inch the mercenary, the soldier of fortune he was. Except for his eyes; for the space of a heartbeat they were haunted by sorrow for a homeless people and a ravaged land.

"We all do the best we can. It's never enough, is it?" His voice was as hard as ever; the fleeting moment of shared commitment, however unintentional it had been, was gone like a puff of thistledown on the wind.

"Is that what you believe? That one person, no matter how hard he tries, can't make a difference?"

"I'd say that's what about ninety-nine percent of the people in this world believe," he responded, answering obliquely but meeting her questioning gaze head-on. It might have been her imagination but it seemed to Rachel as if his expression had softened slightly. "You're one of those very few dreamers who are willing to back up their beliefs with damned hard work."

"I'm not a saint."

"No. You're a woman."

"Why are you here?" She couldn't let the conversation get any more personal.

Brett continued to watch her, his expression non-committal, any emotion in his eyes hidden by shadows cast by his thick, dark lashes.

"We're on our way to Chiang Rai to arrange for a final shipment of teak to be brought out before the rainy season."

"Only teak?"

His frown was back, darker, angrier than before. "Do you think I'd tell you if there was more?" The expression in his eyes was easy enough to read now. It was contempt. Rachel felt the chill of it all the way to her bones.

"I didn't mean..."

"Yes, you did. Surely, your brother...at the Census Bureau...warned you not to ask too many questions of a man in my profession?"

"Actually, he told me to stay the hell away from you. Period."

To her surprise he laughed. "He's smarter than I thought. You should stay away from a man of my reputation, if you value your own."

"Bullsh...feathers." Rachel had the satisfaction of seeing Brett Jackson blink in surprise. "Don't you think I can make my own decisions about people? And why didn't you ask me Micah's opinion of your trustworthiness. He's supposed to be your friend."

"I didn't have to ask about Micah." His voice was lower, less rough.

"He said I could trust you with my life."

"Yes." Brett said softly.

Rachel couldn't believe they were having this conversation, in the middle of the main camp thoroughfare, with people all around. She felt as if they were alone, the last man and woman on earth. She didn't know what to do with her hands. She stuck them in the pockets of her gray cotton shorts. She didn't know what to do with her eyes. She looked down at her worn, dusty canvas shoes.

"And which of your brothers do you believe?" There was an extraordinary, intimate note of challenge in his voice. Awareness raced across her nerve endings, as though he had touched her with his words. The sun dropped below the horizon and the light grew dim and hazy around them, sealing them more tightly into a world of their own.

She looked up, directly into his eyes, daring her demons, risking what little composure she had left in their hard blue depths. "Both of them."

"So, there's bedrock common sense beneath the missionary meekness."

"I'm not meek. And I'm not a missionary. Look, I apologize if I offended you. Although, with your reputation, I'd imagine you'd be used to others being suspicious of your motives by now." To her utter amazement he smiled, then laughed, a deep, rich laugh that warmed her heart.

"You don't back down, do you, Rachel McKendrick Phillips? You know what is right and what is wrong and anyone in the middle be damned."

"That's not true. I'm very open-minded. And I never pretend."

"No," he said thoughtfully. "You don't pretend. You adapt, you survive, you do what's necessary to stay alive."

She shivered, despite the heat of early evening, assailed by sharp-edged bits and pieces of memories of the past. He spoke as if he knew firsthand what forces had shaped her, made her what she was. "Once I did all those things," she said so quietly he had to lean toward her to hear the words. "Now I do what I want to do. Because *I* want to do it."

"I know that, too." He lifted his hand, touched her hair very lightly. His palm grazed her cheek, a fleeting caress, over in a heartbeat, yet Rachel felt as if he'd reached out, surrounded her with his arms, held her captive with the mere strength of his will. The smell of his pipe tobacco was evocative, masculine. It tickled her nose, momentarily overpowering the smell of dust and chickens and wood smoke that pervaded the camp. She closed her eyes, willing her thoughts free of the sensual pull of the man before her.

"How long will you be here, Rachel?"

The question surprised her. Her eyes flew open. "I have a little over a year left of my commitment to Father Dolph." He didn't move closer, didn't touch her again, but still Rachel felt bound by his nearness.

"Do you have plans to come south?"

"No." The denial was bald; she softened it. "I mean, I haven't made plans. I don't have leave until June."

"The rainy season—not the best time to see the city, or the country, for that matter."

"I'm not a tourist," she reminded him, glad to hear her voice didn't tremble.

"I know that." He straightened to his full height, giving her space, a moment to order her thoughts. "I want you to come to Bangkok."

He'd thrown her off balance again. "I...I don't know."

"I want to spend some time with you," he said, moving back, moving away, setting her completely free, she thought with relief, until he spoke again. A single word that sent her rushing off into the gathering dusk without even saying goodbye. "Alone."

CHAPTER FIVE

BRETT STOOD BY THE WINDOW in the main room of his home, a large Thai-style house, airy and open, with soaring rooflines. The house stood in a neighborhood that had once been a small village outside the city and still maintained aspects of its old identity. Bangkok was a city of contradictions; its commercial district had traffic tie-ups and noise pollution as bad as any modern city in the world, yet an age-old atmosphere of serenity infused the serious business of making money. *Sanuk,* the all-pervasive sense of fun and lightness that was an outgrowth of Buddhism, enabled the Thai people to conduct their lives and their businesses with both ambition and serenity.

Along the distant skyline, the gold-crusted *chedi* soared toward heaven, shoulder to shoulder with concrete and steel office towers, temples to other, less benevolent beings than the Buddha. Yet, even the occupants of those strongholds of capitalism would not think of neglecting to raise a spirit house outside their doors, a dollhouse-size temple for the devotion of the faithful.

There were other contrasts, too. Great wealth and even greater poverty in the same neighborhood, magnificent museums and art collections only blocks away from bars where nude dancers, some barely into their teens, gyrated to everything from Elvis to The Who. Some of the girls were there of their own free will. Yet most were driven to Patpong Road and its environs by need and necessity, and still others, a few, were there because in this part of the world some men still trafficked in human flesh. Brett turned away from the window with a disgusted snort.

"Preach on, Brother Jackson." The corner of his mouth turned upward in a bitter smile. The rain was causing him to turn philosophical, it seemed. Sometimes that happened about this time of year, although he usually didn't mind the monsoon all that much. There were fewer tourists crowding the flooded streets, less hassle at the restaurant, more time to travel, to read...to think about where his life was going.

The answer to that one was easy. His life was going to go nowhere in a hurry if he didn't quit spending so much of it thinking about things he couldn't change...and women he couldn't have. He should be concentrating on the details of his next meeting with Khen Sa, not comparing the color of the sky after a thunderstorm to the color of Rachel Phillips's eyes.

Today the sky looked like gunmetal, nothing more or less. And it was going to keep on raining, as it had rained the entire month of June and most of July, and would keep on raining until the cool, trade winds of autumn finally chased the clouds away for good.

Brett walked into the breakfast room, his footsteps echoing across the bare polished teak floor. The house was authentic Thai, made entirely of that precious wood, the roof of glazed tiles, but inside he'd taken some liberties with the traditional floor plan. Privacy didn't mean a lot to Thais; staying cool did. Most

Thai-style houses used only partitions and screens to mark the boundaries of different rooms. Brett's house had walls, at least in the sleeping and bathing areas. It was also air-conditioned. Living with high humidity and sixty inches of rain a year was one thing; living with rampant mildew was something else again.

He sat down at the breakfast table. Like magic the houseman, Nog, appeared at his elbow with fruit, black coffee and a soft-boiled egg.

"Shall I set a place for Mr. William?" he inquired.

"No."

Billy was late. He should have been back in the city last night. Yet Brett had been unable to reach him at his home. No one at the Lemongrass had seen him or heard from him for a week. Brett ate his breakfast without tasting it, staring out at the timeless peace and serenity of the Chinese garden, Nog's special pride and joy, seeing nothing.

Billy could take care of himself. He'd been in Southeast Asia damn near as many years as Brett. But dealing with a man like Khen Sa, a throwback to the Dark Ages, tended to make you paranoid. A spot of car trouble, a washout on a northern road that necessitated an unexpected detour, any of those things could have delayed his friend. Nothing more.

Still, he looked up with relief when the Japanese rice-paper screen that served as a wall between the living room and dining room slid open and Billy stepped inside, his tall figure silhouetted briefly against the light background before he moved toward the table. He looked dirty, tired and hungry enough to eat a horse.

"Nog. Get me some coffee."

"Certainly, sir." Nog was Chinese, from Hong Kong, and his upper-class British accent made him sound like a royal duke. He was a shade under five feet tall and somewhere between seventy and a hundred years old, as far as Brett could tell. He'd served with the British army during World War II and had lived in Bangkok since the end of that war. He knew everything there was to know about the city and what it took to get things done.

"I expected you back last night." Brett cracked the shell of his egg.

"Got any more of those, Nog?" Billy asked, indicating the egg when the houseman returned with his coffee. "I'm starved. Last time I ate...was noon...the day before yesterday."

"That bad?"

"Khen Sa's lieutenant, Ben Hua, he wanted to give me a goin'-away feast. All the best stuff—roast dog, fried bat, cobra's blood." Billy scowled down at his coffee. Nog clicked his tongue against his teeth to indicate his sympathy. Brett grinned. "Put me off my food the rest of the trip."

"I can imagine, sir. Although I remember in Burma during the war we had a cook who did cobra in a rather tasty curry dish." Nog left the room shaking his head, still talking to himself.

"What else did you find out?" Brett asked when the old man was out of earshot. He pushed his egg and plate of fruit in Billy's direction.

"I'm too old to sleep on a dirt floor in the middle of the monsoon." Billy inhaled his first cup of coffee and reached for the ceramic pot Nog had placed by his elbow.

Brett ignored the comment. "The meeting?"

"Not too bad. Khen Sa's no dummy."

"He wouldn't have lasted this long if he was."

Billy nodded agreement. He chewed thoughtfully on a bite of egg. "He's got a real setup there. His base camp is in Burma, like we thought, just across the border in Shan State. I didn't get invited up there. Probably won't, unless you're along." Brett nodded. "The factory, though. It's in Thailand. Closer to the poppy fields."

"Factory?" Brett didn't like the way Billy said the word. Most opium-refining labs were hole-in-the-wall operations in the jungle. Billy nodded again.

"We're not talking nickel and dime hits here, buddy. He's set on refining the stuff down to pure heroin. China White. It'll be worth—" he shrugged broad shoulders "—maybe a hundred million, if it gets to California or New York."

"Was the harvest that good?" Billy was talking almost a ton of refined opium, ten percent of the Golden Triangle's entire harvest. Acres and acres of poppies, maybe a hundred tiny, remote villages under Khen Sa's thumb.

"In the region Khen Sa controls, yes."

"And all of the opium being refined in one central location." Brett drummed his fingers on the tabletop. "He's the only one who could have managed this, that's for sure."

"Khen Sa wants to go big time. His troops are getting restless."

"The Burmese government troops are harassing him in the north. I got a report...from our friend in the palace while you were gone."

"Khen Sa's Shan troops hate the Burmese, that's no secret. He promised them a free Shan State. They're tired of short rations and forced marches. He's going to have to let them go after the government troops, and soon. For that, our self-proclaimed general needs guns. And to get guns, he needs money. Cold, hard cash."

"Did you set up another meeting?"

Billy poured a third cup of strong, black coffee. He shook his head. "They'll be in touch. I let them know we were real interested, but not overanxious. My guess is the general won't stir out of his redoubt up there in the mountains till the rainy season's over. We'll just have to sit tight till then." He tipped his chair back on two legs, folded his hands behind his head and balanced there. "He's gonna want a hell of a lot of money. He's gonna want it in gold."

"That goes without saying." Brett pushed his chair away from the table, walked to the window, leaned his hand against the frame and stared out at the rain.

"Can your guy in the palace come up with the rest of the up-front money to satisfy Khen Sa?"

"If we can promise him the entire crop, I think he can. He'd damn well better be able to," Brett added under his breath.

"Maybe it's time you talked to Alf Singleton face-to-face."

"Not unless we have to. Any help we get from the U.S. government has to be strictly on the QT."

He'd been working on this deal for almost two years. It had taken a lot of time, a lot of risk to bring the wily warlord this close to striking a bargain. If he did manage to bring it off without getting himself or

Billy killed, they could call it quits, get out of the mercenary business. Retire. Settle down.

"Then all there is left to do is wait for the rains to quit."

Both men watched the torrential downpour beyond the window and were silent.

"I'd best be gettin' along. I drove most of the night," Billy announced, letting his chair ease back onto all four legs. Brett was being pretty close-mouthed this morning. But Billy decided not to push him. This deal was the biggest thing they'd ever done. It was also way out of his league. Brett had never said so but Billy knew he was feeling the strain, too. Khen Sa wasn't your ordinary two-bit criminal. Hell, the man fielded a goddamn army up there. It wasn't like rousting some small-time pusher on Patpong Road, or setting up some greedy fool running drugs on the side, like the Vietnamese colonel—what was his name, Ky?—they'd engineered into taking a fall the year before. No, it wasn't the same at all. Khen Sa was big time with a capital T.

"Any problems along the way?" Brett turned away from the window. He hooked his thumbs into the waistband of his slacks and stared at Billy with narrowed eyes.

"Nope. Why'd you ask?" Billy knew perfectly well why his friend wanted to know where he'd been. He'd been due back yesterday. He waited, keeping his thoughts to himself.

"What took you so long? Bad roads?"

"No. I made a little stop on the way back from Chiang Rai, that's all."

"What kind of stop?"

"Just a little visit to Father Dolph's camp."

"Why?"

Billy blinked at the cutting edge in Brett's voice. "I thought I'd say hello to Ahnle. See how her English is comin' along."

"Ahnle? The Hlông girl who works with Rachel?"

"Yeah, Ahnle. What about it?" Billy was on the defensive and he knew it.

The strange thing was he really hadn't had any intention of detouring off the main road to the camp. He'd just done it. He hadn't been able to get the girl out of his thoughts, and it bothered him. He'd spent less than an hour in her company, exchanged only a few words. She was young enough to be his daughter, for God's sake. Yet he still woke up most nights in a cold sweat, hard and aching, dreaming of Ahnle.

"Nothing, man. It's just not like you to blow off the plan that way."

"Yeah, I know." Billy stared down at his empty coffee cup. He'd had no business trying to see Ahnle again. He'd done it to convince himself to recognize her for the child she was. It hadn't worked.

"What did you two have to talk about?"

"Nothing."

"Nothing? I would have thought her English would have improved considerably by now, with Rachel Phillips as a tutor."

"It probably has. I didn't talk to her." Here was the hard part. "She wasn't there, man, and neither was Rachel."

"Where are they?" Brett asked.

No one knew Tiger Jackson better than Billy Todd. Still, he could detect little emotion other than natural curiosity on his friend's hard-edged features. Maybe he was wrong in thinking Brett was as interested in Rachel as he was in Ahnle.

"Down near Surin somewhere. At one of the camps on the Kampuchean border."

"What the hell are they doing there? The Khmer Rouge are stirring things up all around there, on both sides of the border."

"That's what I wanted to know. I hunted up that French doctor, Reynard. He said there was cholera." The word hung in the air between them. Cholera, a disease as deadly today as it had been throughout the centuries, capable of killing hundreds in a few days' time.

"Why the hell did Rachel go?"

"She nursed some Vietnamese nationals through an outbreak during the war. She volunteered to go and took Ahnle with her to help out. Dr. Reynard was against the idea but Father Dolph let them go."

"He probably couldn't have stopped her if he'd tried." Brett turned back to the window as if Billy's explanation answered some unspoken question of his own. He looked relaxed, at ease, but his hand on the window frame had curled into a fist. "How long have Rachel and the girl been there?"

"Three, four weeks."

"Has anybody heard from them? Are they all right?"

Billy knew why he was asking. The camps on the border were crowded, grim settlements as large as cities. Crime and violence were common, and there was always the threat of attack by the Khmer Rouge or other antigovernment factions who crossed the border almost at will.

"Doc says Rachel won't let Ahnle near any of the cholera patients, and they're both all right." He couldn't keep the relief out of his voice. She was just a kid, dammit. He shouldn't care so much.

Brett swung his head around to eye him sharply. "Do Rachel's brothers know where she is?"

Billy snorted, halfway between a laugh and a hoot. "No way. The Doc said Rachel told Father Dolph she'd pin his ears back if he gave them so much as a hint of what she was doing."

Brett shook his head. "Poor old Micah. She's some woman," he added, almost as if to himself.

"Maybe she'll stop over in the city on her way back north."

"Maybe." Brett didn't sound as if he expected her to do any such thing. Billy wondered what was going on between the two of them. His old friend sounded as off balance as he was. Women. Hell. They'd gotten along fine without them for twenty years. Now. Bam, they were on your mind day and night.

How hard had Tiger fallen for Rachel's blue-gray eyes and that sad, pretty smile? Hard enough to risk the deal they'd been working on all these months? Billy didn't know for sure. He didn't ask either, even though it did seem to him that Rachel Phillips was worth the risk. She was just the kind of woman Tiger Jackson needed.

SUNSHINE. REAL SUNSHINE.

Rachel woke to the warmth of it on her face, surprised to find she'd dozed off so close to her destination. She looked out the window of her train compartment, blinking against the brightness of the late September morning. The train was slowing its headlong pace, moving into the outskirts of Bangkok. The change in speed was what must have awakened her. She stretched and yawned, kneading a kink at the back of her neck with her fingers. Sleeping sitting up was never comfortable.

"Good morning," Ahnle said.

"Good morning." Rachel smiled at her young friend. "Ahnle, look. Elephants." She pressed her face to the window. Outside, a family of work elephants moved alongside the track, trunk to tail, baby placed protectively between mother and aunt, as their trainer maneuvered them into position beside a pile of railroad ties. Rachel watched them for as long as she could.

"There are elephants everywhere here," Ahnle said, shaking her head. "I think you should be used to them by now."

"Never," Rachel laughed, pulling a comb out of her bag and running it through her silver-threaded hair. "I love elephants. Although, you're right, there do seem to be a lot of them around."

"Yes," Ahnle agreed dryly. "And also the large, smelly piles of . . ."

" . . . manure," Rachel prompted hastily before any less suitable word came out of her mouth.

"Manure, they leave it everywhere they walk." Ahnle curled her lip. "Ugh."

"I wish we could have stayed in Surin for the elephant roundup in November," Rachel said wistfully.

"We have been in Surin long enough."

"I guess you're right. Ten weeks is a long time to stay away." The danger of the cholera outbreak at the huge camp on the Thai-Kampuchean border was over and they were needed back at Camp Six. She was glad Father Dolph had talked her out of her fear of taking Ahnle along with her. She would have missed the girl sadly if they'd been separated so long.

The train passed over a flooded canal, or *klong*, as the Thais called them. She watched several long-tailed boats streak along the swollen waterway. Perhaps she'd buy a small wooden carving of an elephant to give to Ahnle, to remember their journey by, something she could take with her when she left the camp to start a life of her own.

"I wonder if we have time to do some shopping between trains?" she mused, pulling a timetable out of her bag. "Three hours until the train for Chiang Mai leaves. Would you like to see some of the city?"

Ahnle shook her head. She'd been looking out the window for a long time, watching the city close in around them. "It is too big. I think we would be lost here."

"We would take a taxi," Rachel explained. "And come back to the train station the same way. We wouldn't get lost."

Ahnle shook her head. "No. Please, I will stay here."

"All right. We'll stay here." Ahnle had never ridden on a train before they boarded in Surin. She'd been working long, hard hours under trying conditions during the cholera outbreak. It was understandable that she should be apprehensive of venturing out into one of the biggest, busiest cities in the world.

Suddenly Rachel, also, found herself not so anxious to set off on the proposed shopping trip. She was tired and grubby. Mostly tired, bone-achingly tired, and had been for weeks. But that wasn't the sole reason for her sudden attack of indecision. If she left the station there was the possibility, however remote, she might meet Brett Jackson somewhere in the city. Never mind that the odds were millions to one against just such a meeting. She was afraid to go.

"I would like breakfast," Ahnle said. "I'm not afraid to leave the train. I just do not want to... shop...."

"And I could do with a wash." Rachel closed the snap on her heavy tote and stood up. "I think you're right. Breakfast and a wash is a much better idea than shopping."

She was happy enough to find something to do that would take her mind off thoughts of the mysterious and dangerous Tiger Jackson. Even the nights she fell asleep so exhausted she couldn't find the energy to take off her clothes or shoes, the moment she shut her eyes, his face would be there, silhouetted against the velvety darkness behind her eyelids. A hard-featured face, bronzed, remote, his profile edged in the memory of silvery jungle moonlight. And when she dreamed, she dreamed of him, not the nightmare past or the uncertain future. But those dreams were fantasy, nothing more.

It was true, she was coming to think of this beautiful and exotic land as her home. The cares and concerns of the homeless people she worked with were becoming her own. Yet, she must also face reality. She was no longer young. Her resources were limited. The plain truth of the matter was that she was alone, no matter how much she cared for Ahnle, Father Dolph and the others.

Alone.

As always, the stinging ache of loss assailed her, darkening her mood just as a cloud passing before the sun dimmed the light of a summer day. The pain came less often now as time passed, but still, she mourned the death of her child and knew she always would. She also knew she could never have another child, even if by some miracle she found someone to love.

That, in light of the terror of the past, was the way she'd always expected it to be.

Until she met Tiger Jackson and miracles became a regular part of her dreams.

CHAPTER SIX

AHNLE STEPPED OUT OF the small wooden cottage she shared with Rachel and shaded her eyes against the brightness of the sun. It was October now, Rachel had told her, naming the moon time that her people called the Moon of the Mists because the rains were over and the wet forest steamed in the warmth of the sun.

It was going to be a nice day, she decided. The heat of the sun was strong on her face. Its brightness would help dry up the last of the mud around the cottage. She wondered if this afternoon they could plant the seeds Rachel's mother had sent all the way from America. She smiled as she set her conical-shaped straw hat on her head and tightened the strings. She was anxious to see these Big Boy tomatoes that Rachel was so fond of talking about. She had never tasted one. She was curious to know what they were like.

She dropped to her knees to check the small patch of turned soil in front of the cottage and deemed it ready for planting. In her village in the mountains the soil was stony and thin. Here it was rich and red, but covered over with huts and buildings and trampled down by the comings and goings of thousands of feet. Very little of anything could grow here. Ahnle shook her head. It was very hard to understand how round-eyed Westerners thought. But she was trying. She wanted to go to America, to be free to live as she wished. That could never happen if she remained in Thailand.

And her most secret wish, one she kept close to her heart, was that she could take her son to America with her.

A shadow blotted out the sunlight. Ahnle looked up from her musings, expecting to see Rachel returning from a night spent with Dr. Reynard and a laboring Lao woman whose baby, Rachel had told her, was twisted sideways inside her.

"Little sister."

Ahnle gasped. The figure standing over her was familiar, but not welcome.

"Good spirits, Brother," she said formally. She bowed low before her male relative, the patterns of a lifetime of ritual holding true, although inside she was shaking with fear. "All is well in our village?" There was only one soul whose well-being she cared about in the village she'd left behind. Her baby. Her parents were dead. She'd made the dangerous journey from Laos with her aunt and uncle and three cousins, who had refused to acknowledge her since her disgrace.

"The village remains the same. Not good." Her brother shrugged, staring at her so intently that Ahnle felt a prickle of unease. "You look good. They feed you well here."

"The spirits are kind. There is enough to eat." He continued to look her over appraisingly and Ahnle shivered in spite of the heat of the morning sun.

"My son?" Only the desperate need to know about her baby gave her the courage to ask the question outright. Her brother's cryptic references alarmed her.

Were they starving in her village? Had the rains washed away their fields, ruined their meager stores of rice and vegetables? Did her child go hungry?

"The boy is well. I have found a home for him." Her brother's tone was callous. He was a hard man, the head of her family. He was, after all, the son of her father's first wife, as she was only a daughter of the second. He came and went as he pleased, it seemed, making the long journey down out of the mountains, across the river several times each dry season and even once in a while in the rainy season—if there was extra opium to sell.

"You do not mean to keep my son with you?" Ahnle felt her knees go weak and soft. She couldn't have risen from the damp ground if she'd tried, yet she refused to show her brother how much anguish his words had caused. "Your new wife—"

"Has finally given me a son of my own. But Chengla and his wife have no sons. They will give your child ancestors to protect him. But you must give them money in return."

"I give you all I have." Rachel and Father Dolph gave her a few *baht* each week for the work she did. Twice before this, her brother had appeared in the camp to take it from her. Today she had no money at all. She tried not to think of the sour-faced Chengla and his lazy wife taking her baby. She couldn't let that happen. She tried to look past her brother, hoping that Rachel or Father Dolph would appear and help her.

"The money you get from the unbelievers is not enough. I have found work for you. I have come to take you away."

"Where?" Ahnle was not stupid. She was of no use to him if she returned to the village. Her brother meant to sell her away in the city. It was his right. She had heard from talking to other young women in the camp of how she would be expected to earn money in the city, and the knowledge turned her heart to stone.

"Bangkok. Chiang Mai is too close."

But in Bangkok, so huge and so far away, no one would ever find her.

"When I have earned the money necessary for Chengla and his woman to give my son a good home, I will keep the rest and go to America." She spoke defiantly, despite her dread.

"You can go wherever you want to go."

Her brother was lying and they both knew it. Even if the man her brother sent her to gave her money, it would be only a pittance. She wasn't being hired for a job. Her brother was selling her, and not one of her people would lift a finger to help her, disgraced as she was. Only her new friends could save her and she had no way to tell them what was happening. And they would never know where she had gone.

"I'M SORRY, ASSISTANT Ambassador Singleton is unavailable. If you'll leave your name and where you may be reached, I'll see to it that he gets your message." The very polite, perfectly groomed young woman behind the reception desk of the American embassy looked Rachel over with just a hint of alarm in her green eyes.

"I must see Ambassador Singleton." There was a mirror on the wall behind the receptionist's ornate gilt desk. Rachel didn't even glance into it. She was aware how disheveled and travel-stained she looked. Two days on the road from Camp Six in the cab of a supply truck bound for Bangkok to pick up medical equipment couldn't be compared to traveling first class. Add to that the strain of a week of anxious, sleepless nights filled with worry over Ahnle's safety and no woman would look her best.

"I'm sorry." The young woman glanced toward the two tall young marines standing guard nearby.

"I'm an American citizen. I need help. There must be someone I can talk to." Rachel abandoned any pretense at polite conversation. The woman hesitated.

"The ambassador's assistant, Mr. Bartley, is available."

Rachel brushed her hair away from her cheek. "He'll do." In the jungle he'd been little help to either of them. Perhaps here, in his own element, he would be of more use.

"One moment, please," The woman picked up a telephone and gestured Rachel toward a chintz-upholstered love seat by the window. Rachel was too restless to sit down. Several minutes passed before one of the ornately carved doors along the far wall of the room opened and Harrison Bartley appeared. He was dressed in a spotless white linen suit, white shirt and pale mauve tie. Rachel felt smaller and more disheveled than ever. To combat a sudden rush of insecurity, she moved forward with her hand outstretched.

"Thank you for seeing me."

"Hello, Rachel." His handshake was perfunctory. "What seems to be the problem?"

"I need to locate a missing person, a young Hlông girl who was kidnapped from the camp by her brother. I'm sure she's in Bangkok." He motioned her through the open door into his office. With a wave of his hand, he indicated that she should take a seat in a red leather chair drawn up before a carved mahogany desk, flanked by the flags of the United States and Thailand.

"Are you sure she was brought here against her will?" He rested one hip on the edge of the desk and surveyed his foot in its white leather pump.

"She disappeared from our cottage—she's my assistant—without a word. It took me five days to find someone who had seen her leave the camp. She was with a man, her brother as I said, and she was crying." She clamped her fingers around the straps of her bag. It contained a change of clothes, her passport and what little money she had. Harrison Bartley eyed the woven bag distastefully.

"Young girls are brought down from the hills into Patpong every day." Rachel hated the accepting tone of his voice, the little nod of his head that said, "You get used to hearing such things in this part of the world."

It wasn't as if she hadn't heard the words before. Father Dolph had warned her this was how it would be when she'd told him what she'd learned from the Hlông woman who'd seen Ahnle leave the camp with her brother. "He's most likely taken her to Chiang Mai or Bangkok." The priest's words had been gentle, his tone sympathetic but resigned. "You're too brave and intelligent to hide from the truth, Rachel. Unwanted daughters are often traded away here. Surely that happened in the village where you lived? It's an old custom. We can only pray to God and work to change it."

"It's a terrible practice but it still happens here." Bartley's words echoed Father Dolph's in her head. "Officially, I can't do much. The girl isn't even a Thai national, is she?" He twitched the leg of his pants. "They turn a blind eye to what the hill people do down here. Except for the king. Bit of a reformer, His Majesty."

"Perhaps Ambassador Singleton might be able to give me some more information." She closed her eyes to blot out the sight of Bartley's handsome, vacuous face. The sharp sting of angry, frustrated tears pricked behind her eyelids. "Can you arrange for me to speak to him?"

"He's unavailable, I'm afraid."

"Please." She would beg if she had to.

"I'm sorry, Rachel." The peevish tone was gone. "The ambassador is in conference with the king's minister right now. I couldn't get through to him if my own life depended on it."

"I see."

"Look, why don't you try to get in touch with your friends from the jungle?"

"I don't understand." She was so tired she couldn't think straight.

"Sure, you do." For the first time she heard real anger beneath Bartley's smoothly cultured tones. "Tiger Jackson and that black friend of his. Surely you know it was their camp we spent the night in?" He stood up and walked behind the desk, distancing himself from Rachel and her problem.

"I don't know how to contact them." She could be blunt, also.

"Try the Lemongrass." He sat down behind the desk.

"The restaurant you took me to that day?"

"I've heard you can contact Tiger Jackson there. He's got a damned sight better chance of finding the girl than we do. Our Mr. Jackson has friends in very high places."

"By that you mean he's paid off everyone necessary to ensure he's not bothered by the authorities."

"So do the kind of... businessmen who are interested in young girls like your assistant, if you catch my drift. It's the accepted way of doing business in Southeast Asia." He twirled a gold pen between manicured fingers. "Do you know I couldn't get one single person, including my boss, to listen to me when I told them we spent the night in his jungle hideout? No one. And the fellow who gave me the map? He's gone. Rotated home right in the middle of his tour. There isn't a copy of that map to be had anywhere in Thailand. The one I had with me that day, remember?" Rachel nodded. "It's gone, too. Disappeared. Just like your little friend. And I'm sorry to say, I think you've got just about as much chance of finding her as I do of getting back to that *wat* without it."

"YOU MUST LISTEN TO ME. It's urgent that I contact him. Now. Today."

The voice sounded familiar, feminine, American, sweet and clear. Lonnie Smalley pushed aside the beaded curtain that separated the private rooms and offices of the Lemongrass from the main dining room off the bar.

"Sorry," Ponchoo, the Thai maître d' and occasional bartender, was saying. "There's no one named Tiger Jackson here."

Lonnie lifted a shaking hand and parted the curtain. He needed a fix but Brett had made him promise not to leave the restaurant. He'd gotten some bad stuff last time he'd gone out on his own and it had nearly killed him. Or at least that's what Billy said. He could only remember the dreams, horrible dreams of monsters and blood and then nothing at all. The nothingness hadn't been so bad. At least not till he'd awakened in his bed with the worst hangover he'd ever had in his life.

"Please. It's important." The woman standing in the filtered sunlight near the bar windows was Rachel Phillips. He remembered Billy telling him she'd spent years in a Vietnamese prison camp and a hill village in Laos. He'd thought a lot about her since then, of the things that must have happened to her. Of the things she must have seen and couldn't forget—like him. He wondered if she felt as out of place in the world as he did these days. He wondered how she'd been able to go home again. He never had. Or had she been able to go home again? Maybe not. Maybe that's why she was back in Southeast Asia—because she didn't belong anyplace anymore, just like him.

He thought about going into the bar to ask her but he decided against it. Fire danced up and down his arms, just under the skin, and his head pounded like a kettle drum. He'd better tell Brett she was here. He wouldn't like being interrupted, not while the two bigwigs he was palaverin' with in the back room were there. But Lonnie thought Brett had better know the pretty woman with the sad smile and blue-gray eyes was kicking up a rumpus in the bar.

BRETT HADN'T REALLY BELIEVED it when Lonnie came sidling into his office to tell him Rachel Phillips was in the bar arguing with Ponchoo, but the younger man had been telling the truth. He stood a moment, behind the beaded curtain, watching her. She was wearing a flowered cotton jacket and skirt that was mostly pink and green, and a white blouse, open at the throat. She was thinner than he remembered and her hair had lost the glorious moonlight sheen that haunted his dreams. Her face, reflected in the mirror behind the bar, was tense and exhausted.

Something was wrong, very wrong, for Rachel Phillips to have taken the risk of coming to him. A thousand times over the past months he'd wished to hell he'd never given in to the impulse to let her see and feel, and know of his attraction to her. He'd pushed a little too hard and she'd bolted. But now she was back and he had another chance. He looked back over his shoulder, consigned the two very important and influential gentlemen he'd left cooling their heels in his office to Hades, and walked into the bar.

"I'm sorry I can't help you," Ponchoo was saying in the friendly, polite way all Thais carried on business, and even arguments.

"I have to find Tiger Jackson." Her tone was friendly and polite, also, but tired, with a thread of anxiety snaking along beneath the surface calm. "I was told I might find him here."

"Sorry." Ponchoo picked up a glass and started polishing it. "Do you want a drink?" he asked politely, changing the subject and ending the discussion as far as he was concerned.

"No. Please." The barman pretended not to hear.

"Arguing with a Thai is like trying to wrestle a cloud."

Rachel whirled toward him, her eyes wide with relief, and a hint of wariness. "Brett." As always, the sound of his name on her lips made his gut tighten with need. "He said he'd never heard of you." She looked back at Ponchoo accusingly. He shrugged and smiled disarmingly.

"Sorry, ma'am." He went back to polishing his glassware.

"He has his orders."

A faint hint of color stained her cheeks. "Of course." She wrapped her hands around the straps of the *yaam* she carried on her shoulder.

"What's wrong, Rachel?" He didn't come any closer. He didn't want to frighten her away again. It was late afternoon, the bar was empty for the moment but the early dinner crowd would be arriving soon. He pulled a high-backed bamboo chair away from a small table nearby and held it for her.

"Is it so apparent something's wrong?" she asked, brushing nervously at her hair where it lay against her cheek.

"Yes. And I know you wouldn't come to me unless you needed help." He held her gaze with his own. She didn't flinch or look away, just smiled sadly.

"It's Ahnle. She disappeared over a week ago. I think she's been brought here against her will. I just got here today—I came in a supply truck. I tried the embassy first. I thought...Ambassador Singleton might help. He's a friend of my brother, Simon." She made a helpless little gesture with her hands as she sat down.

"Since you're here, he obviously didn't." He signaled Ponchoo to bring her something to drink.

"Juice is fine," she said when the bartender appeared at her elbow. "I never saw the ambassador. Harrison Bartley suggested I try to contact you here."

"Out of the goodness of his heart, I imagine."

She smiled, just a hint of a sparkle in her tired eyes. "I don't think so." Her smile disappeared. "Brett, can you help me?"

"You're looking for a needle in a haystack." She flinched when he said it.

"I have to try to find her." He hadn't been wrong in thinking Rachel was growing very attached to the young Hlông woman that day at the camp.

"Khob khun," she murmured as Ponchoo set the tall glass of iced juice in front of her. "She didn't come here of her own free will. I know she didn't." Rachel curled her hand tightly around the glass and looked down. "She's lost everything, Brett. Can you understand that? Her family...her identity..." She was silent a moment, then looked up at him with such sorrow in her blue-gray eyes that he was shaken to the very center of his soul. "She's lost everything dear to her. I can't stand by and see her lose her freedom...her self-respect." Her voice grew stronger, determined once more. "I have to find her."

"In a city this size..." he began, choosing his words carefully. He didn't want to build up false hopes.

There were people he could contact, but it would take time. If Ahnle had been gone over a week already, there was no telling what might have happened to her.

"Surely there are places I can look for her?"

"No, not alone."

She reached out her hand, as if to touch him. He leaned back in his chair, away from her. If she touched him, he didn't know what would happen. He'd sure as hell want to touch her back, and he'd probably be tempted to go off with her on some damn fool search of the seedier bars off Patpong Road. He couldn't do that, not now. He was too close to talking the gentlemen in his office into giving him the extra quarter-million dollars in gold bullion he needed to ice the deal with Khen Sa. The search for Ahnle would have to wait.

"You won't help me?"

"I can't leave here now."

"Why not?"

"I don't like to publicize this fact, but I own the place."

"I see. Business first." She squared her shoulders. The hand she'd reached out to him just moments before curled into a fist. "You don't have to tag along with me. Just tell me where she might be. Surely you know what kind of places take young girls like Ahnle."

"Not firsthand, if that's what you're implying." He was angry, too. His reputation had never bothered him. He did what he had to do and the rest of the world be damned. But seeing the contempt in Rachel's eyes flicked him on the raw.

Rachel closed her eyes briefly. "I'm sorry. I didn't mean that. I just thought..."

"A man with my reputation would frequent dives like that."

"Brett." This time she did touch him, a butterfly caress on the back of his hand that rocked him with the force of a mortar shell going off beneath his feet. "Forgive me. I'm tired and I'm scared to death for Ahnle. I have to find her. I know...I know what it's like to be forced into..." She broke off and took a deep breath. "Please help me find her."

For twenty years he'd been able to put duty and necessity before his own needs. Never had it been harder to do than at this moment.

"Where are you staying?"

"I...I don't know."

He recalled her disjointed explanation of Ahnle's disappearance, the method of travel she'd used to get to the city. She probably didn't have more than a few dollars to her name.

"There's a place you can stay nearby." She started to object but he cut her short. He couldn't afford to delay the stalled negotiations in his office much longer. "It's a guest house. Clean and cheap. Lonnie can take you there. I'll put out some feelers on finding Ahnle. I should know something in a day or two." Or sooner than that, if he could find Billy and head into the Pat-pong district himself later that night.

"A day or two? I can't wait that long." She stood up. So did he. Rachel leaned forward, rested her hands on the table. "I intend to go looking for her today. Now."

"That's out of the question." He kept his voice low. One or two patrons had begun drifting into the bar. "Patpong Road is no place for a woman alone."

"I'll manage."

"I said you're not going. That's an order." He'd made a mistake saying that. She stood taller, her shoulders thrown back, her chin high. She looked brave and determined and scared to death.

"No one tells me what to do. No one." She started to walk away. Brett was aware of curious looks, suspended conversation around them.

"Rachel, wait." He ran his hand through his hair. He'd rather face Khen Sa and a hundred of his men than argue with a woman, especially this woman. He wanted to make love to her, not fight with her.

"No." She shook her head. "Don't you see, I can't wait? I waited half a lifetime for someone to come for me. I'm not going to let that happen to Ahnle if I can help it."

"Dammit." Brett watched her walk away, back straight, her hips swaying gently beneath the soft cotton skirt. What the hell was he supposed to do? Ponchoo couldn't leave the bar. Billy wouldn't be back for hours. He'd have to let her go for the time being. Right now he had to get back to the men in his office. They were all taking a risk just meeting here, but time was getting short and he needed the gold Khen Sa demanded as earnest money, and damn soon. He watched the door close behind Rachel, then turned and walked back through the beaded curtain to his office, a grimly determined look on his face.

Women. For twenty years he'd managed to stay pretty much free of them. Now, in a matter of months, in a number of meetings he could count on one hand, Rachel Phillips had managed to turn his life upside down. *Hell,* he thought, twisting the knob on his office door with a great deal more force than necessary, *she was making a wreck of his life and he hadn't even gotten around to kissing her.*

RACHEL STOOD ON THE SIDEWALK outside the Lemongrass, looking for a bus stop. She simply didn't have enough money to bargain for a taxi, although it would be faster. At least the Lemongrass was close enough to the Patpong district that she shouldn't have to transfer. It hadn't been so convenient getting to the restaurant from the embassy on Wireless Road.

"Hi." The hoarse, ruined voice belonged to Lonnie Smalley. "Need a lift?" He was leaning out of the open window of a very battered VW of indeterminate age and color.

"I'm going to Patpong," she said, fishing in her *yaam* for her sunglasses, "not some guest house your boss picked out for me."

"I figured that when I saw you march out the door. I overheard some of what you told him," Lonnie said without embarrassment. "You're makin' the colonel real mad, ya know."

"It can't be helped." She leaned down and looked at him.

"Get in. I'll take you where you want to go."

"I don't want you getting in trouble for helping me."

"Don't worry about me. I know some of the places you'll need to go look for your friend. Get in," he repeated, opening the door.

"Do you think we can find her?" Rachel asked, as he maneuvered his way through the heavy traffic.

"We can try." He handled the car competently enough, although his hands were shaking and his face twitched uncontrollably. He needed a fix, Rachel realized, badly. He turned his head, saw her watching him. "Don't worry. I'm not going to dump you to go off looking for some China White. I'm tight. Okay?"

"Okay," Rachel said doubtfully. She hadn't considered the complications of Lonnie's addiction when she'd agreed to accompany him. She wondered what had happened to make him lose control of his life.

"Patpong is no place for a lady."

"I've been in worse places," Rachel said quietly.

"Yeah," Lonnie said, nodding his head. "So have I."

The days were getting shorter. It was almost dusk before they arrived at the entrance to the Teak Doll. It was a bar on a narrow, twisting side street called a *soi* off Patpong Road. Behind them, the noisy main drag of the so-called sex center of the city was busy and well-lighted. Here, where she stood with Lonnie Smalley, it was relatively quiet. The neon signs were smaller, many with burned-out letters above ramshackle bars and massage parlors.

The come-on girl outside the third bar they'd stopped at had directed them this way, after first ascertaining that her boss couldn't see her talking to the *farang* woman and her man. Lonnie had reached over and slipped a ten-*baht* bill inside the almost nonexistent bottom of her bikini. "Try Teak Doll," she said in heavily accented English. "Many new girls, young girls, sent there."

Rachel looked to Lonnie for guidance. "We might as well give it a shot," he said, hunching his bony shoulders against a spasm of shivering. They set off, following the directions the girl had given them. It was still very hot but Lonnie continued to shake. Thunder rumbled off in the distance, promising a quick, drenching shower before the night was over.

Rachel's hands were shaking as badly as Lonnie's as she pushed open the bar's swinging door, like those in old-fashioned western saloons. The Teak Doll was as seedy and down-at-the-heel as the street on which it sat, dark and smelling of stale beer, cheap perfume and unwashed bodies. It was crowded and noisy and their entrance went unnoticed by most of the clientele.

About six or seven young girls moved around the long, narrow room, laughing too loudly, bending too near the men at the tables. On the teak bar, the room's most prominent feature, four more very young, scantily clad girls gyrated to heavy-metal music, played at ear-numbing levels. Ahnle was one of them. She looked lost and scared. She kept trying to stretch the scrap of red satin bikini that was all she was wearing to cover more of her golden skin. Her long, gloriously black hair hung straight and heavy, almost to her waist. Rachel's heart twisted inside her. Modesty was important to Hlông women. They displayed their bodies to no one except their husbands.

Ahnle's actions obviously displeased the burly German sailor seated directly beneath her at the bar. He reached up, tugging the skimpy material lower on her hips, laughing at her distress. Ahnle pushed at his hand, looking around her fearfully as she did so. The look of utter horror in her eyes so at odds with the death's head smile stretching her lips, made Rachel's blood run cold. How well she knew the sense of hopelessness Ahnle must be feeling, the dread of being so completely at the mercy of a man, a stranger, with nowhere to turn and no one to keep you safe.

The German sailor was getting angry at Ahnle's continued rebuff of his advances. The owner, a skinny pockmarked Chinese, was also taking notice. Rachel felt paralyzed with indecision.

"Is that her? The girl in the red bikini?" Lonnie asked. For a moment she'd forgotten he existed. Now she could feel him watching her, gauging her reaction.

She nodded. "Yes, that's Ahnle." She turned her head. His face was pasty beneath his tan. He was scratching his left arm with an intensity that brought welts to the surface of his skin. That he was in withdrawal was obvious to her and would be to others. The Thai government dealt harshly with addicts. Lonnie Smalley shouldn't be here any more than Ahnle. "We have to get her out of here."

She glanced up once more to find Ahnle looking at her. One crystal tear squeezed out of her dark, frightened eyes and ran down her cheek, smearing mascara and cheap red blusher as it went. Rachel didn't give herself time for any more thoughts. She moved into the bar like a small, indomitable tornado, ignoring Lonnie Smalley's restraining hand.

"Get down, Ahnle," she ordered in as strong and steady a voice as she could manage. "I've come to take you home."

The frightened girl clung to the pole anchored from bar top to ceiling that she'd been "dancing" around. "Ahnle, come down," Rachel said in Hlông, watching the angry German from the corner of her eye. He was a big man, burly and blond.

"She's mine," the sailor roared in German. Rachel didn't have to speak the language to understand what he said.

"She belongs to no man."

Ahnle scrambled down off the bar, as though no longer having to face the big man's hungry attentions had released her from a spell.

"Rachel." For the first time in the months they'd been together, Ahnle ignored the conventions of her people and threw herself into Rachel's arms. "Take me away, please. It is a bad place here."

Rachel slipped off her light cotton jacket and wrapped it around Ahnle's shoulders. The girl was shaking so hard her teeth chattered. "Don't let that man touch me again."

The sailor didn't look ready to give Ahnle up without a fight. The bar owner advanced on them, also, yelling abuse in Chinese, flourishing a very business-like billy club. Rachel took a prudent step backward, dragging Ahnle with her.

"*Nein,*" the German howled, diving for the girl just as Lonnie Smalley stepped into his path. Without breaking stride, the sailor swung his arm and knocked the smaller, lighter man against the bar. Lonnie slid to the floor in a crumpled heap.

"I pay many *baht* for this one." The owner of the bar broke into English. "She not good here. She not dance and laugh. She drive customers away. I lose money. She not go unless I get paid for trouble." He waved the billy club in front of Rachel's face. Then it disappeared from sight, spinning the man half around as it was ripped from his hand.

"We're not paying anything," a low male voice said.

Rachel looked up, startled. Brett Jackson towered over her, holding the billy club, slapping it into the open palm of his other hand. Lonnie struggled to get to his feet and she looked away, kneeling to help him, trying to hide the relief that brought sudden tears to her eyes.

"I lose money," the bar owner whined.

"You'll lose more than that if you don't shut up and let the girl go quietly."

"The same goes for you, buddy." Billy Todd's grin was as menacing as his words. The German sailor looked as if he intended to press his claim for Ahnle, standing, now, in the shelter of Billy's arm. His right hand moved casually toward the knife sheathed at his waist. The German backed away.

"You okay, Lon?" Brett asked, never taking his eye from the disgruntled bar owner.

"Yeah." Lonnie dragged the back of his hand across his mouth. It came away streaked with blood. "He blindsided me."

"Let's get out of here before some of the natives get restless." Unbelievably, only those in the immediate vicinity of the altercation had paid it any heed. For the rest of the customers, it was business as usual.

"Right behind you, Colonel."

"Coming, Mrs. Phillips?" Brett inquired with a twist of his lips that wasn't quite a smile.

Rachel nodded. She couldn't trust her voice just yet. She'd come a long way from the frightened shell of a woman she'd been when Micah and Simon brought her home from Vietnam, but she still had trouble dealing with hostility and anger in men.

"I suggest we blow this joint." Billy was grinning from ear to ear. "Otherwise, I might have to smash somebody's head in, just for the hell of it."

"No." Rachel held her ground, although she was shaking all over. "We should call the police. See if any of the other girls need help."

"We can't do anything for them. Do you want to get us all killed?" Brett's face was as hard as his words. He grabbed her hand, manacling her wrist with a grip she couldn't break. "Move it, Rachel. You're coming with me and this time you'll do as you're told."

CHAPTER SEVEN

"IS SHE SLEEPING?"

Rachel's breath caught in her throat for the space of a heartbeat. She spun around. Billy Todd was standing directly behind her in the dimly lighted hallway.

"I'd appreciated it if you would quit sneaking up on me like that." She smiled up at him but her heart raced in startled reaction.

"Sorry," he said, and grinned. "Force of habit." He glanced through the open bedroom door. Ahnle was lying on a low platform bed of some highly polished wood that Rachel couldn't identify. There was a troubled, haunted look on her face that hadn't smoothed away even in sleep. Billy walked forward, as silently as ever, and looked down at her. "Can she be left alone?" A frown carved deep lines in his high forehead.

"I think so." Rachel took one last, considering look at the sleeping girl and started down the hall ahead of Billy Todd.

"I'll leave the door open. If she wakes and calls out for me, it will be easier to hear her."

"Was she raped?" His hand on her arm stopped her. Billy's question was blunt, as hard-edged as his voice, but Rachel sensed the leashed anger and concern beneath the surface calm.

"As far as I can tell, no, thank God. I guess even the clientele of the Teak Doll balks at carrying off a young girl kicking and screaming and scared out of her wits." Rachel folded her arms beneath her breasts, hugging herself against the sudden chill of memory that struck deep into her heart. They both knew it was only a matter of time until someone would have bid for Ahnle's services. "I think the bar owner got a whole lot more opposition from her than he bargained for." She shook her head, laughing a little to lighten her own darkness.

"She's a spunky kid. She's got you to thank for that."

"Me?" Rachel was surprised by the statement.

Billy nodded. "No Hlông maiden would have dared defy her male relatives that way, no matter what she was expected to do."

"I know," Rachel agreed, "but very few of the Hlông I knew would ask that of their daughters or sisters." Even the ones who had brought disgrace on the family ancestors as Ahnle had done.

"Well, she's free of them now. And believe it or not, there are a lot worse places in Bangkok than the Teak Doll." Billy crossed the main room of the lovely, traditional-style Thai house that Brett had brought them to. *His home,* she realized suddenly, now that she could take the time to consider her surroundings.

"I could use a drink. How about you?" Billy went directly to a bar tucked against the far wall. Dressed in light blue cotton shirt and dark slacks, he looked less dangerous, more civilized than usual.

"Sounds good." She sat down on an overstuffed couch covered in Thai cotton in a pattern of earth tones and dark green. It was comfortable, casual and decidedly masculine.

"Whiskey and soda all right? The whiskey's Canadian. I've been in Thailand for over fifteen years and I still can't get used to their rice whiskey. Too sweet. Tastes like rum."

"I'd like a beer," Rachel said wistfully. "A cold beer."

"One cold beer coming right up." He brought her a bottle of Thai beer and a glass, seating himself on a chair opposite the couch.

Rachel took a sip and let her eyes wander around the teak-paneled room. "This is Brett's house, isn't it?"

"Yeah. He doesn't spend too much time here, though."

"You . . . travel . . . a lot, I suppose," Rachel said, searching for a tactful way to phrase her thoughts. She looked down at her mint-green linen skirt. The skirt and sleeveless white blouse were all the clothes she had, except for what she'd been wearing earlier in the day. She tried futilely to smooth the wrinkles with the palm of her hand.

"We're on the road most of the time." He took a swallow of his whiskey as he glanced around the quiet room. "I like this place. Feels like home, ya know? Maybe someday I'll have a place like it." He leaned forward, holding his glass between his hands, his elbows resting on widespread knees.

"Don't you want to go home, back to the States?"

"I've been gone too long to go back. Bangkok is my home now." He was silent, lost in his own thoughts.

"Where in the city do you live?" She watched the bubbles in her beer race to the top of the glass.

"I got a houseboat on one of the *klongs* off the river. Used to be a nice little place—now the tourists have found it and it's damn near as crowded and noisy as the floating market." He shook his head. "Progress. It's a damn shame sometimes."

A clock in a nearby room chimed midnight with the soft tinkle of tiny temple bells.

Billy stood up. "It's time I headed over to Lonnie's hooch."

"Is Brett with him?" She studied the bubbles in her glass more closely than ever. She tried hard to keep her voice noncommittal.

"Yes, he is." Billy drained the remainder of his whiskey in one long swallow.

"I see."

He bent over and very carefully set the glass on the bamboo table between them. "Don't judge what you don't understand, Mrs. Phillips." There was no mistaking the warning in his words.

"Rachel, please. I'm not judging, Billy." She couldn't keep the tightness out of her voice; her throat just seemed to close up when she tried to say the words.

"The hell you aren't."

"You're both breaking the law, helping to supply his habit." There was no beating around the bush. She knew as well as he did that Brett had accompanied Lonnie on a search for heroin to satisfy his body's craving for the drug.

"We're doin' our best to keep him safe and off the streets. They don't give drug addicts a slap on the wrist and send them on their way round here, you know. If the Thai police pick him up he's looking at hard time."

"That's not the point. You're helping him to kill himself." She watched his face carefully. Surely, he understood how precious life was. He must have seen it cut short too often, as she had. His eyes were bleak, his expression carefully guarded. He ran his fingers through the short, wiry curls of his night-black hair. "Can't you get him into some kind of rehabilitation?"

"Maybe you should be askin' Brett these questions."

"I . . . I can't."

"Then I'll tell ya, so you don't go blamin' him for what Lonnie's like." His Georgia accent grew more pronounced. "Brett's got him in rehab programs, good ones, expensive ones. Three of 'em in the last five years alone. It don't work. He's been hooked too long. For him, it's the only thing that can keep back the past. It ain't gonna be the heroin that kills Lonnie Smalley. It's the war. Even if it takes thirty years to do it, it'll still be the war. Lonnie was too young and too scared and he got hurt too bad to ever get over it. And if you don't understand, then you ain't the woman I thought you were."

"I understand." She thought of Micah and the nightmares in his past . . . and her own. Rachel stood up so suddenly her cotton skirt swirled around her knees. "Lonnie's your friend. In Thailand, if you believe as the Thais do, that makes his health and happiness your responsibility."

"Ain't no one knows that more than Brett. Till the day he dies, he'll believe he's responsible for what happened to Lonnie, 'cause he was his commanding officer. The boy was too young and too green for the kind of missions we were on, but he was the only medic we had. Lonnie did his best to keep the guys alive but most of the time it wasn't enough. He just couldn't take it. Brett's taken care of him ever since. Only there ain't no one to take care of the colonel, except me. We don't need no more complications in our lives.''

"I don't intend to be one." There was no mistaking his meaning. Rachel raised her chin and looked straight into his dark, angry eyes, but he was staring off in the direction of the bedroom where Ahnle slept, not looking at her.

"You already are. Both of you." He turned and stalked out of the room. At the doorway he stopped, twisted his head to look back at her. "Look, I'm sorry I said that. What's between you and Tiger is none of my damned business."

"There isn't anything between us," Rachel said, just a bit too forcefully.

"Yeah, then y'all forget I said anythin'." He didn't sound convinced.

"Billy," Rachel held out her hand. "I do understand about Lonnie. I just wish things could be different, that's all."

"They aren't," Billy said, and left the room.

IT WAS ALMOST 2:00 a.m. The night had cooled down but it was still warm as a midsummer evening back home. Brett couldn't sleep. He gave up pacing around the living room and stepped through the French doors into the garden. Billy was staying with Lonnie the rest of the night, making sure he didn't wander off and get himself mugged or go out looking for another hit to help prolong that first rush of pleasure and ward off the crash that was sure to follow. When he thought about it too much, he hated himself for not being able to halt his friend's slide into oblivion. He'd tried so hard and so long to keep them all safe and it hadn't been enough.

He stopped in the shadows to light his pipe, to shut out the past and the nagging sense of defeat that always came with thoughts of the war. Smoke curled upward in the heavy night air, the aroma of tobacco overpowering the scents of jasmine and honeysuckle.

"Brett? Is that you?" Rachel's voice came from the deeper shadows surrounding the grotto near the spirit house. He didn't answer her for a long moment because he couldn't read the underlying emotion in her voice and he wasn't ready to confront her censure. A woman with Rachel's strong ideals wouldn't condone his behavior in supplying drugs to Lonnie. He didn't blame her. He could barely condone it himself. *Except that you did what you had to do to keep a friend alive.* He hesitated, then stepped forward into the small pool of shifting light, near the fountain, cast by a stone lantern that Nog lighted every clear night.

"You ought to be asleep," he said, watching her shadow dance across the moon-spangled water. "It's been a rough day."

He saw her shake her head, starlight catching in the silvery highlights of her hair. "I can't sleep. Maybe I'm too tired."

"Nog's wife has a great home remedy for that. Would you like me to have her brew you a cup?"

"No," she said firmly. "They've been so kind and helpful already. I wouldn't think of waking them at this late hour."

He glanced at his watch. "You're right, it's later, even, than I thought. I lost track of the time."

"Brett." She spoke his name again. "Is Lonnie all right?"

"Yes." *He's safe and off the streets. That's as all right as he'll ever be.* He braced himself for what she would say next. She surprised him by changing the subject.

"I'm glad." There was a little pause. "I want to thank you for what you did for me this afternoon."

He didn't answer, pretending to be busy relighting his pipe. He didn't want to start an argument by reminding her that she'd disobeyed his orders, putting herself, as well as Ahnle and Lonnie, in danger.

"I know I was wrong going off on my own that way." She moved out of the shadows toward him as she spoke. "And I was wrong allowing Lonnie to go with me. But sometimes I can't stop myself from rushing ahead. I can't sit back and wait while others take the risk."

"Is that why you volunteered to go to Camp Twelve during the cholera outbreak?"

"How do you know about that?"

"Billy checked in at the camp one day last summer. Doctor Reynard told him where you had gone."

"I didn't go running into danger," she said, tilting her head back to bring her gaze level with his. Although she held his look with steady regard, there was a shadow of hesitation, of withholding, in her blue-gray eyes. Or perhaps it was a trick of the light? "I took every precaution, for myself and Ahnle." There was no hesitation in her voice. It was possible he had imagined the other. "There was an epidemic in a village near the hospital where I was stationed in Nam years ago. Most of the young volunteers at Camp Six had never come across the disease, thank God. I wasn't being quixotic. I made the practical choice."

He shook his head. "It was a brave and foolish thing to do just to get out of keeping a date with me."

She looked startled, then smiled delightfully, the darkness receding from her eyes. "You're teasing me. You know I went because they needed me."

"You were running away from me," Brett insisted. "Admit it, I scared you with that remark about being alone together that day we met at the camp gate." His worry and guilt over Lonnie's addiction began to recede. The ever-present anxiety over his scheme to relieve Khen Sa of his opium also faded. For the time being, he was only a man, alone with a fascinating and desirable woman in the timeless peace and beauty of a Chinese garden beneath a tropical moon.

"I don't know if I would have come to Bangkok in June," she answered with the honesty he found so intriguing, if discomfiting. She wasn't looking directly at him now, but staring at the top button of his shirt. He wondered what her lips would feel like brushing across his chest. She raised her eyes slowly, as if sensing his thoughts. She tilted her head sideways and the coquettish smile faded from her lips. She was suddenly totally serious. "I didn't relocate myself into the midst of a possible cholera epidemic merely to avoid being alone with you. I'm not suicidal, only confused."

Brett caught her hands in his as she seemed about to move past him and retreat once again into the shadows. "What confuses you, Rachel?"

"You do," she whispered. Her expression held a question and just a hint of passion buried so deeply within her, he wondered if she was aware of it yet herself.

"Do you ever question yourself?" Rachel asked suddenly. "Is the successful businessman I see standing before me now, the soldier of fortune I met that night in a ruined jungle temple, complete and whole within himself? You're the same, yet different here, somehow, in a way I can't explain. Can you go from one life-style to the other with no shifting of values, or does it tear you up inside?"

"We all conform to some extent to the environment around us. Rachel, I . . ." He didn't know what to say next. There was so little, really, he could say.

She lifted her fingers to his lips. "Shhh." Her skin was cool and smooth, her fingers scented with the petals of flowers. "I don't want to know. I'm tired of always trying to be rational, of weighing each decision I make, of considering and reconsidering the consequences of every word I speak."

"There are very few times in life we can live so heedlessly and not be held responsible for our actions," Brett replied. He knocked the tobacco out of his pipe and ground the coals beneath the heel of his shoe. He knew how she felt. God, how many times had he felt the same?

"Maybe tonight is one of those times?" she said in a small, quiet voice. "I don't care what you've done in the past, Brett. You had your reasons, I imagine, just as I had mine. I don't see everything in black and white the way you think I do, the way everyone expects me to. I know there's a lot of shading, degrees of right and wrong. I'm not asking you to explain why you are the way you are.''

"I couldn't if I wanted to." And he did want to. He was tempted to tell her everything. He'd never cared what others thought of him. During the war, he'd made the decisions necessary to keep himself and his men alive. After the war, he'd attempted on his own to correct some of the wrongs that had been done to Ahnle's people and others like them, when the U.S. pulled out of Vietnam and left them to fend for themselves. In a lot of instances that meant arming them against their enemies. He'd done that without a qualm. Micah understood what drove him and always had. He wondered if Rachel would understand, also, but he couldn't find the courage to tell her. Instead, he took her in his arms.

She didn't pull away from him, as he half feared she would. She stood quietly as he held her, then slowly, reluctantly, as though she were fighting against herself, her arms crept around his waist and she pressed closer. His breath caught in his chest, the earth tilted on its axis, then righted itself slowly as he absorbed the sweet, reluctant promise of her body. He tipped her chin up with his knuckles so that he could see her face. Her skin was pale, ivory in the moonlight. Her eyes were closed, her breathing shallow and quick. She trembled against him and he felt her resistance and her desire, like a heartbeat echoing his own, a faint, steady counterpoint beneath the fear.

"Don't be afraid," he said in a husky voice that sounded strange to his own ears. He hadn't asked Micah the details of her long imprisonment, but he knew she couldn't have escaped either physical or emotional abuse at the hands of her captors. Her scars would be deep and lasting. "I don't intend to ask anything of you that you're not prepared to give." He stayed still so as not to frighten her more. She was like some small, exotic bird in his arms. One wrong move, one jarring note, would be enough to send her winging away from him forever.

"It's been so long." Tears welled in her eyes, drowning the moon in their blue-gray depths. "I haven't been in a man's arms in years." She shuddered, closed her eyes, fighting off the past, then opened them again. "It's been much longer than that since I've wanted to be."

"All I'm asking for is a kiss." One crystal tear escaped and rolled down her cheek. He wiped it away with the edge of his thumb. He lowered his head so that their lips almost touched. "I've waited months for it, you know."

She moaned a little as his mouth closed over hers, a sigh somewhere between desperation and surrender. Brett held her close, tasted her lips, inhaled the delicate herbal fragrance of her hair, clean and shining once more. He didn't tighten his hold on her slender waist, although he was amazed at the effort of will it cost him to keep from doing so. He wasn't used to being this aroused by a kiss.

Rachel shuddered as she felt his body's reaction and he cursed his inability to control the surge of passion that swept through his veins. He ignored her hands as they pushed against his chest but kissed her again, not so gently this time, urging her mouth to open beneath his, teasing her lips with the tip of his tongue until she melted against him and returned his kiss with warmth and passion of her own.

When it was over she laid her head against his shoulder. She was breathing heavily and he could feel her heart pounding against his chest. "I have to go," she said so softly he strained to hear the words.

"Don't run away from me." He stroked her hair and felt her draw a deep, trembling breath.

"I'm not ready for this. I may never be ready for this." He caught her hand in his and wouldn't let her go.

"Don't be afraid." Brett could only keep repeating those words to help her banish the terror of the past, a talisman against memories that only time could erase.

Rachel shook her head. She stayed within the circle of his arms, quiet but trembling. "I'm not afraid of you," she said very softly. "I'm afraid of myself. I'm afraid of what I'm feeling because I haven't let myself feel anything like this for so long." Another tear rolled down her cheek and soaked into the cream-colored linen of his shirt. "Can you understand? Feeling means coming back to life and that hurts. Sometimes it hurts too much to bear."

"Don't think, don't try to reason it out. Isn't that what you said you wanted earlier? Go ahead. For a little while just feel. Nothing more, nothing less." He bent his head to kiss her again and tasted the salt of tears on her lips. Hatred for the men who had done this to her welled up inside him so strongly he could taste the bitterness of it at the back of his throat. Some of that anger must have communicated itself through his kiss.

"Brett. No." She pushed at him in a flurry of panic, but he held her still, his hands just below the soft curve of her breasts, his thumbs moving softly, caressingly against them.

"Shhh, be still, Rachel. Only as far as you want to go, only what you want me to do. I promised you that." She sucked in her breath and clamped her hands over his wrists to stop him. He ignored her silent plea, increasing the pressure, grazing her nipples with the pad of his thumb. "Don't think, don't remember. I'm only asking for what you're willing to give. No more. No less."

"I can't give you what a man wants from a woman. I can't."

"Then this is enough." He moved his hands, skimming the soft cotton of her blouse to cup her breasts. Her bra was as flimsy as her blouse. He could feel her nipples tighten beneath his touch. She strained against him then, pushing close, winding her arms around his neck to bring him closer still.

"Kiss me again," she said, looking up at him with tear-bright eyes. "Help me feel again, help me remember, a little, what love is like."

CHAPTER EIGHT

RACHEL LAY QUIETLY, listening to the sound of Brett's even breathing in the predawn darkness. She turned her head on the pillow to look at him in the dim glow of a night-light shining through the open bathroom door. She had never thought she would lie beside a man again and be comforted by the warmth of his body, and aroused by the promise of his love and strength in the night. She closed her eyes as a faint nightmare image of a faceless man's hands and body pushed for recognition. *She would not remember.*

She opened her eyes again, willing away the terror. As she watched, a slight frown drew Brett's brows together. She let her eyes wander lower over the arrogant jut of his nose, the line of his jaw. His skin was bronzed, stretched taut over well-defined muscles. A pulse beat slow and strong at the base of his throat. Lower, the silver tracery of old scars snaked across his shoulder and disappeared in the dull gold hair covering his chest. Her eyes, disobeying her will, followed that arrowing line of gold to his belt buckle, then skittered away, obedient at last, returning to the endlessly fascinating study of his face.

He slept with the same fierce intensity of purpose that characterized everything he did. As though he used sleep as a tool, renewing his body and mind to face whatever challenges the new day might bring. Certainly he didn't sleep to escape life as she'd done so often in the past, nor did he sleep to court dreams.

A sound from the hallway caught at the ragged edges of her thoughts. She sat up, slowly pulling her blouse together, buttoning the buttons with fumbling fingers as her mind refused to let go of the memory of Brett's mouth on her nipples and his hands on her breasts. She had hated him a little for proving her body could still be pleasured by a man's touch. Even now, hours later, she shivered with the sheer arousing power of that memory as she swung her feet over the edge of the low bed.

A slight ghost-like shadow flitted down the hall ahead of her. Rachel furrowed her brow, trying to bring the figure into focus in the near darkness. "Ahnle?" she whispered so quietly she didn't think the girl heard her at first. "Stop."

Ahnle halted and turned very slowly as Rachel caught up with her and urged her into what turned out to be the kitchen. Outside, a security light shone through the window, illuminating a small rectangle of glazed tile floor at their feet. The girl was dressed in the clothes Nog's wife had provided for her, a plain, dark skirt and short-sleeved, pale yellow blouse. She carried her sandals, also provided by the servant, in her hand. Her long, gloriously black hair was twisted into a haphazard knot on top of her head.

"Where are you going?" Rachel asked under her breath. She didn't know where Nog and his wife slept, so she kept her voice pitched low.

"Home," Ahnle whispered back. There were tears in her voice as well as on her face.

"Back to the camp?" Rachel asked, somewhat bewildered.

Ahnle shook her head. "Home," she repeated. "I must go home."

"You can't." Rachel spoke sharply, too sharply. She lowered her voice to a whisper once again. "Your village is in Laos. There's been a lot of unrest along the border these past weeks. You know that. Father Dolph read the warning from the government last month at the staff meeting, don't you remember?" Had Ahnle's recent unnerving experiences affected her more than she had realized? Rachel didn't know what to think.

"I don't care," Ahnle insisted. "I must go home." She clasped her sandals so tightly to her chest that her knuckles gleamed pale in the yellow glow of light.

"Why?" Rachel asked the question to gain time to order her thoughts, but she already knew the answer.

"My son. Now he is disgraced twice over. Chengla and his wife will not want him. They will think they have been tricked into taking him if there is no money for them."

"We can work something out." Rachel tried to sound encouraging.

The girl shook her head. "My brother will have to make good or he will lose much merit. I must return and take my baby away before he comes back to the Teak Doll and finds me gone from there." In her anxiety she spoke in Hlông and Rachel answered in that language.

"You will have to give Chengla and his wife something for their kindness in fostering your son."

"I have this." Ahnle held up a crumpled one-hundred-*baht* note. "That man, the *farang* with yellow hair, pushed it into my clothes when I was dancing. Other men did that, too, but the owner of the bar always took the money away. Is it enough?"

Rachel looked at the note consideringly. In Ahnle's remote village, the money, less than five American dollars, might be enough to allow Chengla and his wife to save face and return Ahnle's son to her.

But she had nothing for the long journey north. And Rachel, herself, had very little more.

"It is enough for Chengla and his wife, perhaps. But not to go home. It is many days' walk." Rachel tried to translate the hundreds of miles into terms Ahnle could relate to.

"My brother brought me here on a..." There was no Hlông word for bus. Rachel supplied it in English, all the while straining her ears for sounds of awakening from the other occupants of the house. "I know buses go all the way to Chiang Khong where my aunt lives." Ahnle held out the money. "This is not enough for both the journey and for Chengla and his wife?" Fresh tears glittered in her dark eyes.

Rachel shook her head. "Ahnle," she said, hesitating. "I will help...."

"What's going on here?" Light flooded the room. Rachel ducked her head, lifting her hand to shield her eyes from the sudden brightness. Brett stood in the doorway in his bare feet, his slacks riding low on slender hips. Ahnle took a step closer to Rachel, closer to the familiarity and security she represented.

"Ahnle woke up. She's still a little confused. She's afraid her brother might find her," Rachel said, sticking as close to the truth as she could. She'd been doing that for almost two years now, skirting the truth about a lot of things. She was getting very good at telling half-lies.

Brett didn't come any closer. His blue eyes were narrowed, focusing on the trembling girl at Rachel's side. "She needs something to eat. Nog will be starting breakfast soon. Ahnle," he raised his voice very slightly and spoke carefully and slowly in Thai. "Why don't you go back to your room for a little while, let Rachel and me get bathed and dressed and we will share tea and rice at my table."

Ahnle glanced pleadingly at Rachel. "Do as he says," Rachel said in Hlông. "I will come with you. Wherever you go." Hope gleamed in the ebony depths of the girl's eyes.

"To the gate of my village?"

"Yes. But first we must do as he asks." She smiled just a little. "He has my shoes."

Ahnle giggled. "Thank you," she said in English, bowing formally to Brett. He returned the salute and stepped out of the doorway, still watching the girl. He waited for Rachel to precede him down the hallway, back to his room, to the bed they'd shared, yet hadn't made love in.

Dawn was coming up over the city. But the view of the garden faded abruptly into darkness when Brett switched on a bedside lamp. "Your things are here," he said, indicating her *yaam* and the clothes she'd been wearing the day before, now neatly cleaned and pressed. "Nog's wife brought them in last night."

Rachel felt a stain of color surge into her cheeks and was amazed to realize she could still blush.

"She evidently decided I'd be able to get you into my bed a lot sooner than I did." He continued to watch her closely. Rachel looked down at her bare feet.

"Brett . . ." She felt torn. Part of her wanted to be here with him, part of her wanted to be with Ahnle, where her duty lay. And part of her wanted to be somewhere dark and safe and quiet, where she didn't have to face any choices, especially those thrust on her by her reawakening body and its needs. There were too many demons at large inside her soul. She didn't want to remember why they were there. Brett opened her up, made her remember. It frightened her.

"Shhh." He took her in his arms and her senses swam with the heat of his nearness and the hard strength of his body so close to hers. A low, coiling ache of desire began deep inside her and she pressed against him, ignoring the clamoring warnings of her brain and the panicked beat of memories in the icy darkness at the center of her heart. "It's too early in the morning for long-winded discussions." His mouth was so close that his breath stirred her hair. "It's too early for anything but crawling back between the sheets and taking up where we left off last night."

She jerked away, but he'd been expecting her to bolt and tightened his arms around her. "I know. You're not ready for anything more. But I can dream, can't I?"

"Dreaming is sometimes the most dangerous thing of all."

"Maybe that's why we belong together, Rachel, because we know we can't trust our dreams." He kissed her then and she responded with every fiber of her being, despite the warring emotions swirling around inside her. If he had pulled her down with him on his hard, narrow bed, she couldn't have denied him whatever he wanted of her. And then it would be too late.

Brett stopped kissing her, looked down into her eyes for a long moment, then rested his forehead against hers. "When you're ready for me, Rachel, I'll be waiting."

"Don't say that." Her voice came out all squeaky and broken into little bits. She swallowed hard against the sudden constriction in her throat. "Don't say you'll wait. I might never be ready."

She felt him shake his head very slightly. His lips were still close to hers; she had only to tip her head slightly and their mouths would meet again. She resisted the urge and found it harder than she'd imagined it would be.

"You'll be ready, someday. But not today." He stepped away, leaving her feeling absurdly cold and forlorn. "I'll get cleaned up. You can use the shower in Ahnle's room. We'll have breakfast and you two can do some shopping. We'll make an early night of it and tomorrow, when you're both rested, we'll start making arrangements for Ahnle's future. How does that sound?"

The temptation to agree to the plan was so great Rachel bit her lip to keep from doing so. She couldn't let herself fall any further into his debt, or under his spell. She owed Brett Jackson too much already, and, even more dangerously, she could too easily remember how to fall in love with him. That was the last thing she could afford to do because then she would remember everything about herself she'd betrayed to stay alive.

"Rachel? Are you okay?" He held her at arm's length, watched her without smiling.

No, she wanted to scream. *Help me, I'll never be all right again.*

"I'm fine. I just need a shower to wash away the cobwebs." She tried to smile and succeeded. He looked as if he wanted to kiss her again so she stepped back hastily.

"Don't disappear on me," he said, and Rachel couldn't be sure he wasn't serious. "I promised to show you Bangkok, remember? We'll have that few days alone I asked you for. Just the two of us, at least at night."

She wished he hadn't said that. It made her hands shake and her toes curl when he talked like that. "Go take your shower."

He walked into the bathroom and closed the door. Rachel stayed where she was, not even turning around when she heard Ahnle in the doorway. She couldn't stay. That much was obvious.

"Rachel?"

"I'm ready." She sat down on the edge of the bed and slipped on her shoes before looking at the girl. Her heart was pounding with anticipation and with dread.

"Do we go now?"

"Yes." Her gaze slid to the bedside table. Beside the telephone was Brett's wallet, a money clip and a set of car keys. "We can go now." She picked up the money clip and marveled at the amount of cash it contained. She slipped out some of the bills and wrote an IOU on the pad by the phone. For a moment she hesitated, her hand hovering over the car keys. Then she picked them up, as well. Might as well be hanged for a sheep as a lamb.

"I do not understand," Ahnle said, casting anxious glances at the bathroom door where the sound of running water from the shower could be heard.

"Nothing. We must go. Quickly." Rachel folded her clothes into the *yaam,* pocketed the money and the car keys and turned her back on the room she'd shared with Brett.

She couldn't explain the forces that drove her any more than he had been able to explain himself to her. All she knew was that she was bound to Ahnle and because of that bonding, she must help her recover her child. It meant going back into the jungle alone, without Brett's help. It meant facing the hill country of Laos that had haunted her days and nights for fifteen years. But at least those terrors were familiar, the skills needed to fight them easily recalled. In so many ways, this journey was less dangerous and frightening than the one Brett had asked her to make with him.

BRETT STOOD CONCEALED behind the beaded curtains that separated the private section of the Lemongrass from the main bar and dining room as the evening dinner crowd began to arrive.

"Man, somethin' smells good in the kitchen tonight," Billy said, coming up behind him. "How's the room?"

"Usual Saturday night crowd." Brett watched as Ponchoo escorted group after group of well-dressed, well-heeled Europeans, Japanese and Americans to their tables.

"The kid's got the touch." Billy was as proud of Ponchoo as Brett was. Twelve years ago, when they'd opened the restaurant on a shoestring budget, Ponchoo had been a snotty-nosed street urchin, picking pockets and panhandling on the street outside. Neither of the men had wanted to see him hauled away by the police, so they'd offered him a job washing dishes. Ponchoo had been smart enough to see a good deal when it was offered to him and headed into the kitchen.

"He told me he had a 3.9 GPA this semester," Billy announced as proudly as any father. "We'll get this place a five-star rating before you know it." Ponchoo was studying hotel and restaurant management part-time at Thammasat University. He spoke English with an American accent and ran the dining-room staff with an iron hand.

"How's the newest member of the team working out?" Brett asked.

"Not too bad," Billy replied. "The little Chinese girl is a real worker." Over the years they'd helped other street kids work their way into the mainstream of Thai life. Their newest employee was an ethnic Chinese girl Lonnie had dragged home from a massage parlor where she was being trained to replace her mother, who, at twenty-seven, was considered over the hill.

"Well, well, here comes Ambassador Singleton. You two had any heart-to-heart talks lately?"

"No. But we're going to have to get together very soon." Brett watched as the ambassador and his party were seated at one of the prime tables near the windows overlooking the Chao Phraya River and the city beyond.

"I take it it's time to call in the big boys?" Billy asked with no more curiosity than if he were inquiring about tomorrow's weather report.

"We're going all the way to the top." If Alf Singleton couldn't talk his Thai counterpart in the palace into delivering the rest of the money he needed, Brett would probably have to mortgage the restaurant to come up with it. He wasn't about to let Khen Sa and one hundred million dollars' worth of heroin slip away, if he could help it.

"We better come out of this lookin' like the heroes we are."

Brett merely grunted.

"The police found Lonnie's car," Billy said a few moments later.

"Where?" Brett swung away from the scene beyond the beaded curtain. Billy's hair and shirt were wet from an early-evening thunderstorm. Behind them, the increasing noise of conversation in half a dozen languages masked their words.

"On a side street near Hualamphong Station."

"They took the train north?"

"Looks like it. There was no sign of foul play. The old bug was locked with the keys inside."

Brett ran his hand through his hair, stirring the heavy gold waves with agitated fingers. At least she had left the city safely. "They should have been back at the camp two days ago. Where the hell are they?" He could read most men and their intentions like a book, but Rachel's actions were a complete mystery to him.

"Your guess is as good as mine." He felt Billy watching him, and for the first time in twenty years, he deliberately avoided confiding in his friend. That's what falling for a woman could do to a man, twist him all up inside until he didn't know whether he was coming or going.

He'd known Rachel was frightened and confused by the feelings he'd aroused in her the night she'd spent in his arms. Yet, surely there was more to her disappearance than a reluctance to enter into a physical relationship with him? It was out of character for her to keep running away. In most other circumstances she'd faced her challenges, even rushed headlong to meet them, regardless of the consequences. Except with him. There had to be something more, something about her he didn't know.

"My guess," Billy said, breaking the silence that stretched out between them, "is that they're headed for some other up-country destination besides Father Dolph's camp. As far as I can figure it, the only logical place that could be is Ahnle's village, across the border in Laos."

"What the hell would they do that for?" Brett growled. He'd been angry, scared, frustrated, most of the time all three at once, since he'd walked out of his shower three days ago and found that Rachel and Ahnle had cleared out of his house. They'd vanished between one minute and the next, taking Lonnie's wreck of a VW and most of his pocket money, leaving nothing but an IOU, signed with Rachel's initials. He didn't know what he'd want to do first when he found her again, kiss her or wring her neck for not trusting him enough to ask for his help.

"Who knows with women? But you can bet it's somethin' important. I remember her face that first night Lonnie and me came across her and that embassy flunky, Bartley, stuck in the mud up there in the hills. Rachel's scared to death of that jungle. She wouldn't go back there unless it was for a damned good reason."

"You're right." Brett made his decision. "See if you can get a call through to Father Dolph. I'll tell him what we know about the car. And this time he damned well better not beat around the bush telling us what he knows, or I'll have his hide, priest or no priest."

"MCKENDRICK HERE." Micah waited for the caller on the other end of the line to identify himself. Outside, an early November snowstorm wrapped the cabin in white isolation. Inside, it was warm and cozy and behind him, Carrie was playing with their son in front of the fireplace. The static on the line sounded as if the connection stretched halfway around the world. A shiver ran up his spine that had nothing to do with the north wind howling around the cabin.

"Micah? Can you hear me?"

"I hear you," Micah said tersely, his suspicions confirmed even before he heard the caller's name.

"It's Tiger Jackson."

"What's wrong?" There was no reason for his old friend to call, except with bad news.

"Rachel's disappeared. She's been gone almost a week."

"How did it happen?" Micah felt like shouting into the telephone. Had there been a border raid? Had she been kidnapped by bandits?

"The last I saw of her was at my place in Bangkok. She stole my friend's car and most of my pocket money and took off north on the train with a young Hlông girl she'd befriended at the camp."

"Damn." He punched the top of the desk with his fist. Behind him, Carrie stopped playing with the baby and scooped him up onto her lap. He turned slowly, knowing the anguish he was feeling would show plainly on his face. "What the hell was she doing in Bangkok? What the hell was she doing with you?"

"It's a long story."

The connection wasn't getting any better. Micah tried to figure out the time differential. He glanced at his watch. Four o'clock on a lousy early November afternoon. That meant it must be about four in the morning—tomorrow—in Bangkok.

"Father Dolph, at the camp, thinks she's probably headed into Laos, back to the girl's village to help her retrieve her baby son." Surprisingly, something like anger laced Brett's words. "I'm sorry, buddy. I didn't know about the girl's baby. Father Dolph seemed to think it was none of my business at first. I would have stopped them if I'd had any idea what they were up to."

"You couldn't know, man. And I doubt if you could have stopped my sister if you'd tried. She's got this thing about kids." He glanced lovingly at his wife and son, the baby Rachel had delivered, here, at the cabin. He thought of the way she'd risked her life to save Annie's daughter, Leah, when her Vietnamese mother had attempted to abduct her. Of the baby Rachel had lost so long ago. "I'd only be surprised if she didn't try to help the girl."

"Khen Sa is on the move in those hills." Brett's words were hard-edged, matter-of-fact. Micah didn't expect to hear anything else. Emotions got you killed in Tiger's line of work.

Carrie had come forward, holding their son to be comforted and to give Micah comfort, as well. He held her close in the circle of his arm.

"Micah, you still there? This is a damned lousy connection." Once again, an uncharacteristic lacing of anger underscored Brett's words.

"Yes, I'm here. The trouble's probably on this end. It's snowing to beat the band up here. Always plays hell with the phone lines."

"I just wanted you to know I'll do everything I can to get her back to Father Dolph safe and sound, you know that, man." Micah didn't for a moment doubt that he would. "I'll call again as soon as I have some news."

"Tiger, wait."

The line went dead.

"Damn." Micah stared at the phone, then cupped the receiver in his hand as he began flipping through the phone book.

"Who are you calling now?" Carrie asked. His son watched him also, as she held him in her arms. His eyes were warm and bright with lively intelligence. Micah loved him, loved Carrie more each day.

"The airline," he said, blessing her for not asking for details just yet, for letting him act first and talk over the decision later. "Think you can manage here alone for a few days until Reuben can get back up here from Ann Arbor?"

"Of course." She dismissed his question with the disdain it deserved. "Micah, where are you going?" she asked more quietly, her voice once again filled with concern.

"Bangkok," he said, still holding her close against him, "by way of Chicago. This is one time having a brother with Simon's contacts is going to come in handy."

CHAPTER NINE

RACHEL STOOD ON THE dusty main street of Chiang Khong and watched the evil-smelling diesel bus they'd been riding in for so many long hours drive off. It was a hot, muggy morning, the third since they'd run away from Brett's house. She wondered briefly if he'd found Lonnie Smalley's VW, but she was really too tired to think about it much. She'd tried very hard to park the car where it would be safe and not too difficult to find before they boarded the train north. At the time, it had seemed the best thing to do.

She stopped thinking of what was done and beyond repairing and looked around her. Several people had stopped outside businesses and shops to stare, politely and unobtrusively, but curiously, nonetheless. Their arrival, it seemed, was creating a small stir of interest. There had been only three other passengers to get off the bus, all men. Several others, including two women with live chickens headed for market, had boarded the bus for the return trip to Chiang Rai. The male passengers had already disappeared into one of the hotels, leaving Rachel and Ahnle alone in front of the bus stop.

Once Chiang Khong had been a busy border crossing into Laos, a half mile away across the Mekong River. But the Pathet Lao had closed the border years ago and there were few boats on the river. Now the entire town appeared as dusty and dejected as its main street.

"We should move out of the street," Ahnle said, staring at the potholed pavement beneath her feet. It wouldn't do to draw too much attention to themselves.

"Yes," Rachel agreed. They were both wearing dark cotton slacks and light-colored blouses, bought in the market in Chiang Rai. Flat straw hats covered their hair. Rachel wore sunglasses as well, to hide her eyes. "Do you know where the home of your mother's sister and her son is located?" She spoke carefully in Hlông. Ahnle looked so exhausted, Rachel was afraid she might collapse, the result of two and a half days of hard travel, added to the strain and fear of the week before.

The girl looked around her in confusion. "It is near the river," she said at last. "My cousin brought us here by boat. It was a fishing boat with a motor." She furrowed her brow, trying to remember. "He met us at a place along the river. It was very early in the morning and I was very cold. Everyone was afraid. If a border patrol found us, or bandits . . ." She left the sentence unfinished. "I hid my face. I did not like crossing the river. It is very big and very deep. No one in my family could swim." She looked up and down the street, undecided.

"If we walk toward the river, do you think you can recognize your cousin's house?"

"I will try." Ahnle shouldered her *yaam,* filled with supplies and sweaters and blankets they'd bought along with the clothes they wore. She started walking in the direction of the river. "We stayed here for two hands of days. Then men from the government came. They said we must go to the camp, that we could not stay here with my aunt. We could not say no to them or they would send us back." She was quiet for a long while, looking at houses and looking into the past, also, Rachel suspected. "What if my cousin will not take us across the river?" she asked.

"Then we'll find another way. I didn't commit grand larceny in a foreign country to give up now," Rachel said grimly, as she shifted the weight of her woven bag higher on her shoulder. She ached with fatigue, every joint in her body protesting the long, tiring days of travel and almost sleepless nights.

She knew they should stay here in Chiang Khong, at one of the cheap hotels, if not with Ahnle's relatives, and rest. Yet, neither of them was prepared to accept the delay. Ahnle's brother would surely be on their trail by now, and Rachel knew they couldn't take the risk of allowing him to catch up with them.

Not Ahnle's brother—or an equally angry Brett Jackson.

"I do not know how much opium my uncle offered him to cross the river for us. My brother bargained for our passage," Ahnle said. Rachel had heard the whole story before, of course, on the bus ride north, but she listened patiently. It had come in disjointed bits and pieces that first time, as they pored over a map of the Golden Triangle Rachel had purchased at Chiang Mai, trying to pinpoint as closely as possible the area of Ahnle's village in Laos. Anything she might remember by telling the story again was worth listening to.

"It doesn't matter how much opium your uncle paid for the crossing. We haven't got any." As always, Rachel tried to empty her mind of anger toward the hill people, who grew opium poppies as they had for generations only as a medium of exchange, nothing more. It was the dealers, the middlemen and pushers who made life miserable for so many, not subsistence farmers, who only followed age-old patterns of trade and barter.

"Do we have enough money?" Ahnle's voice was barely a whisper. They had heard others talking on the trip north, stories of bandits and of Khen Sa coming down from Burma to deal for the opium crop and the danger there was to villagers and strangers alike, traveling even on government buses, when he was in the area.

"We're doing fine," Rachel reassured her. Actually, they had a little over a thousand *baht*. About fifty dollars. Not much, but it would have to do. She was hoping in the depressed economy of Chiang Khong, she'd be able to get Ahnle's cousin traded down to a reasonable figure, not from family feeling—he sounded every bit as opportunistic as Ahnle's half brother—but because she was offering something even more valuable than raw opium: cold, hard cash.

They trudged through the muggy heat, Ahnle peering carefully at each rickety house, all on stilts, most leaning at precarious angles along the water's edge. The air was filled with the heavy smells of river mud, garbage and raw sewage, relieved sweetly and unexpectedly by the occasional scent of honeysuckle or jasmine. Small children laughed and ran beneath the houses, ran in and out of the river, naked and care-free, chasing scrawny chickens and being chased by equally scrawny pigs.

A hundred yards farther on the village began to peter out. The houses were farther apart here, even more dilapidated, the children quieter, as though they didn't have the energy to run and play. Even the pigs and chickens and occasional goat were quiet, dispir-ited. Rachel shivered despite the heat. This was where the hill people and Lao refugees made their homes, slightly apart from the rest of the village, balanced precariously on the edge of poverty.

"There," Ahnle said suddenly, her voice filled with relief. "That is the sister of my mother. There, work-ing in her garden." She hurried forward, stopping outside the rickety fence of bamboo stakes and bowed low, dropping to her knees to show respect to her aunt, who was kneeling among a row of cabbages. "Mother's sister," she said, steepling her fingers be-fore her in greeting. "It is I, Ahnle. I have come from the missionary's camp."

"Sister's daughter," replied the wizened old woman, who Rachel knew was probably only a de-cade older than she was herself. No trace of surprise showed on her face at Ahnle's sudden, unexpected appearance on her doorstep. "Do the spirits leave you well?"

"I am well, Aunt, no evil spirit troubles my body."

"Good. But why do you come here, Niece? I have nothing extra to spare for you."

"I ask nothing of you, Aunt. I seek your son, Bohan." Ahnle continued to stare at the ground between them, not at her aunt's weather-beaten, almost toothless face.

"He is within." She gestured with her head at the house behind her. "What do you seek from him?" Her straw hat shadowed her face; her voice held no inflection.

"I...I must return to my village."

"For the child?" The older woman's expression didn't change. She never even looked in Rachel's direction, although Rachel, too, had dropped to her knees to show the proper respect to one older and wiser than herself.

"You know of my son?" Ahnle bowed lower, then straightened her shoulders and raised her eyes almost level with her aunt's, showing that she considered herself, in this matter at least, to be her equal.

"We know. Your brother came here when he took the child across the river."

"Was my son well?"

"A fine boy for one without ancestors." Ahnle hung her head, then lifted her chin.

"We wish to bargain for passage to the other side of the river."

"Bohan will not bargain with a girl, one who has disgraced our family." The old woman returned to her weeding, effectively dismissing Ahnle's gesture of defiance.

"I will bargain with your son, Wise Mother." Rachel removed her sunglasses and looked at Ahnle's aunt, focusing on a point at eye level, somewhere near her ear. To have made eye contact while arguing would have been interpreted as a sign of contempt.

"A *farang* woman who speaks our tongue and who knows our customs." She paused, considering. "I have heard of one such as you from the traders who sometimes come here with my son. I did not believe you existed. I thought they talked of poppy smoke dreams."

"I exist, Wise Mother."

"I will tell Bohan that you wish to see him." The old woman made a *wai*, returning Rachel's earlier greeting. "Times are hard here. He will take you across the river if you bargain with him."

"We have sufficient means to bargain, but not to be taken advantage of," Rachel said firmly, but politely.

Ahnle's aunt nodded. "Good. You will do well with him and I will remind him to show respect to my sister's spirit, even though her daughter has not." She gave Ahnle another hard glance, then nodded toward her home. "Come inside."

RACHEL AND AHNLE paused on the ridge above the tiny village of thatch-roofed huts. Smoke curled in thin, lazy spirals from holes in their roofs and from larger fires scattered around the settlement. The scent of wood smoke was heavy in the thin, humid air. Outside the dozen or so huts, women and children went about the chores of daily life. Two water buffalo were penned in a bamboo corral in the middle of the village, protected from prowling animals and marauding Pathet Lao irregulars. A few straggle-tailed chickens and tiny, Vietnamese pigs scratched and rooted under the oxen's feet. One woman was milking goats. Four or five young boys were practicing with bows and arrows, a favorite Hlông weapon.

Smaller boys and girls raced along behind one lucky youngster who was hurtling down the muddy street on what appeared to be a board with wheels attached. Their screams of laughter and delight echoed off the hills and floated upward to Rachel and Ahnle.

"Is this your village, Ahnle?" Rachel asked softly. There were no men to be seen; most likely they were off hunting in the hills around them. She was surprised they hadn't been seen and stopped already by one of the keen-eyed hunters. A small field of poppies filled the only level space around the village, while the huts clung precariously to the hillside. It was too early for the poppies to be in bloom at this altitude. The field was deserted.

"Yes," Ahnle replied. "This is my village. We have found it. We will go down, and I will speak to my uncle, the *dzoema*. He makes all the decisions in the village. He will say if I can take my son away, or not."

"Yes." Rachel's heart was pounding in her chest from excitement and anticipation. It didn't seem possible to her that the nightmare journey she'd set out on with so much dread was almost at an end. Everything had gone well. She'd bargained Ahnle's cousin down to eight hundred *baht*; three hundred when they reached Laos, the rest when they safely returned.

Crossing the river had been easy. Bohan had merely taken his boat downstream on the Thai side of the river, then angled across to the Lao side at a place where the great river narrowed and curved between marsh-lined banks. There he had replaced the Thai flag above the motor with the Pathet Lao flag, cut the engine to something like trolling speed and drifted on downstream. They met only one other boat, as rickety and unprepossessing as Bohan's, on the Lao side of the river. The fishermen in it, occupied with their lines, barely gave them a second glance.

Several kilometers below Chiang Khong, Bohan nosed the boat into a tributary stream almost completely hidden by the drooping branches of a willow-like tree, then continued upstream, fishing lines trailing astern. An hour later, somewhere near midmorning, they stopped. The stream had narrowed considerably. Along the shore the ruins of several small huts and two or three derelict rowboats were all that remained of a fishing village. Bohan guided the boat ashore.

"I go no farther," he announced, spitting dark red betel-nut juice into the water. "Pay me now."

Rachel reached into her *yaam* and produced the money, a bundle of ten-*baht* notes. If Ahnle's cousin intended to rob them and strand them on this inhospitable shore, she had no idea what she would do to stop him. She could only rely on the Hlông superstition that to harm a defenseless woman would bring the evil *phi* spirits down on you with a vengeance.

Bohan took the money without touching her and waved them out of the boat. "To find the village, follow the stream to the waterfall. Above that there is a trail, very faint. It is two days' walk for women. I will come back in five days at sunrise. Only once. If you are not here when I return you will have only the spirits to guide you back." He'd smiled then, an ugly, gap-toothed smile out of a mouth stained red from betel juice.

"And you will be five hundred *baht* poorer than you are today." Rachel refused to be cowed.

"Five sunrises." He backed away from the shore, waiting until the stream widened sufficiently to turn the boat around. The current was swift. He was soon lost to sight.

"We must go," Ahnle said.

"Yes." Rachel took a moment to look around her. She was back in Laos, a country that held only memories of hardship and terror and loss for her. Yet the scene before her was peaceful and serene. The huts were derelict, long abandoned, housing only rodents, or more horribly still, cobras. The boats were equally derelict except for one which, while just as weather-beaten as the rest, appeared to be well-patched, with a pair of oars laid beside it where it was overturned in the reeds at the stream's edge.

A smuggler's skiff, Rachel decided with a shiver of returning fear, used to transport opium out to the river where it could be transferred to larger river-worthy craft. If this was indeed an opium transfer point, it was no place to linger.

"We must go." Ahnle repeated. "Not good here." Rachel shouldered her *yaam* and started walking away from the stream into the trees.

They stayed within earshot of the water, catching glimpses now and then of the stream growing narrower and wilder as they climbed into the hills. They ate dried fruit and cheese from their stores as they walked. Darkness came early and they camped above the waterfall Bohan had described to them, in an outcropping of rocks that offered some protection, however slight, from the rare tigers, or more likely, wild boars and snakes. They rigged a tiny lean-to from a square of plastic draped across tree branches and ate boiled rice and tea they made in an aluminum pan over a fire.

Rachel fully expected the sounds of the jungle to keep her awake, the horror of other nights spent lost in the limitless rain forest to haunt her dreams, but she was wrong. She slept restlessly, it was true, because the night was cold and damp and they had only the cheap Chinese blankets from the Chiang Mai market to cover themselves. She didn't dream at all and woke with the dawn to a dreary, overcast sky and the threat of rain.

Now it was late afternoon. They followed narrow trails into the hills all day. At the top of a steep ridge they looked down to find the village Ahnle recognized as her own spread out below them on the other side. Rain clouds piled up behind the hills, ringing the far side of the valley, and thunder rumbled in the distance. The rainy season might have ended, officially, but that didn't mean the rain was gone for good.

"We go down, now," Ahnle said, leading the way. Her expression was strained and Rachel's heart ached for the anxiety she must be feeling over their upcoming confrontation with the village elders and the couple who had custody of her son. "We will go in through the spirit gate. We do not want to enter the village any other way and anger the *phi* spirits. Or my uncle."

"Certainly not." As far as Ahnle was concerned, her uncle was almost as powerful as the spirits themselves.

"Do you think my uncle will see us at once?" Ahnle pulled a square of gaily colored silk from her bag to tie over her hair. Rachel did the same.

"I hope so." As Rachel spoke it began to rain.

AHNLE SAT, HER LEGS folded under her, in the near darkness of the women's side of her brother's house. It was still raining outside, softly, as if the sky were weeping. The feeble light from a kerosene lantern cast strange, misshapen shadows on the mat walls. They had been in the village for several hours and she had not been allowed to see her uncle or her son. Her brother's second wife, with her new baby son, had welcomed her to their section of the house, but her brother's first wife had not so much as spoken a word of greeting.

The others were all asleep, including Rachel, curled up in her blanket on a mat near where Ahnle sat. In the morning her uncle would see her and hear her plea for the return of her son.

She wasn't brave and fearless as Rachel was. She would not have had the courage to stand up to the terrible men in the bar to save another as Rachel had saved her. She could not have stolen the car and the money from the dangerous man they called "Tiger," as Rachel had. She could not have come back into the jungle where she had been held prisoner for so many years to aid another. She was not nearly brave enough and it shamed her.

All she could do was speak from her heart of how much she loved her baby and wanted him with her. That would be enough.

She lay down on her woven mat and pulled the blanket close around her. A man's face crossed the dark space behind her eyelids where the spirits painted dreams and pictures and recalled you to scenes from the past; a dark face with white teeth that gleamed when he smiled. She liked the man called Billy Todd very much. He had been kind to her; he had protected her from the men in the Teak Doll. She remembered his voice in the darkness of the room in the dangerous Jackson's house that was like the palace of the Thai king to her. She had pretended to be asleep while she listened to his rough, strong voice. She wished he had touched her, stroked her hair. She reached up, touching her silk-wrapped head in surprise. A maiden shouldn't think such things. Then she remembered she was a maiden no longer, but a woman full grown. And she had no time to be thinking of men when she needed to be planning on how to regain her child.

Anua, her brother's second wife, who was two seasons younger than Ahnle, let her hold her infant while she washed the dust of the day from her elaborate silver-bangled headdress. Once a girl became a woman in the Hlông world, she almost never took it off. She even slept with it on. And baby girls wore caps from birth to accustom them to the weight and restrictions of the headdresses they would don later in life. Ahnle's brother had taken her headdress after she became pregnant. She had never seen it again. She no longer mourned its loss.

"Your son cries much," Anua had told her with a sad shake of her head, "especially at night." Chengla's fat, lazy wife was losing much of her beauty sleep.

Anua thought Chengla's wife could be persuaded to take the money to return Ahnle's son. Chengla had a new, young second wife who would surely give him a son within the year, and his fat first wife would be comforted with the silver bangles she could buy with Ahnle's gift. All Ahnle had to do was persuade her uncle that she could give her son a better life among the unbelievers.

A tear rolled down her face and she brushed it away, furious with herself. Rachel had told her time and again that she could do whatever she wanted to do in her new life. Right now, the most important thing in that life was retrieving her child from her old one. She would not give up. She would not fail. On that fierce and uncharacteristic resolve she willed herself to sleep.

"AHNLE, DAUGHTER of my younger brother's second wife." Ahnle bowed courteously to the wizened old man sitting on a pile of woven mats in the center of his four-room house, by far the grandest in the village. "You have come to petition for the return of your son, born to you by a man who was not your husband."

"Yes, Uncle, to my shame," Ahnle replied formally, in a very small voice, but Rachel sensed a new pride and determination in the girl-woman and let a small sigh of relief sift past her lips. She had woken in the middle of the night and been unable to fall asleep again from worry over the outcome of this meeting, but so far Ahnle was holding up well.

"Your brother brought the child back to us before the rains. He said you could not care for him."

"I thought I could not but now things have changed." Ahnle didn't raise her head but spoke to the floor.

"Why have things changed? You are still Hlông. They do not honor our people across the river."

"The unbelievers in the camp honor all who work hard to succeed. I have work that I do there. They pay me *baht*. I will be able to give Chengla and his wife a gift for their kindness in caring for my son all these months."

"Does she speak the truth?" he asked, turning bright, dark eyes on Rachel.

"She does, Honored Father. She is my helper. I work for the missionary's doctor at the camp."

"You have lived among us. You know our ways and our language. I believe what you say is true." He took a deep puff of his cigarette. He was very old and very wise, but whipcord strong and capable of working long days in the fields, or hunting in the hills.

"Why did you return without your brother to guide you and protect you?"

Rachel held her breath. She wasn't certain how much honor and respect Ahnle's brother commanded in the tiny village. He was, after all, almost their only contact with the outside world, the source of their gunpowder and ammunition, the canned food that supplemented their meager stores of rice and corn and wild game. He was also, most likely, the dealer for their small cash crop of opium. To make accusations against him in his absence was risky.

"My brother did not honor me." Ahnle lifted her head, still covered by the brightly patterned silk scarf, but kept her eyes averted from the old man's. "He sent me to the city. He sold me to a man who made me dance for the pleasure of strangers, with my head uncovered and my hair unbound." There was a murmur of disapproval from the women sitting along the wall, as well as from several of the men squatting around the smoky fire in the middle of the hut, their machetes and old-fashioned, muzzle-loading rifles beside them.

IT'S FUN! IT'S FREE!
AND IT COULD MAKE YOU A

MILLIONAIRE

If you've ever played scratch-off lottery tickets, you should be familiar with how our games work. On each of the first four tickets (numbered 1 to 4 in the upper right) there are Pink Metallic Strips to scratch off.

Using a coin do just that—carefully scratch the PINK strips to reveal how much each ticket could be worth if it is a winning ticket. Tickets could be worth from $10.00 to $1,000,000.00 in lifetime money.

Note, also, that each of your 4 tickets has a unique sweepstakes Lucky Number…and that's 4 chances for a **BIG WIN!**

FREE BOOKS!

At the same time you play your tickets for big prizes, you are invited to play ticket #5 for the chance to get one or more free book(s) from Harlequin. We give away free book(s) to introduce readers to the benefits of the Harlequin Reader Service®.

Accepting the free book(s) places you under no obligation to buy anything! You may keep your free book(s) and return the accompanying statement marked "cancel." But if we don't hear from you, then every month we'll deliver 4 of the newest Harlequin Superromance® novels right to your door. You'll pay the low subscriber price of just $2.74* each—a saving of 21¢ apiece off the cover price! And there's *no* charge for shipping and handling!

Of course, you may play "THE BIG WIN" without requesting any free book(s) by scratching tickets #1 through #4 only. But remember, that first shipment of one or more books is FREE!

PLUS A FREE GIFT!

One more thing, when you accept the free book(s) on ticket #5, you are also entitled to play ticket #6, which is GOOD FOR A GREAT GIFT! Like the book(s), this gift is totally free and yours to keep as thanks for giving our Reader Service a try!

So scratch off the PINK STRIPS on all your BIG WIN tickets and send for everything today! You've got nothing to lose and everything to gain!

*Terms and prices subject to change without notice.
Sales tax applicable in NY

© 1991 HARLEQUIN ENTERPRISES LIMITED

Here are your **BIG WIN** Game Tickets, worth from $10.00 to $1,000,000.00 each. Scratch off the **PINK METALLIC STRIP** on each of your Sweepstakes tickets to see what you could win and mail your entry right away. (SEE OFFICIAL RULES IN BACK OF BOOK FOR DETAILS!)

This could be your lucky day – GOOD LUCK!

FOLD AND DETACH ALONG THIS DOTTED LINE—RETURN ALL GAME TICKETS INTACT.

THE BIG WIN

1 Scratch PINK METALLIC STRIP to reveal potential value of this ticket if it is a winning ticket. Return all game tickets intact.

LUCKY NUMBER

1M 793739

THE BIG WIN

2 Scratch PINK METALLIC STRIP to reveal potential value of this ticket if it is a winning ticket. Return all game tickets intact.

LUCKY NUMBER

3F 791342

THE BIG WIN

3 Scratch PINK METALLIC STRIP to reveal potential value of this ticket if it is a winning ticket. Return all game tickets intact.

LUCKY NUMBER

9H 726959

THE BIG WIN

4 Scratch PINK METALLIC STRIP to reveal potential value of this ticket if it is a winning ticket. Return all game tickets intact.

LUCKY NUMBER

5R 723921

FREE BOOKS

5 We're giving away brand new books to selected individuals. Scratch PINK METALLIC STRIP for number of free books you will receive.

AUTHORIZATION CODE

130107-742

FREE GIFT

6 We have an outstanding added gift for you if you are accepting our free books. Scratch PINK METALLIC STRIP to reveal gift.

AUTHORIZATION CODE

130107-742

YES! Enter my Lucky Numbers in THE BIG WIN Sweepstakes and when winners are selected tell me if I've won any prize. If PINK METALLIC STRIP is scratched off on ticket #5, I will also receive one or more FREE Harlequin Superromance® novels along with the FREE GIFT on ticket #6, as explained on the opposite page.

(U-H-SR-01/91) 134 CIH ACEF

NAME _____

ADDRESS _____ APT. _____

CITY _____ STATE _____ ZIP _____

Offer limited to one per household and not valid to current Harlequin Superromance® subscribers.
© 1991 HARLEQUIN ENTERPRISES LIMITED.

PRINTED IN U.S.A.

Carefully detach card
along dotted
line and
mail today!

Play
all your
BIG WIN
tickets
and get
everything
you're
entitled to-
including
FREE BOOKS
and a
FREE GIFT!

BUSINESS REPLY MAIL
FIRST CLASS MAIL   PERMIT NO. 717   BUFFALO, NY

POSTAGE WILL BE PAID BY ADDRESSEE

HARLEQUIN READER SERVICE
THE BIG WIN SWEEPSTAKES

3010 Walden Ave.
P.O. Box 1867
Buffalo, NY 14240-9952

I...II.I..I.I.I..II...II.I.I.I.I..I.I..I.I.I..II

NO POSTAGE
NECESSARY
IF MAILED
IN THE
UNITED STATES

"To set a woman to a task is not against our beliefs," the old man pointed out. "But to display her for the enjoyment of unbelievers, I do not approve of. I have heard of life in the city. It is far away and dangerous for such as we. How did you come to leave that place?"

"My friends," Ahnle made an unconsciously graceful gesture as she pointed to Rachel.

"You are brave for a woman." Rachel could feel him studying her.

"I have spent many seasons with The People. I have learned courage from you," Rachel said politely, her eyes downcast, her head like Ahnle's, covered with a brightly patterned silk scarf tied in the distinctive manner of the women of the village where she'd lived with Father Pieter.

"I can see that."

"We also had the help of a man," Ahnle said very softly. "He is the one they call Tiger."

He shot Rachel a hard, searching look as she watched him through her lashes. "Does the girl speak the truth?"

"Yes."

"You have powerful friends. Even here, we have learned of the one they say moves through the jungle like the great cat he is named for."

The old man turned to Ahnle. "Your brother does not know you are here." It wasn't a question but a statement. Ahnle answered as such.

"No, Uncle."

"You were wrong to run away from him, but right to leave the place he had taken you. I will discuss this matter with him when he returns to his home." The wily old man had neatly cleared away the hurdle of Ahnle's running away from the man the village considered her legal guardian. Rachel began to breathe slightly easier.

"I will not be so disobedient in the future, Uncle."

"See that you are not." He was silent a long moment. Ahnle seemed to be holding her breath. Rachel bit her lip. "I have spoken to Chengla and his wife in the matter regarding your child. They have taken him into their home and treated him as their own for several moons. It is very hard for them to give him up."

"I am most grateful to them but my heart will always ache with pain and sorrow if we are separated longer." Ahnle reached into the pocket of her loose cotton slacks. "I have brought them a gift to show them my gratitude for keeping the child safe and well." She held out the money. Changed into small bills and coins, the hundred *baht* made an impressive offering. "I give you all I have in the world, and this I have only from the goodness of the spirits," she added formally.

The old man held out his hands. Ahnle handed over the notes and coins without touching him. "I will talk to Chengla and his wife today. I will give you my decision in the morning."

Ahnle looked over her shoulder at Rachel, stricken.

"Honored Father," Rachel interjected, bowing low. "We have only a little time left. Ahnle's cousin will be at the edge of the river at sunrise in two days' time. We do not wish to hurry your decision, but we must be gone from the village at first light tomorrow."

"Yes. I see that there is a problem. Very well, you will have my decision at sunset. If Chengla and his wife agree to give up the child, you will have time to prepare the little one for the journey.''

''Thank you, Honored Father.''

He nodded very slightly. ''Go,'' he said, including all the women in the command. ''We men have business to conduct.'' As they filed out of the smoky hut, Rachel saw the pipes being brought out. A pipe of opium would help the old man think. He believed it brought him closer to the spirit gods and made his decisions stronger and wiser. She followed the other women out into the sunshine and walked beside Ahnle, back to her brother's house, and began to help chop vegetable greens for the evening meal, as if nothing important had occurred, *as though she'd never left her own hill village at all.* The thought made her shiver and seemed to take the brightness from the sun.

For the remainder of the day, she did her best to keep the darkness of her own thoughts at bay, as well as encouraging Ahnle to keep her spirits up. They played with the children, who, once they got over their shyness at seeing Rachel's round eyes and pale skin, turned out to be imps of mischief. They helped to weed the poppies, and Ahnle showed her the burying ground where her parents and two younger sisters were laid to rest. Rachel's baby was buried in just such a place, watched over by the mountains and the spirits that inhabited them. As the afternoon grew warm and sleepy, they sat beneath a tree on a rise above the village and simply watched life go on around them.

''No matter what happens, I will never return,'' Ahnle said, as the sun slid behind the hills, bringing instant twilight to the tiny valley and its scattering of dusty, untidy huts.

"Your uncle, the *dzoema,* is a good man. His decision will be wise and just." Rachel wanted to tell the girl she would look after her, take her to America and help care for her child, but she could not. Her own life was in too great a state of disarray to make promises she might not be able to keep. And what if the old man decided against Ahnle? What if Chengla and his wife really had grown so attached to the baby that they could not bear to give him up? Rachel rested her head on her knees and tried not to think of anything at all.

"Rachel. Look!" Ahnle touched her sleeve very gently. "There is my uncle coming along the street to my brother's house. He is not alone," she said, suddenly breathless.

"No." Rachel narrowed her eyes to bring the small procession into focus. Ahnle's uncle was followed by a short, stocky man Rachel had never seen before, and behind him a respectful two steps was an even shorter woman, heavyset for a Hlông—and she was carrying a child. "He is not alone."

"They are bringing my son." Ahnle stood up in one swift, graceful movement and started running along the steep path leading back down to the village, Rachel only a step or two behind. The path was rocky and potholed. She had to keep all her attention on her feet or she would surely fall and twist an ankle, but she wanted to warn Ahnle, say something to prepare her, just in case Chengla and his wife had only come to return her gift of money in person and not to give her back her son.

"Ahnle, wait," she called, panting from altitude and exertion. "Wait for me." It was too late. The girl had already climbed the rickety steps into the hut where the others had entered just moments ahead of her. Rachel could only follow, praying silently to God and Buddha and all the spirits, hoping for the best.

Inside the hut it was dark and smoky and crowded with people: Ahnle's brother's first wife and her two small daughters, his second wife and her infant son, Ahnle and the visitors. Rachel took her place along the wall with the other women and listened to the old man's voice over the pounding of her heart. He was holding the baby, an infant no longer but a small, bright-eyed toddler. She glanced at Chengla's wife but her pudgy face was hidden by the rows of hanging coins draped around her elaborate silver headdress. Her hands were folded in her lap, her body language conveying no emotion.

"Chengla and his wife have brought the child for you to see that he is well," the old man said, and Rachel clasped her hands together in her lap to keep them from trembling. The dark mood of earlier in the day hovered just beyond her immediate consciousness and she fought to keep it at bay. "They are honored with the gift you have brought to show your appreciation of their care of your son. They have agreed to return him to you."

He handed the baby to Ahnle.

"May the spirits bless your house and bring you many strong sons for your kindness to my child," Ahnle said, bowing low to Chengla and his wife.

"A baby already grows within my new wife," Chengla replied smugly. "It will be a son."

"This boy cries too much," his wife answered, lifting her face to look at Ahnle's baby. There was no sorrow at losing him that Rachel could see in the woman's placid eyes. "The new child will not cry, I hope. We have named him Domha—the traveling one. I will pray to the spirits for him and I will buy a silver coin to wear in memory of him."

"Thank you," Ahnle said, her eyes bright with tears. "I will honor your memory by keeping the name you have given him."

"Good." The old man rose. "We will leave you now so that you may eat your evening meal with your brother's wives and prepare for your journey back across the great river. My youngest son, Nouvak, will guide you as far as the marshlands near the ruined village but no farther. May the spirits allow you to pass safely beyond the gate of our village."

"Thank you, Uncle." Ahnle remained on her knees as the old man uttered his blessing.

"Safe journey," he said, nodding slightly to Rachel as he passed.

"Thank you, Honored Father," she replied, accepting the gesture for the compliment that it was. They had done what they set out to do. Now they had only the return trip to the river between them and—home. Rachel sat quietly for a long moment and watched Ahnle rock her son.

IT WAS ALMOST THE LAST quiet moment they had. The baby truly did cry a great deal. He immediately threw up the goat's milk they tried to feed him from a bottle that Ahnle had stored in her *yaam*. He objected to the shape of the plastic nipple on the bottle, refused the

powdered milk they tried next and only barely toler-
ated the rice gruel they finally spooned into his mouth.

During the night he was colicky and wakeful. Ahnle
and Rachel took turns pacing the floor, rocking him
in their arms. More than once Rachel caught the girl
staring down at the baby with a puzzled look in her
eyes, and she knew that Ahnle hadn't been prepared
to see a year-old toddler in the place of the infant that
had been taken from her.

"A child should know its own mother," she whispered, cuddling the fussy little boy against her breast,
as daylight began to lighten the sky above the hills.

"Give him time," Rachel said comfortingly. "We
must leave now. We have a long walk ahead of us."
Outside the hut their guide, Nouvak, a boy barely into
his teens, was waiting for them. He carried a small
leather pouch and a vintage rifle, nothing else. He
walked ahead of the women.

"Everything will be right when we are back in the
camp." Ahnle settled the baby in a sling over her
shoulder, his weight resting on her hip. "We will start
a new life, Domha and I."

The trip back went wrong almost from the moment
the village was out of sight. It started to rain, a steady,
soaking rain that seemed as if it had gotten lost from
the rest of the monsoon and only now caught up.
Nouvak seemed oblivious to the discomfort, even offering to carry one of the shoulder bags when they had
gone far enough to ensure no one from the village
would see him doing woman's work. But it was sill
slow going.

The baby cried himself into exhausted sleep late in
the afternoon and only woke long enough to take a

bottle of powdered milk and rice gruel, as they sat around their small, smoky fire that night. Far off in the jungle a tiger roared. Although no night hunters came near their camp, Nouvak slept with his hand on the gun and Rachel didn't sleep at all.

They were going too slowly. There was too much distance to be made up if they were to arrive near the abandoned fishing village before the next night. Rachel roused them in the still, misty darkness of predawn and they walked all day with only two short halts to feed the child.

They almost made it, but an hour past the waterfall where they'd camped their first night in the jungle, Ahnle stepped on a loose stone and landed painfully on her knee as she twisted to protect the baby. It slowed them down and even though they walked an hour after nightfall, until their young guide refused to go farther along the steep, dangerous path above the stream, Rachel knew it was not far enough.

She sat up again that night, cuddling the baby so that Ahnle could rest, keeping him warm, trying to stave off the cold terror of her own thoughts. They were going to miss the rendezvous, no matter how early they started, no matter how fast they walked. They were simply too far away from the abandoned village.

Still, they left two hours before dawn, bidding their silent young companion farewell as they came out of the hills and into the marshlands bordering the stream. The women hurried on alone, slowed by the baby and Ahnle's bruised knee. When daylight came, the sun was hidden by fog that grew thicker as they reached the water's edge. The ruined huts rose around them, misty shapes in the gloom.

Ahnle's cousin and his boat were nowhere in sight, but very faintly, far away and muffled by the fog, Rachel heard the sound of a motor.

Moving away from them, back toward the river and freedom.

They were stranded.

Bohan had kept his word and returned, but now he was gone, also as he had promised, and Rachel was once again on her own in an enemy land.

CHAPTER TEN

"THERE'S SOMEONE IN THE back room I think you might want to meet," Billy said, materializing in the doorway of Brett's office at the Lemongrass.

He looked up from the sophisticated topographic map of the Golden Triangle he'd been studying. Khen Sa was on the march, down from Burma, moving at will among the hill villages south of Chiang Saen. Somewhere up there Brett was going to have to find the right spot to waylay him.

"Ahnle's brother?" It didn't take more than a quick glance at Billy's grim features to guess his week-long vigil outside the Teak Doll had paid off. Brett's preoccupation with Khen Sa's whereabouts was overshadowed immediately by his concern for Rachel. The sudden shift in concentration gave him a jolt. He'd always been able to compartmentalize his feelings, keep his personal life separate from his business dealings, but it had never been this hard.

The trouble was, he couldn't afford to lose his concentration or his objectivity at this stage of the game. The financing was all arranged, thanks to Alf Singleton's influence with a powerful man in the palace. The only thing left to do was meet with Khen Sa himself, and deliver the first installment of gold. Billy didn't know it yet but they were heading north, themselves, in the morning.

"Yeah. He wasn't too sold on the idea of comin' with me. He took some persuadin'. I think I got everything we need out of him already, but I don't want him hightailin' it back into the hills and gettin' to the women ahead of us." Billy's expression was still grim, but satisfied. He rubbed the back of his right hand with his left, as though his knuckles might hurt.

"What did he say?" Brett stood and picked up the map, as well as a classified air force spy satellite blowup of the same area. Both of the maps had been supplied by the U.S. embassy. Once Alf Singleton had gotten the go-ahead from Washington to back his plan, the ambassador's cooperation had been unstinting. Brett rolled up the charts and slid them inside a wall safe, next to a velvet jeweler's box containing a string of matched South Sea pearls. He closed the door and the safe disappeared into a section of carved panel on the wall.

"He thinks Ahnle might be headed for her aunt in Chiang Khong." Something in his friend's voice alerted Brett to be on his guard. "Except that he can't believe his sister would be fool enough to cross back into Laos just to get her kid." He waited, tense and silent in the doorway for Brett's response.

"She probably wouldn't try it alone. But with Rachel along, she might just take the chance."

"You knew Ahnle had a kid?" Billy's voice was low and controlled, and filled with hidden anger.

Brett stuck his hands in the back pockets of his slacks. Turning, he surveyed his friend's belligerent stance through narrowed eyes. "I didn't, until a day or two ago. Father Dolph told me."

"Why the hell didn't you tell me?" Billy's hands clenched into fists at his sides.

"I told you, I just found out myself." Brett felt his own temper flare. "You've been camped out at the Teak Doll for damned near a week. There hasn't been a lot of time for chitchat." He stopped talking for a moment. "Before that, I figured Rachel had taken the girl back to camp with her because she was running away from me. I didn't look for any other reason."

"Rachel running away from you?" Billy raised his arm above his head and rested it flat against the door frame. "What in hell happened that night at your place?"

"Nothing. Look, forget it, man. I'm sorry I blew up at you." His anger at Billy died away, redirecting itself internally where it belonged. He'd frightened Rachel away with his insistence on a physical relationship. *What had happened to her in the past, in that Vietnamese prison camp, that had frightened her so?* When Micah McKendrick showed up in Bangkok, as Brett was certain he soon would, he intended to learn everything the man knew about those lost and terrifying years of Rachel's life.

"You should have told me about the baby."

"How the hell was I supposed to know you cared that much about...Ahnle?" Brett leaned forward over the desk, resting his weight on his hands. "That's it, isn't it? You're soft on the girl. God, I've been blind." He ran his hand through his hair, stirring the thick, dull gold waves. "I thought you were staking out the Teak Doll to help me find Rachel."

"I was, man," Billy said defensively. "Ahnle's just a kid. I feel...sorta responsible for her."

"Responsible?" Brett gave a snort of laughter that contained no humor at all. He straightened, walking out from behind the desk. "Look at yourself, buddy. You're halfway in love with the girl already."

"You ought to know what it feels like," Billy threw over his shoulder as he headed in the direction of the storeroom, stopping Brett in his tracks.

"What's that supposed to mean?"

Billy twisted on his heel, his broad shoulders blocking out most of the light in the narrow hallway. His face was lost in shadow, hiding his features, the expression in his eyes, putting Brett at a disadvantage in their verbal skirmish. "I may be halfway gone on that little Hlông girl, but buddy, I'm in a hell of a lot better shape than you are. You're in love with Rachel Phillips and you're too damned stubborn to admit it, even to yourself."

AHNLE CLIMBED ONTO THE upended boat and curled her legs under her. She cuddled the baby, in his hand-woven carrier, close to her breast and stared at Rachel, dry-eyed and frightened.

"What shall we do?" she asked in a small voice. "My cousin kept his word. He came for us but we are late. He has gone. I do not think he will return."

"We don't know that for certain." Rachel let the strap of her *yaam* slip down off her shoulder to lie in the grass beside the smaller one Ahnle had carried. She tried to steady her jumping heartbeat and consider their options. They were limited, and panic beat dark wings against the back of her mind. "The fog delayed him, as well as it did us. He said he would stay only a short time, yet he was still here a few minutes ago. Perhaps, if we stay here tonight, he'll come again tomorrow."

"No." Ahnle pointed to a spot near one of the ruined huts. "Men have been here since we passed this way before." Rachel looked where Ahnle had indicated. The panicky wings beat stronger, making her catch her breath. The remains of a fire pit with several empty, still shiny, tin cans strewn around it was ample proof of Ahnle's words. It had not been there five days before. "We can't stay here."

"You're right." Rachel wanted to turn and run, find a safe, dry place to hide and cry her eyes out, waiting and hoping for someone to come and rescue them. But there was no one to come for them, no one who even knew where to look. They had only themselves to rely on. She stared at the small boat Ahnle was sitting on. It wasn't the long-tailed Thai boat one grew used to seeing here. It was a very ordinary-looking boat, shaped something like a wide, flat-bottomed canoe. And it possessed a pair of oars. "We can't stay here. Get off the boat."

Rachel pulled the spindly, narrow-bladed oars away from the boat while Ahnle scrambled down off her perch. "Help me turn it over," she instructed the girl, suiting action to words, "and watch out for snakes."

The fog was beginning to lift as they struggled to right the boat. The sun was a dull metallic ball hanging above the horizon, almost devoid of warmth and light. The grass underneath the boat was dead but didn't seem to have attracted a cobra or the even more deadly krite to take shelter beneath it. With Ahnle's help, Rachel shoved the righted craft into the water, tying one end of her length of Thai silk through an iron ring in the prow. She gave the other end to Ahnle.

"Hold it here while I find something to bail with," she said, moving away as she spoke. The thinning fog, threatening to expose them to anyone watching from the hills, added urgency to her words. "Wooden boats always leak."

"We cannot cross the river in this toy boat." The baby, sensing his mother's distress, whimpered fretfully.

"We can't stay here." Rachel made her voice as firm as she could manage. She picked up two of the biggest tin cans from the rubbish pile around the fire pit. "The men who were here were opium traders or bandits or soldiers. I can't tell which, but they will return. I think that's why your cousin didn't wait for us. It doesn't matter who they are. We're not sticking around to find out."

Ahnle took one look at Rachel's white, set face and did as she was told. She clutched the baby so tightly to her chest he grunted in protest. Ahnle soothed him in hushed tones. "I cannot help you guide this boat, Rachel. I am sorry."

"Don't worry. Your job is to bail out the water and keep us from running into rocks and snags. You can do that, can't you?"

"Yes." Ahnle nodded. "I can do that."

At Rachel's bidding she took the square of plastic that served as their rain shelter and tied the bags inside it to keep them dry, while Rachel struggled to fit the short, stubby oars into the unfamiliar oarlocks of woven rattan.

The current in the tributary stream was swift. Rachel didn't try to row, she just did her best to keep them in the middle of the stream, using the oars to avoid occasional rocks and to fend off snags. It was late in the morning when they reached the mouth of the stream. Rachel had been rowing steadily for the last thousand yards, as the waterway widened and slowed its course. Angling the boat toward the shore, they slipped beneath the overhanging branches of the willows lining the bank. Hidden from view, they stopped to rest.

Beyond them, the great river was still shrouded in fog. Rachel tried to remember every detail she could of their previous crossing. The Mekong was narrow here, but deep and swift-running below the placid surface. The crossing would be dangerous but possible to accomplish, if she could keep them from being swept too far downstream, where they might be waylaid by bandits, or even worse, carried on deeper into Laos where the river grew wild and treacherous and there would be no hope of rescue.

They took time for Ahnle to feed her son and reline his carrier with the soft, absorbent moss that served as diapers for Hlông babies. "Rachel?" Ahnle asked very softly, although they hadn't seen or heard anything to indicate they were not the only two women left in the world.

"Yes?" Rachel drew her gaze away from the foggy water.

"If I . . . do not reach the other shore. You will save my son?"

"Don't say such things," Rachel said sharply, quelling a superstitious shiver of her own. "You will

invite evil spirits into the boat with us and they will
bring us bad luck.''

"You are right." Ahnle looked stricken. Her dark
eyes were fever-bright, her cheeks flushed. Rachel
wondered if she were ill, then dismissed the niggling
worry. She would deal with it in its own good time. "I
shouldn't speak of such things." Ahnle looked down
at the sleeping baby in her lap. "I think we should go.
Domha is quiet and I will be able to bail much easier
now." She eyed the inch of water in the bottom of the
boat with trepidation.

Rachel slipped her compass out of the pocket of her
loose cotton slacks and checked their position before
pushing away from the bank with the blade of her oar.
Without a map or set landmarks to follow, it was the
only navigational guide they had. Almost at once the
current drew them out onto the river, spinning them
around until Rachel managed to head them downstream, prow first. From that moment on, she had no
time to think of anything else but keeping their frail
little boat from being swamped.

She rowed until her muscles burned like fire and her
hands were blistered, raw and bleeding. Every ripple
and eddy in the great river set the primitive craft to
rocking. There was no wind or the low-riding boat
would have been swamped within a hundred yards of
shore. For over an hour she battled the current, making some headway but always being swept further
downstream, away from Chiang Khong. The smell of
the river was thick around them, the fog blanketed
everything, making it impossible to tell how far they
had come, but thankfully, perhaps, also veiling how
far they had to go.

Twice they narrowly avoided being hung up on snags, great tree trunks floating just below the surface, that were impossible to see in the fog. Once Ahnle thought she heard the engine noises of another boat, but Rachel could hear nothing beyond the sound of her own labored breathing. She kept rowing because there was nothing else she could do, and they were not seen.

By the time Ahnle glimpsed the Thailand shore, the boat was leaking so badly Rachel could barely keep them steady in the current. She was so tired she no longer cared how far downstream they were swept, if she could only stop and rest. But she did not stop. She kept rowing doggedly, for Ahnle's sake and the baby's, as well as her own.

Suddenly the river twisted around a headland, spinning them out of the mainstream and into the quiet backwaters of a small cove, where a wide stream, much like the one they'd followed on the Laotian side, emptied into the river. With the last of her strength, Rachel rowed the waterlogged skiff into the stream mouth, out of sight of the main channel, and sat slumped over the oars while Ahnle tied them fast to a sapling's trunk with the length of silk.

"Where are we, Rachel?" Ahnle asked, offering her a drink of water from a plastic jug. Rachel lifted her head and looked around. Ahnle sat quietly, cuddling the fussy baby to her breast. Rachel blinked. She couldn't remember him making a peep before that moment.

She glanced at the compass, frightened of what she might see: that the river had only swept them in a great half circle and they were back on the Laotian side. "I have no idea," she said truthfully, but with a small, tired smile. "But we are in Thailand." They were by no means home free, safe and sound, but they were no longer stranded in an enemy country that had been the setting for her nightmares for more years than she wanted to recall.

"I will never be afraid of riding in a boat with a motor on it again," Ahnle said fervently.

Rachel choked back a laugh that was half a sob. "Neither will I." She leaned over to trail her blistered hands in the cold water. "We can't stay here. We have to head north, find a village or a road that leads to Chiang Khong or some other town."

"We must start soon," Ahnle agreed, looking around her. "The hills are very steep. They come all the way down to the river bank to sip at its waters."

"We'll only walk far enough to find shelter for the night." Rachel studied Ahnle's face more closely. "Are you ill?"

"No. Only tired."

Rachel forced herself to climb out of the boat, stiffening muscles protesting every move she made. "Hand me the bags, and then the baby. We'll fill the water bottles a little farther upstream and look for some kind of pathway into the hills." To head south from their present position would lead them into the bandit-controlled areas around Nan. They couldn't take that risk. If they headed north, toward Chiang Saen or Chiang Khong, they might be lucky enough to come across a party of "trekkers" doing one of the hill country jaunts that operated for tourists out of Chiang Rai.

Or they could meet up with the warlord, Khen Sa.

"I'll take the baby for the first bit," Rachel said, still worried at Ahnle's feverish appearance. If the girl was coming down with malaria, they must find shelter, and soon. "Untie the silk from the boat. We..." She stopped talking abruptly.

"What was that?" Ahnle was looking into the hills where the echo of gunfire had broken the pattern of bird calls and rushing water.

"Guns." Rachel took the baby from Ahnle's slack grasp. She'd been deceiving herself that all would be well, now that they were back in Thailand. Desperate, ruthless men stalked these hills, just as they did in Laos, and unless they were very lucky indeed, they were about to come face-to-face with some of them.

BILLY TODD DROPPED into a crouch behind the trunk of a great teak tree where Brett was already concealed. He was dressed in camouflaged fatigues, as Brett was, and sweat ran freely down his face and neck. He was breathing hard from his rapid descent down the hillside. He rested the butt of his gun in the soft, mossy soil around the tree and took a few deep breaths.

"How many are there?" Brett asked, his eyes raking the dense forest cover on the other side of the narrow trail in front of them.

"Six or seven. The usual."

"Thai Rangers?" Brett took his eyes from the jungle a moment to make sure his friend was all right.

"Border patrol." Billy nodded, his eyes narrowing, as he spied a smear of blood on Brett's forearm. "Jesus, you're bleedin'."

Brett shook his head. "It's a scratch, really. Rico-chet. Tree bark, probably."

"Who the hell do they think they're shootin' at?" Billy took him at his word about the wound on his arm.

"Us," Brett said, his voice devoid of humor.

"Don't they know whose side we're on?"

"'Fraid not."

Billy's head snapped around. His eyes bored into Brett's. "What the hell does that mean?"

"No one knows we're out here. At least, no one who's going to do anything about it if we're caught."

"Oh, Christ. We haven't even met up with Khen Sa yet and the whole damn deal's about to go down the tubes. What the hell's the use of havin' all them friends in high places if we get our heads blown off six hours out on the trail?"

"I don't think they're going to put up much more of a fight. If we can keep 'em pinned down until dark, we can slip away. How about the ponies?" The last thing he needed was for Khen Sa's gold to fall into the wrong hands.

"There's a cave, sort of, up on the hill above the trail. Lonnie's there with the ponies. Naga and Chan are up there, too. They'll all keep an eye on each other."

"Then we might as well make ourselves at home." Brett didn't move from his crouch behind the tree but pointed with the barrel of his rifle. "They're there, and there and there." Billy nodded, sharp, jungle-trained eyes noting the small disturbances in leaves and branches that betrayed the presence of the Thai Rangers. "If we don't give them anything to shoot at, my guess is they'll melt away an hour or so before sundown.''

"And if they don't?'' Billy prepared to move himself to a vantage point about twenty yards away.

"Then do what you have to do to stay alive.''

RACHEL AND AHNLE MOVED cautiously along the steep, faint path leading up into the hills. It was little more than an animal track but it was the only route they had to follow. They had heard no more gunshots, but Rachel couldn't tell if they were walking into the cross fire or not. It really didn't matter. The hillsides were too steep and littered with moss-covered boulders to attempt straying from the dubious safety of the slippery path. They could only move north and west—they had no other choice.

And Ahnle needed to rest. She was feverish and growing weaker with each step, although she denied it. The baby was also starting to fuss again. Rachel hitched him higher on her hip, balancing the heavy *yaam* on the other side, and crooned softly in Hlông under her breath. They needed to find shelter. The day had grown uncomfortably warm but the night would be damp and cold in the higher elevations. They needed warmth and food and some kind of roof over their heads.

The track they were following disappeared in a stand of bamboo nearly as big as pine trees. Rachel stopped a moment, listening, and Ahnle almost walked into her. She turned and studied the girl's fever-bright eyes and pasty complexion. "We have to keep going.''

"I know." Ahnle swayed a little where she stood. "I will not hold you back."

Rachel pushed into the bamboo, hoping to pick up the narrow track on the other side. It didn't branch right or left to skirt the stand, at least not that she could discern. It simply disappeared. When the bamboo thinned, she understood why. It wasn't an animal track they had been following. It was a smuggler's trail down to the river. In front of her was a wider track, better traveled, with evidence that men and horses had recently passed by. Which way to turn? Which way to go? Did danger lie to the right or to the left?

As before, Rachel knew there was no real choice. They had to keep moving toward the more populated areas. She turned right, onto the steeply rising path and started walking once again, putting one foot in front of the other and praying that Ahnle did the same. She'd given up praying for help to come. They were on their own.

LONNIE SMALLEY STOOD JUST inside the entrance to the big, rock overhang and kept his hand on the pack ponies' muzzles to quiet them. A quarter of a million dollars in gold and only five men to guard it. What if Khen Sa just took the money and ran, cut them down where they stood? He'd be glad when this whole deal was over and done. Maybe then he'd take one more stab at getting his life in order, kicking the habit. He stroked one of the rough-coated little mountain ponies and listened for footsteps outside the cave. Chan and Naga were reconnoitering the trail above them, look-

ing for a way past the patrol of Thai guards that had
Brett and Billy pinned down on the slopes below him.

This whole deal was too risky. He wished Brett
would tell him what it was really all about, but he
couldn't be trusted with the details. Brett knew that
and so did he. It was too easy to talk when he was
high, even easier when he was on the way down and
looking for a fix. It was better for all of them if he just
went along for the ride, like he always did. That way
he didn't have to think too much or fear too much.
That was the way he'd lived his life for a lot of years.
It got him through the days and the China White got
him through the nights...and the nightmares...
gave him other dreams to replace them. And he liked
those dreams.

Voices. Lonnie swung his head in the direction of
the sounds. The ponies nickered, stamping restlessly.
He soothed them with an absent hand. Was it Brett
and Billy coming back or Naga and Chan? Or was it
the Ranger patrol? Or Khen Sa? Had his friends all
died while he stood here in the half darkness of the
cave? A baby started crying somewhere close by.

"What in hell?" He muttered into the pony's ear.
"There ain't no babies out here." He pulled his gun
out of its shoulder holster and released the safety. His
hand shook and he made a conscious effort to still the
tremors. He pushed back the fall of vines and creepers
that hid the scooped-out opening in the side of the hill
from the view of the trail directly below it. It had been
one hell of a scramble getting the ponies inside. He
looked out, cautiously, at the stretch of trail visible
from the cave mouth.

What he saw gave him quite a start. Two women
and a baby were being dragged along the trail by Naga
and Chan. One of the women looked ready to collapse, the other, the one carrying the baby in a sling on
her hip, looked ready to put up a fight. Naga silenced
her protest simply and effectively. He merely pointed
his gun at the baby and jerked his head in the direction he wanted her to walk. The implicit threat
worked. The woman started to climb.

Lonnie felt sweat break out on his face and under
his arms. He knew them. They weren't two hill
women, somehow lost in this unpopulated area. The
first woman, being half shoved, half carried up the
slope by Chang, was the young Hlông girl from the
Teak Doll. The other woman was white and her face
was even more familiar. *Rachel Phillips.*

"Jesus," he said reverently. "What a mess."

He crouched in the opening of the cave mouth,
ready to lend a hand when they got close enough. The
sooner he got them under cover, the better the chance
none of the Thai Rangers on the trail would spot
them.

Gunfire erupted from below. There were shouts in
Thai and some dialect Lonnie couldn't understand,
horses neighed, and behind him in the cave, their own
ponies whinnied uneasily. The Hlông girl whimpered
and fell to her knees, skidding backward on the steep
path. Lonnie scrambled farther down the slope, hoping to God that the Thai Rangers were too preoccu-
pied to take the opportunity to fill him full of lead. He
motioned Naga to help Chan carry the girl into the
cave. He held out his hand.

"Get a move on, Mrs. Phillips." She didn't budge, although another burst of automatic weapon fire shattered the jungle calm.

"Lonnie Smalley?" Her blue-gray eyes were big and scared-looking. She stared at him as though he were a ghost.

"Yes, ma'am, and if you'll pardon my French, get your sweet ass up this hill before you get it shot off."

BRETT WAS BEGINNING TO wonder what in hell else could go wrong that day. The trouble was, he knew exactly what else; either he or Billy or both of them could get their heads shot off. The godforsaken stretch of jungle trail in front of him had turned into rush hour, Thai hill-country style. The fifteen or twenty armed men and half a dozen heavily loaded mountain ponies now engaged in a firefight with the hapless Thai Rangers had literally come out of nowhere. Brett sprayed the trees above the Rangers' position with a burst from his M16 just to let the newcomers know he was friendly. He didn't have to wonder who they were. Only one man could command uniformed, armed patrols of that size other than the king of Thailand: Khen Sa.

He worked his way toward Billy's position at a crouching half run. "What do you think?" he asked under cover of the double barreled blast of the sawed-off shotgun that Billy preferred above any other weapon.

"I just got a glimpse but I'd swear the guy with the AK-47 down there is one of Khen Sa's lieutenants. He sat across from me at that banquet last spring.

Remember? The one with the roast bats and cobra's blood."

"You sure?"

"Sure as I can be from this distance." He ducked as a stray bullet ricocheted in the trees above their heads.

"My guess, too. Those ponies are probably loaded with raw opium. It ought to be to our advantage if you've met the man in charge," Brett said consideringly, weighing their options, planning his strategy with one part of his brain while the other stayed alert to the danger surrounding them. It was a skill a line officer learned early on in Vietnam or he went home in a steel-lined box. Or his men did.

"I'm thinkin' if those Rangers down there value their hides, they'll be fadin' off into the jungle pretty damn soon and quit tryin' to be heroes."

"Let's hope so. In the meantime, we've got to make an impression on Khen Sa's lieutenant or he may not stop shooting long enough to figure out we're not with the good guys."

"Dang, and I left my black hat back home."

"Don't get cocky," Brett growled.

Billy grunted a wordless curse and shoved two more shells in the chamber of the shotgun. "You're walkin' a mighty fine line." He pulled the trigger and the branches of the tree above where two of the Thai Rangers were hidden disintegrated into a shower of leaves and bark. Before Brett could answer, more gunfire followed from the direction of Khen Sa's men on the trail.

"We've got no choice, man. This bunch is headed back to the general's main camp and the refinery. We're going to get ourselves invited along."

"You're crazy, man," Billy said, shaking his head. Someone shouted an order in Thai to fall back. Just to reinforce it, Billy emptied the shotgun into the jungle canopy in the general direction of the shout.

"Got any better ideas, Sergeant?"

"No sir, Colonel." Billy's face was stony but excitement sparked in his eyes. "None at all."

Brett gave a curt nod. "When the shooting stops we'll go down and introduce ourselves. With any luck at all, we'll be in Khen Sa's camp in time to join the general for dinner."

CHAPTER ELEVEN

RACHEL SAT WITH HER BACK to the outside wall of the teak clapboard hut and watched the men sitting around the bonfire in the center of the small village. Laughter and crude jokes, recognizable despite the unfamiliar language, a mixture of Thai and Burmese, carried clearly on the cold, damp mountain air. Her stomach rumbled and growled but so far the three harried women, serving food to the twenty or so men, hadn't offered her anything to eat. And she was just too tired to go serve herself from the kettles of rice and vegetables cooking over smaller fires nearby.

Behind her, inside the hut, Ahnle stirred restlessly in her sleep. Rachel held her breath a moment, hoping the baby wouldn't wake, also. She would go and see that he was properly covered just as soon as she rested a little longer. She pulled her knees up under her chin, curled her arms around her legs to warm herself and watched the men.

She could easily pick Brett out of the crowd. He was taller than most of the men who comprised this segment of Khen Sa's private army, of course, although that wasn't as apparent when they were all seated. Rather, it was his dull gold hair that caught the firelight and set him apart from the dark-haired, dark-eyed Shan and hill tribesmen, like a gold coin among iron filings.

Rachel closed her eyes, resting her forehead on her knees, letting fatigue settle over her like a heavy cloak. She and Ahnle and the baby were no longer on their own in the jungle hills, it was true, but how much better off in this situation were they? She still had no idea where, exactly, they were. They were not bound or gagged or locked up in a cage, but, as far as she was concerned, they were virtual prisoners of a ruthless warlord. And a very angry Tiger Jackson.

· The aroma of rice and cooked vegetables and roast meat teased her nose. Rachel raised her head from her knees and found herself confronting Brett. He balanced easily on the balls of his feet, his face level with her own. His expression was stony; his hooded blue eyes held not the slightest flicker of emotion. She thought he might be tired, too, but the fatigue didn't show, wouldn't be allowed to show. He looked fit and hard and dangerous, a man well able to hold his own with Khen Sa or anyone else. Rachel shivered and wrapped her hands more tightly around her knees.

"I brought you something to eat." He set the bowls of food and chopsticks on the floor beside her.

"Men don't bring women food in this part of the world." She made no attempt to pick up the food, although her mouth watered at the sight of it. When they had first arrived in the camp, one of the women had given her some kind of ointment. Her blistered hands were still sore but no longer so stiff she couldn't bend them, so at least she could feed herself.

"They do when the women are a business investment." Brett rested his forearm on his bent leg, watching her. He nodded toward the food. "The meat is wild boar, not dog."

"Did you think I'd refuse it, if it was?" She looked him straight in the eye. "I've eaten it before. When you're hungry you eat anything that's put in front of you. Anything." She was surprised at the venom in her voice. To cover the lapse, she picked up the vegetables and dumped them over the rice. Her hands were shaking. She willed them to stop. She had to be so careful around this man. The temptation to tell him secrets she'd kept for years was strong, even when he was so angry with her. "What did you tell our host about us, anyway?"

"That Ahnle and the baby ran away from her brother with your connivance. *Farang* missionaries have been interfering in people's lives in this part of the world for the last hundred and fifty years."

"Did he believe you?" If she didn't look at him, she wouldn't remember how it felt to be touched by him, to be held and comforted and loved by him.

"I think so." He sounded faintly pleased with himself. She risked a glance from the corner of her eye. "I told him we came across you just before the patrol of Thai Rangers jumped us. I hadn't planned on looking for the two of you until we completed our business here, with the general. By the way, for the record, I'm taking Ahnle back to her brother for a good beating and you back to the mission camp for Father Dolph to deal with. It's always better to stick to the truth whenever you can."

Rachel stirred the rice in her bowl with the chopsticks, not brave enough to meet his eyes. *Don't remember how he held you and comforted you. Don't*

remember how close you came to rediscovering your-
self as a woman with him. Just stick to the truth as
much as you can. It had become her private motto
over the past two years. "Sort of like killing two birds
with one stone?"

"Not to mention doubling up on my...recovery fee.
Khen Sa appreciates that. He's quite a capitalist at
heart." The corner of his mouth twisted upward in a
hard smile. He brushed at a patch of dried red mud on
the pants of his fatigues. His hands were big, the
knuckles dusted with gold hair. His wrists were strong,
his forearms corded with muscle. They could hold a
woman so easily, make her feel so secure....

"There's blood on your arm."

Brett glanced at her sharply. There was panic in her
voice and nothing she could do to hide it. She clutched
the rice bowl so tightly she thought the cheap pottery
might break from the pressure. She would not touch
him, reach out to offer comfort, to be comforted by
the rock hardness of his muscled arms. *She could not.*

"It's just a scratch." He dismissed the wound.

"I don't have anything to treat it with. Only the
ointment one of the women gave me for my hands."
She turned her palm upward, looking down at it un-
thinkingly.

"How the hell did you get those blisters?" He circled her wrist with his fingers, holding her still.

"Rowing across the Mekong."

"I'll be goddamned." She had the satisfaction of
hearing the disbelief and respect in his voice. It
brought her back to herself.

"I had no choice. My date left without me." She
tried to pull her hand away. He let her go. "I'll get the

ointment. Out here...infections..." Her voice trailed off as he tipped her chin up with his knuckles to make her look directly at him.

"I'll take care of it later. I promise. Stop worrying."

"I'm not."

"Yes, you are."

"At least you didn't tell Khen Sa I was your mistress when you made up your cock-and-bull story about why the three of us were wandering around out here alone." *Whatever had possessed her to say that?* Was the brush of his hand on her skin enough, now, to make her lose what little sense she had?

"I have to admit I considered doing just that." He picked up her discarded chopsticks, popped one of the untouched pieces of meat into his mouth and chewed. "It was the first thing that came to mind when I saw you sliding down the hill behind Lonnie. Then I saw Ahnle and the baby and I didn't know what else to say."

"Lucky for me, you think fast on your feet."

"Why is that?" He popped another piece of meat in his mouth and offered one to her. It smelled delicious, hot and spicy. He tilted his head, watching her eat. She looked away, focusing on the patch of tanned skin at the open collar of his shirt. It seemed so intimate and sensual an act to accept food from his hand. But so was looking at him. She wanted to kiss the spot at the base of his throat where his pulse beat slow and strong. Rachel swallowed too quickly and almost choked.

"You didn't answer my question," he reminded her, offering a sip of slightly muddy-tasting water from a gourd hanging from the porch railing.

"No reason, really." He waited with the patience of the jungle cat he was named for. "It's just that you might find it very awkward sharing this hut with Ahnle and the baby and me, that's all," she finished lamely.

"If I'd told them you were my mistress, our hosts would have arranged for us to have a hut to ourselves. I would have insisted on it."

"Brett...don't." She felt tears of humiliation and desperation push against the back of her eyes and tighten her throat.

"Why did you run away from me? How did you come to be wandering around in these hills by yourself with a sick woman and a baby?"

"Ahnle was frantic to get her baby back. I...I had to help her."

"By robbing me and running off? You could have trusted me, Rachel." His words were quiet, evenly spoken, but she knew, then, beyond a shadow of a doubt, how much she'd hurt him.

"I'll pay you back, every cent," she said, the words tumbling over themselves to get out. "Lonnie's car's all right. He told me so. He won't press charges. I...apologized for stealing it," she added, feeling like a child caught with her hand in a cookie jar, instead of a woman who had betrayed the only man she had been able to care about for what seemed like a lifetime.

"To hell with the money."

Rachel had never heard such cold anger in his voice, yet she refused to flinch.

"I would have helped you find the baby."

"I had to do it myself." Rachel rose to her knees. How did she explain the need to challenge the mountains and the jungle that had held her captive so long? That by doing so, she also challenged the darkness and the cowardice within herself? "I have to go. Ahnle is still feverish. The baby will be waking soon and he'll be hungry."

If she stayed beside him much longer she would throw herself into his arms and cry away the terror that had pursued her for so many days. She couldn't do that. She didn't know what she wanted. She never would find herself if she could mask those fears, her memories, her reluctance to face the past in his arms. She would lose herself. Brett was addicting, like Lonnie's heroin, and every bit as dangerous to a bruised and battered soul like her own.

He stood up, pulling her with him. The softening in his expression had disappeared. He jerked her abruptly upright, scattering her thoughts. The diamond-hard edge was back in his voice, in his eyes, in the jut of his chin. He had sensed her withdrawal, read her reluctance in her eyes. "Don't get any more ideas about running off. The sentries in this place will shoot you down, women or not, baby or not. Understand?"

"What *is* this place?" she asked in a whisper that was no more than a breath of air between them. In the background the party seemed to be breaking up. Shadows moved about the fire, shouts and laughter in the unfamiliar mixture of Burmese and Thai carried to them.

"It's Khen Sa's main base camp on this side of the border. He's a wanted man. We're his guests but that doesn't mean he's going to stand by and let us do anything to jeopardize his safety."

"What are you doing here?"

"Don't ask, Rachel." It wasn't a request, it was an order.

"I don't think you brought him in a shipment of guns," she said, deliberately provoking him because she wanted him so desperately to tell her what was going on. "Two ponies couldn't carry enough guns to make the trip worthwhile. But they could carry enough money...." She recalled how heavy the oblong bundles seemed to the men unloading them. "...or gold."

"Rachel." There was a warning in his voice she found hard to ignore.

"Did you come prepared to trade for something else? Something even more deadly?"

"Shut up and get inside." He raised his voice and took her by the arm, not hard enough to bruise but enough to let her know who was boss.

She lifted her chin and opened her mouth to tell him to go to hell. His refusal to answer her was as damning as a confession of drug smuggling.

"I said, no more of your mouth." He raised his hand as though to strike her. Rachel stared openmouthed, so angry she thought she would explode. Instead of hitting her, Brett gave her a shake. "Inside, woman. I won't tell you again." She saw movement from the corner of her eye. A man was standing by the porch, observing them, watching, waiting.

"A woman is often better for a good beating," he said conversationally in heavily accented but passable English.

Brett never even looked in his direction. "We do not beat our women. At least not in public."

The other man laughed. Rachel risked a glance at him from beneath lowered lashes. Instinct had taken over. This man held power, the power of life and death over all those around him, including herself, including Brett. He was small and compactly built, his face weather-beaten and pockmarked. He was wearing fatigues, clean and well-mended. His air of command was unmistakable, like Brett's.

"That is why you have so much trouble in your country. Women in America do not know their place." He stood, rocking on the balls of his feet, watching the scene before him with interest.

"Perhaps you are right, General." Had Brett emphasized the title every so slightly to give her a clue to the man's identity? If so, she didn't need it. She was face-to-face with Khen Sa, the Opium King. That was why Brett was here. That was why the village was here, to collect and refine the raw opium gum into morphine base or possibly even heroin.

Brett was a part of it.

"Let me go." She twisted in his grasp. He released her so abruptly she took a step backward, coming up against the wall of the hut.

"Get inside and get some sleep," he said. "We're leaving first thing in the morning."

She went. This was no time for theatrics. Or heroics. She had a part to play and she was good at make-believe. Especially when her life, and the lives of others, depended on it.

WALKING AWAY FROM RACHEL was one of the hardest things he'd ever done in his life. If he got out of this deal alive, got all of them out alive, he'd tell her everything. *If he made it out alive.* Until then, he couldn't afford to confide in her. Even less could he afford to admit he was in love with her. There was too much at stake.

Khen Sa was speaking. He pulled his thoughts away from Rachel and the frightened, accusing look in her eyes and made himself concentrate on what the warlord had to say.

"One hundred villages, five tribes bring their *jois* of opium gum here to me to be made into the best heroin there is," he said, banging the handle of a riding crop against his palm. A *joi* weighed about three and a half pounds. Ten kilos of raw opium reduced down to about one kilo of morphine base. After that, it required only the addition of simple chemicals to refine the morphine into pure heroin. The process could be carried out in a room no larger than a bedroom. Khen Sa's refinery filled a barn-size building. "Would you like to see what your down payment of gold has bought you, Mr. Jackson?"

"Yes."

Billy had joined him, walking at his side, a beautifully worked Shan knife stuck in his belt.

"Lonnie's lookin' out for the ladies," he said quietly after nodding a respectful greeting to Khen Sa, who ignored him.

"Do you feel your women must be protected from my men, Mr. Jackson?" Khen Sa stopped suddenly, the riding crop tapping against his pant leg. He rocked back and forth from toe to heel. He was barefoot and came barely to Brett's shoulder, but the air of menace he exuded was unmistakable.

"I do not trust the women, sir. I have spent enough time tracking them down." Brett waited patiently for the self-styled general to resume their walk.

The warlord watched him for a long moment. Billy stood quietly, waiting for Brett's cue as to how to proceed. The night sounds of the village settling into sleep around them countered the silence between the three men.

"The *farang* woman bears watching," Khen Sa agreed, suddenly resuming his strolling pace toward the windowless building hidden among a stand of huge teak trees, draped with streamers of moss and vines as big around as a man's arm. "She is either extremely brave or extremely foolish."

"I don't think she's foolish, General."

The refinery was a barn-like structure, open on the side facing the compound. A guard was stationed at each corner of the building. At a sharp command from Khen Sa, the closest one jumped to kickstart a small electric generator. Naked overhead bulbs began to glow dimly at intervals along the length of the building. The paraphernalia for reducing the raw opium into pure heroin consisted of three or four huge iron woks, a number of pots and kettles, plastic jerry cans of chemicals, barrels of water and back in a corner two or three small drums of what was probably gasoline to power the generator. Brett took it all in with one swift glance and kept walking.

Looking over Khen Sa's shoulder, Brett saw *jois* of raw opium stacked several feet high. Kept dry and under cover, it could be stored indefinitely. But directly in front of him was something far more valuable, and far more deadly.

"One hundred kilos of pure China White, Mr. Jackson," Khen Sa said, making no effort to hide the satisfaction in his voice. "And I can promise you one hundred more at date of delivery." He made a sweeping gesture that indicated the as yet unprocessed raw opium beyond them.

Five hundred pounds of heroin, ready to be shipped to London, Hong Kong, San Francisco, New York, with a street value of over a hundred million dollars. Brett felt his heartbeat quicken, then slow to a heavy thudding in his chest.

"When can we take delivery?" Brett asked.

"In about three weeks," Khen Sa replied. "You will, of course, bring the rest of the agreed upon price in gold at that time."

"You'll have your money." Brett said grimly.

"Good. Good. I have need of new weapons for my men, and the...businessmen...I am dealing with are growing impatient for payment. With those weapons I can rid my people of their Burmese oppressors forever." He signaled for them to precede him out of the building. Brett didn't like turning his back on the man. He sounded like a megalomaniac, like a little two-bit Hitler. He wished he could turn around and pound him into the ground. But he'd have to bide his time, get the heroin, preferably without turning over any more of his backer's money, and then step back and watch the tyrant take his fall.

Once outside, Khen Sa barked a sharp command in Shan to the nearest guard and the generator sputtered into silence. The lights died, leaving them in near darkness once more. "The gasoline to feed that monster is almost as precious as the poppy dust," he said with a chortle. Brett didn't bother to join in the laughter.

Above them, through a break in the trees, the moon floated high and distant, bathing them all in cold silver light. "Shall we seal our bargain over a glass of whiskey, gentlemen?" Khen Sa suggested, including Billy in the invitation with a curt nod, as though only noticing him for the first time that very moment.

"Thank you, General." Brett had no intention of getting drunk surrounded by fifty or sixty of Khen Sa's men, but it would be a major miscalculation to refuse to drink with the man at all.

With a wave of his riding crop, Khen Sa led the way to his private quarters. "Has it occurred to you to wonder why I have chosen to sell my opium to you, Mr. Jackson?" he asked conversationally as they walked.

"The thought has crossed my mind," Brett said cautiously. He had no idea how much Khen Sa knew about his previous dealings in the business, that all the other producers he'd dealt with in the past two years were either dead or in prison.

"You were not the only buyer to approach me, of course."

"Of course. A man with your reputation for quality product must have many customers."

"This is true." The little man actually preened, like a banty rooster. Brett felt his lip curl in derision. "But I do not have the time to make separate deals with every buyer in the Golden Triangle. It diverts my attention from my people's fight for liberation from the Burmese.''

"Of course." Brett gritted his teeth. What Khen Sa wanted was to get the Burmese off his back so that he could set up his own little empire. And by the looks of things, he was pretty close to doing just that.

"You, however, were the only one to offer me gold. I have need of gold. And you were the only American." He stopped outside his large, airy hut. "I particularly prefer to sell to Americans. You have been my best customers since 1968.''

CHAPTER TWELVE

RACHEL LIFTED THE WIGGLING, squirming baby from where he was playing, naked on the sun-warmed stones, and deposited him in a big copper wok filled with water from the well at the center of the temple courtyard. He drew his legs up against his chest, a comical look of surprise and disbelief pulling his mouth into a rounded O of consternation when his toes touched the water. But he was soon splashing happily in his makeshift tub, as she lathered his chest and shoulders with a small cake of soap she found crumbling in the bottom of her faithful *yaam*. She looked up as a pair of shadows reached across the courtyard to fall at her feet. Billy and Lonnie were standing a little distance away, watching her bathe the baby. "Come on over," she called, laughing, as Domha splashed water into his eyes and wrinkled up his face to let out a piercing howl, disturbing the ravens in the trees outside the sheltered courtyard. Several brilliantly colored red and green parrots also took exception at the unfamiliar cry and took wing above the ruined *wat*. Rachel wiped Domha's face with a cloth and cooed comforting words in Hlông. From a shaded nook a few feet away, Ahnle looked on and laughed at her son's display of temper.

"He is truly one of The People," she explained, coloring prettily when she spied Billy and Lonnie advancing on their little group. "We do not like water, unless it is in a cooking pot where it belongs."

"My granddad used to say that about drinking the stuff," Lonnie said, hunkering down on his heels and holding out a finger for Domha to grab onto. "The only time he touched a glass of water was if it had a double shot of whiskey in it."

Rachel laughed and Ahnle smiled but Billy only grunted. He sat down by Ahnle, his legs pulled up, his wrists hanging loose across his knees.

"Come to think of it," Lonnie continued, playing to his audience, "he didn't bathe in it any more than he had to, neither."

Rachel shook her head and smiled; Ahnle laughed merrily, pleased to have gotten the joke, and this time even Billy smiled. Rachel glanced at her young friend, noticing the faint blush of color on her pale cheeks. The trip down from Khen Sa's mountain stronghold had been long and arduous, starting before sunup and ending after dark. When they reached the temple, Ahnle had fallen onto her pallet and slept the clock around. Late that morning she'd awakened, free of fever and well on the road to recovery.

Rachel lifted the baby out of the cooking pot and wrapped him in a length of worn and faded saffron-colored cotton, left behind by one of the young monks. She'd been sad to learn that the Acharya had died during the winter and his young followers had been called back to Chiang Mai by the abbot of their order.

"Here you go." She deposited Domha, fresh and sweet-smelling, in his mother's lap. "Do you think he wants his bottle?"

Although the little boy was small for his age, and slightly undernourished, he was bright and alert and already beginning to creep around on all fours. She had the suspicion he would be toddling around their small, cramped hut at the camp before either she or Ahnle was ready for it.

"I have his bottle right here," Ahnle said in careful English. "Please?" She held the baby out for Billy to take, so that she could fetch the bottle from her woven bag.

Billy was too surprised by the gesture to say no, Rachel decided, but his brows drew together in a thundercloud frown. "I haven't held a baby in twenty years," he muttered, his hands inches away from the dangling Domha.

"It is a skill easily recalled," Ahnle said, not daring to look at him.

"Where's the boy's father?" he asked abruptly, taking the baby and settling him gingerly on his knee. Rachel held her breath, hoping the infant didn't decide to do what babies often do after their baths. A wet pant leg would be the last straw, as far as Billy Todd was concerned.

"He has gone to Germany." She still didn't look at him. Hlông women very seldom made eye contact with a man. Rachel wished Ahnle would overcome that particular tribal taboo. She was going to have to be more aggressive if she wanted to break down the barricades Billy was throwing up between them.

"He didn't marry you?" Billy seemed intent on watching the baby, who was trying to rip the breast pocket off his shirt to see what was inside.

Ahnle lifted her head, looked at Billy for the space of two heartbeats. His head swung in her direction and their eyes clashed, then skipped away. "No. He did not choose to make me his wife."

"Jackass," Billy mumbled under his breath.

"My brother took Domha back to our village when he was very small. He said I could not care for him in the camp. After I met Rachel I grew stronger within myself. I knew I must get him back. My friend helped me." She looked at Rachel sitting cross-legged by the wok, washing Domha's black pants and shirt, and smiled. Rachel smiled back, her throat tight with tears. The baby started to fuss. Ahnle looked away. "I think you hold him too tightly," she said, hesitant once more.

"Yeah." Billy eased his grip on the little boy and began to dandle him gently on his knee. Domha started to giggle. The adults all smiled, one more reluctantly than the others.

"You are good with him. Do you have children in America?"

"If I had any children they'd be older than you are," Billy growled. Lonnie glanced at Rachel and winked. The two of them might as well not have existed, as far as Ahnle and Billy were concerned.

"Here it comes," Lonnie whispered, breaking off a long blade of grass that was growing between the cracks of two paving stones.

"Do you have a wife?"

Billy stopped bouncing the baby, who immediately took exception to his ride ending. "Not anymore."

"Good. But I would not mind a lot if you did have a wife." Ahnle looked at her hands but Rachel saw the edges of a smile curve her lips.

"What the hell do you mean by that?" Billy was starting to look concerned. Lonnie stuck the blade of grass in his mouth and started to chew. Rachel squeezed the water out of the baby clothes and smoothed them over the warm stones surrounding the temple well to dry, then sat back to see what would happen next.

"Nothing," Ahnle said sweetly, too sweetly. Rachel began to realize there was more grit to the girl than even she had suspected.

"Ahnle. Forget it." Billy sounded trapped. Lonnie gave a snort of laughter that earned him a sharp, harried glance from his comrade-at-arms. "I'm too old for you."

"Too old?" Ahnle sounded genuinely surprised. "Oh no. You are just the correct age for taking a second wife."

"Second wife?" He thrust the baby into his mother's arms and rose to his feet in one hurried movement. "Where the hell did you get a crack-brained idea like that? The last thing in the world I want is to be tied down with a wife and kid. With a wife who's a kid herself." He turned on his heel and marched out of the courtyard, leaving the rest of them sitting in stunned silence.

"Oh dear, what have I done?" Ahnle sounded close to tears. "I have shamed myself and Billy, too." She lifted Domha to her shoulder and sniffed back a tear.

"You sure ruffled the old rooster's feathers." Lonnie's cheerful voice made Ahnle lift her head and look at him.

"I should not have been so bold. But my brother is not here to arrange a marriage for me. I only wanted to let Billy Todd know that I would consent to be his second wife. But he says he has no other. I would be a good wife. I can cook and plant corn and sew and weave. I have proven that I can bear a child." She looked puzzled and sad and Rachel realized that although she'd come far in her understanding of Western ways, she still had a lot to learn.

"*Farangs* don't pick their wives for the same reasons that The People do," Lonnie said, before Rachel could voice her thoughts. "Most of the time they marry for love."

"That is not practical," Ahnle said, hushing Domha by offering him a bottle of powdered milk. He nestled into the crook of her arm and suckled greedily.

"You've got that right, but it's the way we do things. I'm not sayin' old Bill don't have it bad for you, but he thinks he's too damned old to be a good husband. I guess it's up to you to change his mind."

"Is this true?" Ahnle asked Rachel, her tear-bright eyes beginning to sparkle with new hope, and something more, something she'd only just admitted to herself, Rachel suspected. The strange, inexplicable feelings she'd been harboring for Billy Todd were not all practical considerations of choosing a husband according to custom. She was in love. Rachel saw the realization dawn on her face like an explosion of light beneath the surface of her skin.

"It is true. But you cannot make another love you," Rachel cautioned, as she held out her hands to take Domha, so that Ahnle could go in search of Billy and do battle for his reluctant heart.

"I know that. But I can try." She hurried out of the courtyard, leaving Rachel and the baby alone with Lonnie.

"I bet they'll be married inside a month." He looked enormously pleased with himself, happy, relaxed, and Rachel knew he was high. She hesitated momentarily before handing him the baby he'd reached out his arms to take, and hated herself for doing so.

"Don't sweat it," he said, sensing her reluctance. "I'm about as straight as I can get anymore. I won't hurt him."

"I didn't think you would." She watched as he settled the baby in the crook of his arm and gave him his bottle. "Lonnie, why don't you get some help for your addiction?"

"I have. Brett's got me in three or four rehab centers, but no luck. I'm hooked, Rachel."

"If you tried again I'd help... we'd all help."

He shook his head and there was a world of sadness in the matter-of-fact gesture. "I can't, Rachel. And maybe, deep down, I don't want to. There's too much there to remember, stuff I don't ever want to think about again. That's how I got hooked. I saw what it did for the other guys, how it took away their hurtin' and gave them back their dreams. Some nights, when the past is too close...."

"Don't let the past destroy your future...."

"It's the same for you," he said bluntly. Rachel couldn't meet his candid gaze. She watched the baby, instead, as his eyes grew heavy and then blinked open again, fighting sleep. "You've got memories stuffed away, down inside you in a hole so dark and so deep you pray they won't ever get close enough to sneak into your dreams again. Don't you?" he pressed.

"Yes." Rachel continued to watch as the baby, contented and full, drifted off to sleep.

"I've seen it in your eyes when you're around men," Lonnie went on, his ruined voice a rough whisper above the sound of bird song and wind through the palms. "You were scared at Khen Sa's camp and in the Teak Doll. I can guess some of the reasons for that. What I can't understand is why, sometimes, I see those same ghosts in your eyes when you look at him."

Rachel lifted her eyes and saw him staring down at Domha. Sensing her gaze, he raised his head and waited for her answer, his green eyes filled with pain and resignation.

"Because I had a son. He was never strong and happy and healthy, as Domha is. He died a few days after he was born. I hated....the man ....who was his father. And I hated the baby. Until I held him in my arms. And then it was too late." Rachel looked past Lonnie, trying to blink back the tears that came too easily these days, trying to keep the ghosts at bay, and saw Brett watching her.

How long had he been there? Had he overheard her exchange of confidences with Lonnie? What could she say now that he knew about her son? Would he see the rest of her secrets in her eyes? He read people so well.

If she told him her pregnancy had resulted from a random act of violence, as she'd told the others, would he believe her? Or would he know that she was lying?

She'd hidden the truth so well, for so long, she had begun to believe it herself. . . .

"I have to go," she said, so urgently that Lonnie handed Domha to her without another word. "I have to go." She stood up, holding the sleeping baby tightly to her breast, and fled.

THE MOON WAS FULL AGAIN, as it had been the first night Rachel had come to the temple nearly a year ago. Brett sucked on the stem of his pipe to keep the tobacco burning steadily, but he did so absently, his attention fixed on the courtyard below the parapet where he stood.

Behind him, the jungle settled into uneasy sleep. Cicadas sang in the flame trees, birds tittered and argued among themselves as they dozed off. Somewhere off in the distance the roar of a hunting cat echoed through the trees. He noted and catalogued each sound, each silvered flash of movement, with a predator's objectivity, yet his eyes never left the woman bathing at the temple wall.

She was naked and moonlight sparkled in her hair like diamond drops, rippled down the curve of her spine and over the gentle swell of her hips like a lover's caress. She knew he was there, watching, yet she didn't turn around. She wrapped a length of Thai silk, whose color he could only guess at in the moonlight, around herself and tucked in the ends sarong-style above her breasts. Kneeling, she poured fresh water into the copper wok in which she'd bathed Ahnle's baby that afternoon and began to wash her hair. He watched a moment longer, then left the parapet without making a sound to disturb the night and descended the griffin staircase.

Rachel was still kneeling on the flat stones surrounding the well. Her hair was wet and glistening as she poured water from a bowl over her head to rinse out the soap. He dropped to the balls of his feet and touched her shoulder lightly. "Let me help."

She turned her head, looked at him for a long, heart-stopping handful of seconds, then nodded. "All right."

He picked up the bowl and poured the clear cool water over her hair. She smelled of soap and clean, damp skin and wet silk. His fingers brushed across the nape of her neck. Her skin was smooth as velvet and milky white in the moonlight, her movements graceful as she twisted the water from her hair and wrapped her head in another length of silk. She sat back on her heels and took the empty bowl from his hands.

"Thank you," she said quietly. "I feel really clean for the first time in days and days." She let her head drop back on her shoulders and lifted her hand to massage away the tension.

"You've been through a lot." He cupped the bowl of his pipe in his hand and stuck the other one in the pocket of his pants to keep from reaching out to her.

"Ummm." She leaned back a little farther to look at the stars. Brett looked at her, his eyes following the rise and fall of her breasts above the thin silk that obscured but didn't hide what lay beneath. She felt him watching her and looked back into his eyes. "It was worth it."

"I know." He looked away, across the deserted courtyard.

"What are you thinking?" Rachel asked in a voice that stirred his senses almost as much as the sight of her naked had done.

"That when we leave this place the jungle will take back the temple, just as if none of us had ever disturbed its rest."

"That's the way it should be." She shivered a little as an errant breeze swept across the temple clearing, looking for a way back into the treetops. "I was sorry to hear that the Acharya died."

Rachel was looking at the moon shadows in the courtyard, too. He turned his head once more to watch her profile, making no move to touch her or frighten her away. He wanted her here, beside him. He wanted to make love to her, take her with him to a place where there was no one but the two of them, but he had to move very slowly or she would slip through his fingers like smoke.

"He was very old." Her bone structure was delicate, her nose a little too large to be called snub. She made him think of cloud castles and butterfly wings. But there was strength beneath the softness. Her chin and jaw were firm, with a stubborn tilt that hinted at the determination and courage of the woman inside the seemingly fragile body.

"How did he die?" she asked.

"He died of a heart attack, at his prayers."

"You spoke of leaving here. Does that mean you don't intend to keep using this place as your base camp?"

He knew what she was really asking. He answered as truthfully as he could. "We'll stay here as long as necessary, not one day more." He thought of the three-quarters of a million dollars in gold hidden beneath the temple floor. He thought of the five hundred pounds of processed heroin in Khen Sa's camp and the misery and death it would bring in the West. It could never be allowed to leave these hills. But he couldn't tell Rachel that. It was dangerous for her to be here, at all. If he failed, no one would take the blame but him. If he succeeded, no one would know that, as well.

"I see." She was silent. She reached out and let her hand trail along the fronds of a fern growing at the base of the well. "Perhaps, someday, you'll trust me enough to tell me why you're doing this."

"Perhaps, someday, you'll tell me your secrets, as well."

The delicate fern snapped beneath the convulsive tightening of her fingers. Her breasts rose and fell as she sucked in her breath to deny his words. He didn't touch her, although his hands itched to reach out and pull her close. His heart beat heavy and hard in his chest. His blood surged through his veins and he felt himself grow hard and aching with need and desire.

"You heard what I said to Lonnie this afternoon." She reached up and pulled the square of silk from her hair. Her hands were shaking, he could see that, even in the half-light of the high-riding moon.

"Yes." He wondered if she would fight him if he took her in his arms. She had been hurt badly in the past. He wanted to be the man who helped her get beyond that pain. Perhaps tonight was the night to try. Yet he sensed she wouldn't welcome his lovemaking and that was what he wanted more than anything else. He wanted her to turn to him, to come into his arms, willing and desiring. He wanted it with such intensity it scared him.

"It was a long time ago." She looked down at her hands, saw that she was twisting the silk, and began, instead, to smooth it between her fingers.

"I'm sorry that your son died. I've never fathered a child but I've lost friends and family. I can understand something of your pain."

"I don't want to talk about it." Her words were stiff, her jaw set. She began to twist the silk again. "I've learned to cherish my memories of him and to blot out all the rest—the pain and the fear. Don't make me remember it again." It was a plea but he ignored it.

"You haven't learned to trust me at all, have you?" He ground the coals from the pipe under his heel. The smell of tobacco smoke momentarily overpowered the smell of the jungle and dusty stones and the warm sweetness of Rachel's hair and skin.

"Yes, I have. But I can't trust myself where the past is concerned." There were tears in her eyes, making them sparkle like diamonds. She blinked them back with an effort. "I've worked so hard to keep from remembering." She held out her hand. "I do trust you." She looked at him with wonder on her face and haunting questions darkening her eyes. "But I don't know you, not really. And I'm afraid of you because you make me feel too much. You make me look too deeply inside myself, into those places that I fear, just as much as Lonnie said I did."

He stood up then, pulling her with him, and she came into his arms with no more hesitation. She pressed herself close; her arms lifted to circle his neck. The feel of her body against his sent a jolt of desire arcing along his nerve endings. She was naked beneath the silk, soft and hot and damp, and he wanted to bury himself in that heat, slip into that welcoming sweetness and take her with him into oblivion.

"There isn't anything you can't tell me." He cupped her buttocks in his hands, molded her close, and the thin silk between them was nothing more than a whisper of sensation. He could feel her nipples harden against his chest and the softness of her belly pressed against his hips. She lifted her face for his kiss and her lips were honey and fire. He let his tongue slide inside her mouth, explore its sweetness, mimic a more intimate joining of their bodies, a coupling he longed for more than anything else.

"I'm not ready to remember." She sounded like a little girl, a kid, lost in the dark.

"Then maybe it's time for us to start making new memories of our own." He lifted her into his arms. His voice sounded hoarse and strange, even to his own ears, so he didn't speak again, just carried her beneath the shadow of the ruined wall into the main room of the temple, echoing and vast, and on into the warren of small rooms beyond.

There was a candle burning on the rough wooden table in the room he'd staked out as his own. He set Rachel gently on her feet. He slipped his hand beneath the heavy, damp layers of her hair and cupped the nape of her neck. He kissed her again, the corners of her mouth, the curve of her cheek and the velvety softness of her eyelids. She was trembling once more, but this time with pleasure, not remembered pain. The knowledge made him realize the power of love, what it could do to your heart and soul and brain. It took you over, possessed you. It was wonderful and it was terrifying.

He opened his eyes and found her looking at him. She lifted her hands, traced the outline of his jaw, the heavy growth of beard on his cheeks. She held his face captive between her hands, searched his eyes, as though she might read his thoughts in their depths. "Do you believe you can forget the past if you have someone to help you?"

"I think love can heal most every kind of hurt. If you're lucky enough to find it." He took a deep breath. He felt as if he'd been running hard, for a long time. He felt as if he were trying to breathe underwater. She shook her head slightly. Her breasts were pressed against him. Her body fit his like a glove. "Let me make love to you, Rachel."

"I don't know . . . it's been so long." She was trembling again.

"It's like riding a bike," he said with a smile. The last thing he wanted to do was frighten her more. Whoever had hurt her in the past had nearly destroyed the passion in her.

"Brett?" She looked around her a little wildly. Her hands clamped over his as he worked at the knot of her sarong.

"Trust me." The length of silk whispered to the ground. He held her close, kissed her again and again until she melted against him, until she moaned with desire that matched his own.

Brett laid her on the rough cotton blanket covering the narrow cot that was his bed. He stripped off his clothes and lay down beside her. He pulled the mosquito netting around them, sealing them inside a gauzy cocoon. For a time he only held her, caressed her, letting his hands move lightly across her shoulders, down her arms, over the curve of her hip. Slowly he increased the intensity of those caresses, moved closer to the swell of her breast, the shadowed, hidden places between her legs.

Rachel shuddered and turned her face into his shoulder. She lay passive for a while but slowly she began to respond; then he felt her lips on his skin. She drew her fingers along the roughness of his jaw, slid her hand behind his neck and urged his mouth down to cover hers. She pressed against him, let her hand slide between them to touch him, a caress so feather light and so explosive he moaned out loud.

Brett pulled her beneath him then, urged her legs apart, refused to see the wariness in her eyes because he knew her body, at least, was ready and willing to receive him. He entered her slowly, resting his weight on his elbows, cradling her face between his hands as he kissed her reluctance away. She stiffened at the unfamiliar feel of him within her, then relaxed beneath him. Her arms curled around his neck and she began to move in concert with him as her body adjusted to his.

He kissed her again and again. He led her on with slow deliberate strokes but old fears held her back, and when his release broke over him, he knew she hadn't experienced her own.

"I'm sorry." She turned her head to the wall. "I told you it had been . . ."

"Shhh." He turned her face so that she had to look at him. Her hair spread out over the pillow and the silver strands among the black caught and held the feeble light of the candle. "Next time will be better. And the time after that and the time after that." He smiled and brushed a damp strand of hair from her cheek. It was silky and soft. The scent of soap mingled with the musky warmth of their lovemaking.

"Do you want to make love to me again?" He felt her tense beneath him. The movement pushed their lower bodies together. He hadn't withdrawn from her and he felt himself grow hard again.

"This time is for you." His mind was swirling with desire and need and the beginning of dangerous dreams. Dreams of tomorrow and the day after and every day for the rest of their lives, when all he really had was tonight.

"Brett?" She sounded breathless, confused, and excited. "Brett, please, help me." Her eyes fluttered shut and she moaned in mingled pleasure and frustration. "Please."

He surged into her and felt her body contract around him, clutching him with velvety strength as the tension built within them. "Let go, Rachel," he murmured, his voice taut with strain and his own aching need. "Let go." She held him tightly, still fighting for control. He wrapped her legs around him and filled her completely.

"I . . . can't." The words were nothing more than a breathless whisper. "I can't."

"You can." He stroked into her again and again and then reached between them to touch her, a feather-light caress that sent her spinning out of control. "Let go," he whispered once more against her lips as he felt her shatter into ecstasy beneath him and felt his own release build to a climax. "Let go and step into the whirlwind."

"IT'S LATE. BETTER get some sleep." Simon McKendrick leaned against the door frame of Rachel's flimsy cottage and swatted at a mosquito singing past his ear. Malaria mosquitoes came out at night. He tried to remember if he'd taken his antimalarial pill that morning and decided he had. They'd been in the camp five days and he was beginning to lose his patience with the slow pace of Thai officialdom. He had no more idea where his sister and her young Hlông friend were now than he'd had eight days earlier when his plane touched down in Bangkok.

"You go ahead. I'm not tired. I think I'll just sit out here and watch the stars." Micah was hunkered down on the wooden plank, supported by two cement blocks, that did duty as Rachel's front step, his back propped against the side of the cottage, his face turned up to the sky. The stars, brighter now that the full moon had set behind the hills, were shimmering points of light in the inky darkness.

"The sky sure looks different here." He sat down on the plank beside his brother. If ever, for a moment, he forgot just how far away from home he really was, all he had to do was look at the night sky. The unfamiliar alignment of planets and constellations might have belonged to an alien world.

"What did you find out today?" Micah crossed his arms over his chest but didn't take his eyes off the sky.

Simon considered what to say. Micah had spent the day helping Father Dolph and Dr. Reynard distribute a shipment of clothing donated by a parish in Louisiana, while he'd spent most of his time in Father Dolph's office, trying to get through to Bangkok on the telephone. It had been a tedious and time-consuming exercise in frustration. The phone system in and around the city was excellent. This far into the hills, it left a lot to be desired.

"DEA doesn't know what the hell your friend Tiger Jackson is up to but it's something big. If the CIA knows, they aren't saying. DEA also says a lot of their usual sources of information have suddenly, and mysteriously, dried up."

"Tiger never does anything halfway. You can't in his line of business and stay alive, you ought to know that." Micah didn't sound as if Simon's words surprised him in the least. It was going to take more than a few rumors of something big going down in the hills north of Chiang Rai to shake his faith in his friend.

"As soon as we get some word on Rachel, we'll go get her."

"What makes you think Tiger won't bring her back safe and sound?"

Simon turned his head. He wished he had his brother's faith in Tiger Jackson's abilities...and integrity. He didn't trust the man at all but he wasn't about to start a fight with Micah over it.

"Okay, I'll rephrase that. When Rachel gets back here, with Tiger's help or with ours, we're going to have to track down your friend and have a cozy little talk. And I don't intend to end the conversation until I have all the answers I need.''

RACHEL WOKE FROM A DEEP sleep in stages, slowly, with a feeling of peace and contentment that faded into familiar and unwelcome sadness as she grew aware of her surroundings. She lay very still, listening to the dawn sounds outside the temple and to the steady, even breathing of the man sleeping beside her. This was the second time she'd awakened in Brett's bed, and this time she had experienced the full measure of his love. She closed her eyes to try once more to capture the memory of his touch but the pleasant fantasy slipped through her fingers and was gone.

She sat up and drew her knees up to her chin. Brett stirred in his sleep and turned on his side, facing her. She saw the silver tracery of old scars crisscrossing his chest and shoulders, the new, angry red line of the graze on his arm, and almost against her will, she reached out to touch him. She felt the solid warmth of his skin, the crisp dusting of dark blond hair, familiar now, beneath her fingertips, and she wanted more.

Brett had made love to her time and again through the night. He'd been gentle and persistent and rough and cajoling by turns. He had teased and tantalized and filled her with heat and longing until the ice inside her melted away and she found herself a woman once again.

He had made love to her and she had loved him in return, would always love him. *Oh, God, what was she going to do?*

Rachel dropped her head onto her knees. *Why now?* Why had she allowed him to show her that the passion and desire inside her weren't dead but only dormant and capable of being brought to life once more? He had taught her to love again. Her joy was in their love and in their sharing; her sorrow was in knowing neither could last. He was the wrong man, in the wrong place, at the wrong time. If she admitted she loved him and something happened to him, she would lose her soul.

She started to push aside the woven cotton blanket that covered them both, only to have Brett's fingers close strongly about her wrist.

"Good morning," he said.

"Good morning." She looked at him because she couldn't stop herself. He was wide awake, completely alert, harder and more dangerous-looking than ever with two days' growth of dark blond hair on his chin.

Dangerous. Rachel shivered.

"What's wrong?"

"Nothing."

"You're lying." He stood up, completely unconcerned by his nakedness, and pushed aside the mosquito netting. Rachel clasped her hands around her knees and stayed where she was. He pulled on his pants and yanked the belt through the buckle. He stood watching her for a long moment. "Do you regret making love to me last night, Rachel?" he asked bluntly.

It wouldn't do her any good to lie. He could see the answer in her face. "Yes."

"Do you want to tell me why?"

Rachel felt him drawing away and knew she'd hurt him. She wished she wasn't naked under the blanket. She wished she could tell him to come back to bed, to love her again, to keep on loving her until the world went away and left them alone together for the rest of time.

"I regret making love to you because it makes it that much harder to leave you."

He went very still for a moment, then snuffed the flame of the guttering candle between his fingers. He came back to the bed and sat down at her feet. "Why do you have to leave?"

"I have to go," she repeated stubbornly. "I'm falling in love with you." The words caught in her throat. She had to force them past the tears that threatened to break free. "I can't afford to love you. If I do, I'll lose myself again. I won't have the strength to find my way back." She leaned forward, drew her hand along the strong column of his neck, let her fingers linger for a moment on the slow, steady beat of the pulse in the hollow of his throat. "I have to leave here today, now." She leaned back, away from him. But she ached to have him hold her close again. She wanted him to touch her, love her, make her feel whole.

"If that's what you want." He didn't beg her to stay. He wouldn't. He had promised her never to make her do anything against her will.

"It's not what I want. It's what I have to do." Rachel looked at him in the pale dawn light inside the monk's cell. She tried to read his thoughts in the twilight blue of his eyes and saw only herself reflected in miniature in their depths. "Can't you feel it?" she asked, her voice low and sad, almost overpowered by the awakening jungle outside. "It's in the air around us. I sense it whenever you're near and it frightens me."

"What? What frightens you, Rachel?" He took her cold, shaking hands in his, warming them with his body heat and with his strength.

"Danger," she said, looking away into the future, into the unknown. "Danger and death."

CHAPTER THIRTEEN

"HAVE YOU AND SIMON been arguing again?" Rachel asked. She'd been sitting quietly in the sun on the step of her hut, half daydreaming, half watching Micah trim his beard.

"It wasn't an argument. It was a discussion." He finished his beard, surveyed himself in a small hand mirror and started to work on his thick head of dark hair.

"I heard your *discussion* all the way down the street." Rachel frowned at the memory and at the mess Micah was making of his haircut. "Here, let me do that." She took the scissors from his hand and started to trim the hair at the nape of his neck. "Sit still." She flicked the scissors a fraction of an inch closer to his earlobe than necessary. He stopped fidgeting and sat still as a stone on the hard wooden chair he'd appropriated from the main room of the hut. "Can't I leave you two alone for a couple of hours without a fight breaking out?"

Finding her brothers firmly entrenched in her small hut when she returned to the camp had produced an emotion blended of almost equal parts of happiness and dismay.

"I told you it wasn't a fight."

"Did you win or lose?" Rachel persisted. Micah didn't flinch again, although the scissors continued to hover very close to his ear.

"Actually, I won. That's why we're talking. Simon's idea was to chloroform you and keep you drugged until our plane landed back in Chicago."

"Don't be ridiculous." Rachel couldn't help laughing at the exaggerated menace in Micah's cloak-and-dagger tone of voice. It was wonderful to hear him tease her as he'd done when they were younger, even about so touchy a subject as her staying in Thailand. "I don't want to go home," she reminded him for the hundredth time.

Somewhere nearby a cock crowed, although it was almost noon. Rachel automatically checked her watch. Hospital rounds with Dr. Reynard had taken longer than she expected, but she was glad to be back at work. Around them, women were lighting charcoal cook fires to boil rice and vegetables for the noon meal. She was hungry, too. Her stomach growled.

"We think it would be a good idea for you to come home with us."

Rachel wasn't sure how much of her heavily edited description of the events of the past two weeks her brothers had believed. She hadn't kept anything back except for their visit to Khen Sa's camp, because she was afraid they might ask her if she could get back there—and she thought, just possibly, that she could. *And she had told them nothing of her involvement with Brett.* It was her memory, alone, not one to share. She had also warned Ahnle not to discuss that part of their adventure with anyone, and Ahnle seemed happy to comply, probably Rachel suspected because Ahnle had fallen in love with Billy Todd. As Rachel had fallen in love with Brett, although she wished she could say it wasn't true. She didn't see much hope of happiness ahead for either of them.

"No," she said firmly, brandishing the shears. "I won't run out on Father Dolph again. And I can't get the necessary papers for Ahnle to accompany me until at least the first of the year."

"Mom and Dad are going to be disappointed if you aren't home for the holidays."

"I stayed home for the holidays last year," she reminded him.

"Father Dolph will look after Ahnle. You can be all settled back in the States by the time the visas for her and the baby come through."

"Micah," Rachel said warningly. "Don't push it. I know how much I owe the two of you. I probably won't ever be able to come up with enough money to reimburse Simon for the pearls." Her brothers had steadfastly refused to disclose the value of the pearl necklace that had bought her and Micah's freedom from the Vietnamese. She'd given up trying to find out—for the time being.

"Forget the pearls. Having you back was worth every cent, you know that."

She squeezed his shoulder. "I know that." A group of young boys in the saffron-colored robes of Buddhist monks strolled by, alms bowls held in front of them as they begged for rice for their noonday meal. Devout Buddhists came to the front doors of their small huts to put balls of sticky rice, vegetables and even bits of meat in the bowls. They were both silent a moment, watching the ritual that underlined how far from home they were, yet made them both aware of how beautiful and unique this country was.

"If you'd let me work out a payment..."

"Rachel," Micah growled.

"Maybe I could forget how much the pearls were worth if you both didn't have families to support and educate." For many months she hadn't even been aware that Micah's Michigan home had been mortgaged to pay Simon his share of the expense of the pearl necklace.

Simon had balked, refused to take the money, but Micah was equally insistent that he did. They had argued for days. In the end Micah won, by the simple expedient of depositing the money into an account in his brother's name.

It made her more determined than ever to find a way to pay them back. "I should have done a book or sold the movie rights...." She stopped talking, knowing she could never go on living her carefully orchestrated lies if reporters or scriptwriters began probing into the darkness beneath the surface of her life.

Micah lifted his hand and circled the wrist holding the scissors. He swiveled around on the chair seat to face her.

"Is that why you're here? Is this some kind of penance?"

"Of course not." She spoke too quickly and he knew it.

Micah nodded, his blue-gray eyes, so like her own, searching for the emotions beneath her carefully shielded gaze. "I know what you're doing here is important to you, but it's not the only reason you're not ready to go home, is it?" He lifted the hand still holding the mirror to stop her automatic protest. "What's keeping you here is your own business, unless it has something to do with Tiger Jackson."

"Don't press your luck or I'll be arguing with you, just like I've been arguing with Simon for the past three days." When she thought about it rationally, it amused her to see her two dominating and aggressive brothers so thrown off balance by her refusal to look at things their way. They weren't used to her asserting herself quite so forcefully. "Bullheaded" was the word Simon had used as he stomped out of the hut just before she left for her hospital duties that morning.

"Tiger was always quite the ladies' man," Micah continued, ignoring her warning. "I remember one time when we were on R&R in Vientiane when he had three..." He seemed to remember he was talking to his sister. "Never mind...."

"Go on," Rachel laughed, enjoying the red stain of embarrassment that crept above the collar of his shirt. She was pleased to hear Micah talk about the war, no matter how disreputable the story. For so long he'd suppressed his memories of the three tours of duty he'd spent with the Ravens in Laos.

"I need to talk to Tiger, Rachel. Take me to him." He looked down at her wrist, still circled by his own strong fingers.

"No." He'd changed the subject so suddenly she was caught off guard. She couldn't meet his eyes, but she felt him looking at her. "I...I don't think I could find my way to his camp. I . . . I told you that when his men brought us back."

"Liar." He said it gently and released her hand.

"Micah . . ." She was trembling and he'd felt it.

"Tiger always did inspire loyalty."

"I'm not involved with Tiger, Micah."

"I think you are. You hide your thoughts pretty well but I think you're in love with him. After all," he said, smiling as he thought of his wife and son back home, "I know the signs."

Rachel remained silent. Anything she said would only be more lies. She couldn't make peace with her own feelings; how could she explain them to another? She loved a man she ought to despise. She'd *made* love with that man and wanted to go on doing so for the rest of her life.

"I don't want to talk about him," she said at last.

"It's the company Simon's been keeping since we got here that's got you scared, isn't it?"

She nodded. "They're DEA, aren't they?" The Drug Enforcement Agency of the United States government kept a low profile, but they were active in Thailand, all the same. And Simon had managed to get himself attached to the district office in Chiang Mai on a temporary basis. Rachel felt as if she had to guard every word she said to him. She hated the awkward position she was placed in by her divided loyalties.

"They're not hard to spot when they show up in a place like this," Micah agreed. "Our little brother is doing what he thinks is right."

"Imagine, Baby Simon, the authority figure in our lives." She shook her head, laughing softly. Micah chuckled, too. She felt so torn. She could confide in Micah, she knew. He had trusted Brett Jackson with his life countless times in the past. He still trusted his friend, and he would go on believing in him until he had undeniable proof of his guilt. She couldn't put him in the position of having to lie to Simon, as she was doing.

She was protecting Brett for reasons she scarcely understood herself. She hated what Brett was doing out there in the jungle. She hated the men he dealt with, Khen Sa and his henchmen and how many others just like them? Brett was involved in criminal activities, and she couldn't condone his actions for a moment. Yet she would go on protecting him as long as possible. It made no sense. Unless she admitted she was in love, as Micah contended. Her heart knew the truth, but saying the words out loud was impossible.

Micah stood up, towering over her. He pulled the towel off his shoulders, gave it a shake and draped it over the back of the chair. "I'll bet Brett Jackson is doing what he thinks is right, too."

Rachel looked into his eyes, narrowing her own against the brightness of the noonday sun. "You knew him a long time ago. It's possible he's a different man . . . it's possible that life has . . . changed him into someone you couldn't possibly know or trust." *Someone living a lie, as she was herself.*

"Not here," he said, touching the second button of her blouse with the tip of his finger. "Nothing could change in his heart, where it counts. You don't change there, no matter what happens to you in life."

"I wish I could believe that." *For the sake of her own sins, as well as for Brett.* "I wish I could."

"You do." Micah handed her the small mirror. He smiled, looking pleased with the result of the conversation and so sure of himself. He ran his hands over his beard and through his neatly trimmed hair. "Got another mirror so I can see the back?"

"Only the one over the sink." Did she believe what he had said about Brett? About herself? She wasn't sure she dared, but later, when she was alone, she would think about Micah's words some more. She gathered up the towel as Micah picked up the chair to return it to the hut. "What do you want for lunch? Rice? Or rice?" she asked with a smile of her own, a little thin and quavery around the edges, perhaps, but a smile nonetheless.

"I've got an idea," Micah said, smiling back at her. "Let's have rice, for a change."

BILLY TODD STOOD BEYOND the small circle of light that spilled from the single window and door of Rachel's hut, a darker figure in the shadows that surrounded him. The woven mats that served as protection against the cool winter nights had been pushed back from the screened openings and he could see the two women moving around inside, talking, laughing softly as they worked.

Rachel's brothers were nowhere to be seen. He'd made certain of that before he ventured this far into the camp. He had already ascertained that they were playing poker with Father Dolph and Dr. Reynard in the priest's quarters at the far end of the dusty, narrow street. The game probably wouldn't break up before midnight. He intended to be long gone by then, back on the road to Chiang Mai, where he planned to spend the night.

As he watched Ahnle through the window, she knelt to place her son in a sleeping basket on the floor. He could hear her singing to the baby, a haunting, mel-ancholy tune that was a Hlông lullaby. Her hair was uncovered, twisted high on her head in an intricate knot. It caught the light from the naked overhead bulb in its ebony depths and he remembered the feel of it beneath his hands, the softness of her body pressed close to his, the taste of her mouth, sweet and shy, the first time he kissed her in the temple courtyard.

His body tightened and hardened and he wanted her in his arms again. He wanted her in his bed so that he could know every inch of her, and beyond that, he wanted to keep her with him forever. He'd never con-sidered having a woman of his own, a family of his own, not for twenty years. He wanted them now with an intensity that sometimes took his breath away.

But if he didn't talk Rachel Phillips into coming back to the temple with him so that Brett could find out what, if anything, she'd told her bloodhound of a brother, they were all going to be deader than a mackerel inside of ten days.

Rachel sat down at a small table along the far wall of the hut's main room and began to write a letter, or work on a report, or something. Ahnle stood up and walked out of his line of sight. Billy waited, his eyes fastened on the hut, the rest of his senses sorting through the myriad of sounds and scents that swirled around him as the camp settled down for the night. A few moments later, Ahnle appeared in the doorway, carrying a small basin. She opened the screen and stepped outside to empty the water carefully over a small plot of plants growing outside the door.

She was wearing a *phassin,* a Thai-style sarong, in some dark color, that she probably slept in. Her feet were bare and she'd taken the pins from her hair. It hung straight and free, almost to her waist.

"Ahnle." He stepped out of the shadows where he'd been standing. He didn't raise his voice because he didn't want Rachel to hear. And he certainly didn't want to disturb the dogs and chickens and people sleeping in the huts around them.

"Who's there?" she asked in Thai. She moved out of the square of light from the doorway. For a heartbeat he lost her in the darkness, then found her again, moving gracefully forward, her face a pale oval in the fading moonlight.

"It's Billy, Ahnle." He came to the edge of the dusty street and a moment later she was in his arms. He couldn't stop himself. He pulled her close, wrapped her in his arms and savored the scent and shape and feel of her against him. When he held her like this, nothing else mattered, not the difference in their ages, their cultures, their race. He was in love with a girl young enough to be his daughter and he didn't give a damn who knew about it.

"Billy, I miss you so." She lifted her face for his kiss. She was a very passionate woman beneath the passive exterior she showed to the world. She learned quickly and the taste of her small, pointed tongue as it darted into his mouth with butterfly quickness made his head reel with desire.

"God, sweetheart, I've missed you, too. How's Domha?"

"He grows like a Big Boy tomato plant. Rachel's brother, Micah, the one who is as big as a water buffalo, calls him that. Big Boy. I like it." She giggled and wrapped her arms around his neck, pressing close. He let her talk. He loved the sound of her voice, the funny little ways she fractured English sentences and rearranged them to suit herself. "He has a small son, also. Not many seasons older than Domha. Rachel says they will play together when we go to America."

She fell silent as his arms tightened convulsively around her. "You're going to America?"

"When Rachel arranges with the head men of the States, yes." She didn't meet his eyes. He couldn't read her expression in the fitful light of the waning moon, but he could feel her resistance. "I...I do not want to go," she said finally, hesitantly.

"I don't want you to go." He could no more have stopped himself from saying the words than he could have stopped the moon from slipping away over the hills.

"I will stay with you." Ahnle wound her arms around his neck and pulled his head down for another kiss. Billy gave in to the bittersweet temptation to feel her mouth on his again, but when the kiss ended, he took her by the shoulders and held her at arm's length.

"If Rachel wants to take you to America you'll agree to go. Do you understand?" He hardened his heart to the pain that blossomed in her face.

"You do not want me? You do not want my son?"

"I may not be around to take care of you."

"We have learned to take care of ourselves," she said with pride.

"I know that." He touched her hair, let his hand slide along the silken fall of it. "What I mean is, I may not be able to take care of you." He might was well say it. Ahnle wasn't some sheltered little Georgia peach of a girl. She was a woman in the eyes of her people, a people hardened to the tragedies of living—and dying. "We go to Khen Sa's camp very soon. If we don't succeed there, I won't come back. Ever."

"Oh, no. Don't go." She wiggled free of his restraining grip on her shoulders and threw herself into his arms. "You will be killed there, sure. They are bad men. I know. I have seen such others in my village." She clasped her hands so tightly around his waist, he grunted in surprise.

"Ahnle..." Inside the hut the baby began to cry. Billy didn't finish what he had started to say. He saw Rachel get up from the table and stoop to take Domha into her arms. She stood up, looked around and walked to the door.

"Ahnle?" she called softly into the darkness. Ahnle put her fingers over his mouth. He knew if he faded into the deeper shadows among the huts across the street, she would say nothing of his being there. But that wasn't the purpose of his visit. It was Rachel Phillips he'd come to see.

He gave Ahnle a nudge. She looked at him, puzzled. "Answer her," he said in a rough whisper only she could hear.

"Over here, Rachel. I...I am with Billy Todd."

He stepped into the oblong of light that spilled across the ground outside the hut, keeping Ahnle close to his side. Rachel looked at them both for a long moment, then opened the door.

"You'd better come inside. The mosquitoes are bad tonight and we don't want anyone coming down with malaria. We've been so fortunate in that respect." She stopped talking abruptly as the door closed with a

snick of the latch behind him. Out of habit, he moved
to a corner of the room where he couldn't be seen from
outside. Rachel noticed the maneuver but said nothing. She handed the baby to Ahnle, who took the little boy with a smile and moved back to stand beside
him.

"What do you want, Billy?" Rachel asked, flick-
ing the ash from a burning coil of mosquito repellent
that was sitting on the table where she'd been working. She straightened a pile of papers before turning
back to look at him.

She was wearing a *phassin,* too. It was cotton, in a
pattern of jungle flowers in pastel shades. Over it, she
was wearing a simple white cotton blouse, open down
the front. Her feet were bare, her hair pushed care-
lessly behind her ears. She was a good-looking
woman, and if Brett was half as much in love with her
as he was with Ahnle, they were both too far gone to
save themselves.

"I came to give you a message from Tiger."

Her dark, arched brows drew together as she
frowned. "I don't think this visit is a good idea. You
know my brothers are here."

"That's what he wants to talk to you about." As far
as he was concerned, it was okay if Rachel Phillips
knew everything there was to tell about the deal with
Khen Sa. If he was going back up into the hills to get
killed, he'd like to have someone know the real reason why, but Brett was adamant that the knowledge
was too dangerous to share with anyone else. And
maybe he was right. "I'll be at the main gate at dawn
tomorrow. Can you meet me there? I'll take you to
him."

She shook her head. "I can't leave again." She drew her finger through a smudge of ash on the tabletop.

"It's important, Rachel." He could see she was waging a battle within herself. Brett should have come and talked to her himself. She'd probably have listened to him, but he couldn't leave the temple. They were waiting for word from Khen Sa. It could come any day, but Simon McKendrick was getting too close for comfort.

He didn't like being this far out on the edge. He'd wanted Alf Singleton at the embassy to warn Simon McKendrick off, but Tiger didn't want anyone else to know about the plan and the ambassador had agreed with him. Not even the local DEA agents were aware of what was going on. The slightest hint of a double cross, the smallest leak, would send Khen Sa so deep into hiding they'd never find him. They needed Rachel's assurance that she'd do nothing to jeopardize the operation. And how the hell Tiger intended to get her to agree to that, when she thought they were a pack of thieves and drug runners, was beyond him.

The baby started to fuss. Ahnle held him close to her breast and shushed him. Billy reached out and touched him, feeling the softness of his black hair, the fragility of the bones beneath the skin. He'd like to hold him, cuddle him, but there wasn't time and he wasn't a goddamned masochist. It hurt to have Ahnle and the little guy so close and to know in a few minutes he'd have to leave them, maybe never see them again.

He looked up. Rachel was watching him and her eyes were wide with fear. Billy felt a superstitious chill race up and down his spine. She felt it too, that the deal was going wrong, that death was waiting for them out there in the jungle. He pushed the thought away.

A door opened and closed somewhere down the street. Men's voices, faint and far away, carried on the night breeze. Rachel heard them, too. He saw her stiffen, tilt her head toward the sounds.

"The game must have broken up early," she said, still frowning, but the fear in her eyes was gone; maybe he'd just imagined it. Instead, her expression was shadowed by indecision and regret.

"Sounds like it. I need your answer, Rachel."

"I can't leave," she repeated stubbornly, and maybe a little desperately. "I won't tell Micah you were here."

"Don't make no difference if you do. I come and go as I please. Anyway, it ain't Micah I'm worried about." Billy put his hand on the door latch. He looked as dark and menacing as a storm cloud. "It's the other one, Simon. He's been stickin' his nose in every nook and cranny from here to Bangkok an' back."

"It's his job." Rachel hated the defensive note in her voice. Simon was working for right and justice and truth and the American way and all the things she'd been taught to revere, all the things she'd sacrificed fifteen years of her life for.

"He's stirrin' things up," Billy said. His voice was cold and grating. "Brett was going to try and convince you to call him off."

"And if I don't—if I can't do that?"

"Then he's goin' to end up gettin' us all killed."

"WHO THE HELL WAS THAT man I saw leaving this place?"

As Simon watched, Rachel squared her shoulders

and set her jaw in a stubborn line he was coming to know all too well. He'd made a mistake jumping her this way, the minute he stepped inside the door, but it was too late now to take back the words.

"Your poker game broke up early, didn't it?"

"Rachel. Answer me."

She raised a delicately arched brow. "A man? I don't know what you're talking about."

"Rachel." This time it was Micah who spoke, reasonably and low enough not to wake the baby, sleeping just beyond the flimsy wall. It was a subtle warning Simon decided to heed.

"Yes, a man," Simon said patiently. "The tall black man I saw come out of this door not two minutes ago. Was it Billy Todd?"

"Yes." Rachel raised her chin proudly, prepared to do battle. She'd sent Ahnle to bed with the baby, Simon noticed. That meant she intended to face his questions on her own. If he just had a chance to get to the girl, he'd bet he could learn what he needed to know in ten minutes' time. But in the two weeks they'd all been living in Rachel's cramped hut, he'd barely had a chance to talk with her alone. His sister had protected her as fiercely as a mother tiger with her cubs, as fiercely as she guarded what knowledge she possessed of Tiger Jackson and his whereabouts.

If she was in love with the man, as Micah surmised, it explained a lot. A few short months ago, she wouldn't have hesitated to tell him. Simon didn't like being cut off from Rachel's confidences, but he didn't see much hope for changing things until they were back in the States.

He might as well tell her the truth, or what he believed to be the truth. "Look, Rachel. This deal is going sour. There are leaks in Bangkok, in Chiang Mai. That's why we're back here early tonight. I just got a call from a source in Chiang Rai. Khen Sa's moving back and forth across the border at will. The guy I talked to thinks it means something big is coming down. He mentioned lots of ponies. Large numbers of men. Gold. Huge amounts of heroin changing hands. For God's sake, Rachel, tell me what you know about what's going on."

"Nothing. I don't know anything," she repeated so forcefully Simon knew she was lying.

"You were in Khen Sa's camp while you were out in the hills, weren't you?" She did look at him then.

"Yes."

"What did you see there?"

"Very little." Her tone was clipped, emotionless. "Women, especially uninvited *farang* women, aren't exactly given the royal tour."

"All right. All right." Simon ran his hand through his hair. If and when they all got home safely, he was going to go ahead and take a desk job somewhere. He was getting too old for this kind of work. "Can you take me back there? Guide me in?"

"No. I'd have no idea of how to get there...from here." This time, too, she seemed to be telling the truth.

"Okay." Simon tried a different tack. Behind him, he could feel Micah's disapproval of his bullying tactics but he remained silent. Simon had never been so at odds with his siblings. He didn't like the feeling,

despite the fact that he knew he was doing his job.
"What did Billy Todd have to say?"

Rachel sat down on one of the uncomfortable
wooden chairs. She straightened an already neat pile
of papers on the table in front of her. Her hands were
shaking. "He told me he knew you were hooked up
with the DEA. He said they knew you'd been sticking
your nose into . . . Brett's business . . . all the way from
here to Bangkok and back."

Simon gave a grudging snort of laughter. "His
sources are probably better than mine."

"I think they are." Suddenly Rachel looked scared
and tired and uncertain. "Simon, please, don't make
me tell you anything else. I don't know anything else."

"Rachel." He dropped to a crouch beside her chair,
bringing his face on a level with her own. "I can't let
the amount of heroin I'm beginning to believe Khen
Sa is peddling up here, heroin Brett Jackson is dealing for, get out of this country without doing my best
to stop it."

"I know." She stood up and he rose also, stepping
back out of her way. He hadn't seen her look so de-
feated, so unsure of herself since her return from
Vietnam. "You're doing a good job. That's what Billy
came to tell me. He said if I couldn't persuade you to
back off, you'd end up getting them all killed."

CHAPTER FOURTEEN

RACHEL SAT WITH HER ARMS folded over the steering wheel for a long minute, trying to ease the fatigue in the muscles of her arms and shoulders. It had been a long time since she'd driven a stick shift and Father Dolph's battered old Chevy pickup didn't have power steering, either.

She glanced at her watch. It was almost 11 a.m. She'd been on the road since dawn. She wondered how long it would take Simon and Micah to figure out where she'd gone and talk Ahnle into showing them how to reach the temple themselves. She only hoped her friend could resist their bullying until she had a chance to warn Brett and the others to get out of there and call off their deal with Khen Sa.

Rachel got out of the pickup and started walking. The jungle closed around her before she'd gone more than a few feet off the road. Rachel pushed the strap of her bag higher on her shoulder and felt absurdly comforted by the weight of the machete she carried hidden within its folds. It was the only protection she had. She took a deep breath and kept walking, waiting for the old fear to settle on her. It didn't. Her heart was beating fast, both from the exertion of the steep trail and the knowledge that she was once more in an untamed and potentially dangerous place. But within herself, she now also carried the certainty that she could survive here, and the knowledge gave her strength.

Jungle greens and browns surrounded her; the only sounds were bird calls and the echo of her footfalls, very faint, against the spongy loam of the forest floor. A red and green parrot flew across her path, startling her. Ahead, a half dozen rooks took wing from the branches of a huge teak tree, as though as startled as she by the parrot's flight.

But it wasn't another bird or animal that had alarmed the rooks. It was a man wearing military-style fatigues. He stepped out of a dense stand of rattan and bamboo and planted himself directly in her path.

"Come," he ordered in Thai. He was carrying a rifle and looked as if he wouldn't hesitate to use it. He jerked his head in the direction of the temple. "This way."

Rachel resumed walking. If this wasn't one of Brett's men, she was in very bad trouble. But only a minute or two later she glimpsed the *chedi* of the temple through a break in the trees. Her heartbeat slowed its headlong gallop in her chest and she breathed a little easier. She entered the clearing ahead of her escort and found herself approaching the avenue of Buddha statues. She walked past them into their shadows and remembered how they had looked in the moonlight when she stood on the temple wall with Brett.

Tonight there would be no moon.

Rachel tried not to think about Brett and what they had shared and might never share again.

A small truck was backed up to a gap in the temple wall and Rachel realized there was at least one more route through the jungle to this place, and probably several others, as well. Escape routes for men who operated on the far side of the law—like Brett and Billy—were a necessity. More men in paramilitary outfits were loading the truck with the same wrapped oblong bundles, seeming far too heavy for their size, that she had seen taken off the ponies' backs in Khen Sa's camp. *Gold bars.* And in this part of the world, gold bought two things more often than anything else. Guns and opium.

"I came to see the Tiger," she said in Thai, when her guard seemed uncertain of what next to do with her.

He grunted and motioned her into the cool shade of the temple proper with the barrel of his gun. "*Farang.* Inside."

It took a moment for her eyes to adjust to the dim interior of the main room. The niches for the Buddha statues in the walls were empty, their sacred images long hidden away and forgotten by the faithful, or carried off and desecrated by the profane. In the middle of the huge, high-ceilinged room stood a central pillar. At its base was a large gaping hole in the floor. It was being refilled with dirt from buckets being carried inside by more armed men. Standing off to one side, Lonnie Smalley directed the replacement of the flat paving stones that covered the temple floor.

He looked up and saw her standing, silhouetted by the bright morning sunlight outside. "Jeez, Rachel." He lifted his hand and ran it through his hair in agitation. "How in hell did you get here?"

"I . . . I stole Father Dolph's pickup," she admitted with a nervous chuckle. "I'm getting pretty good at it, actually."

"Well, I'll be damned. First my poor old Bug and now a padre's truck. You need to think about getting a set of wheels of your own." He looked at her for a long time, then rubbed his hand along the back of his neck. "Why are you here, Rachel?" he asked at last.

"I . . . I've come to talk to Brett." Her mouth and throat were suddenly very dry. "Could I have a drink of water, please?" She was carrying a plastic container of water in her bag but she asked, anyway. She needed time to order her thoughts.

What was she doing here? Did she think Brett would give up this dangerous, illegal and immoral scheme just because she asked him to? She thought of all the bars of gold that must have come out of the hole in the temple floor and were now being loaded onto the truck. How much were they worth? How many times that much opium could the gold buy? Fifty? Eighty? One hundred times?

Lonnie handed her the canteen clipped to the wide canvas belt of his jungle-patterned fatigues. "Here. It's not very cold but it's wet."

"Thanks." She took a sip. "Lonnie, where's Brett?"

With tired eyes, he was watching the men replace the floor stones and sweep away the spilled dirt. He was silent a moment. "He'll be along soon," he said finally. "You know something?"

Rachel shook her head as she replaced the cap on the canteen and handed it back to him.

"Billy owes me a buck." He gave her a sad, weary smile. She noticed, suddenly, that there was a lot more gray in his red hair than there had been when she first met him. He looked old and diminished, although he couldn't have been much more than thirty-five or thirty-six. "I bet him you'd show up sooner or later, no matter what you told him last night."

"I only came to warn you that my brother knows about the deal with Khen Sa."

"We know that, too. The colonel has better sources of information than the DEA will ever have." It was the first time she'd heard him refer to Brett by his military title. It made the man she loved seem more of a stranger to her than ever.

"I figured that, too." Rachel lifted her chin. "I don't want anything to happen to my brothers."

Lonnie nodded. "Come on over here and sit down." The laborers had finished filling the hole and replacing the floor stones. They trooped out of the temple ahead of Rachel and Lonnie, carrying their rifles and buckets and thatch brooms with them. They sat down, side by side, on the wide, shallow steps and watched the activity in the courtyard.

"Are you going with Brett to make the deal with Khen Sa?"

"Yeah." He rested his elbow on his upraised knee and dropped his chin onto his fist. "I'm straight, Rachel. I have been since we talked that day, by the well. Do you remember?"

She pictured the cool, tree-shaded inner courtyard in her mind's eye. It was peaceful and beautiful, even in its ruined state. She longed to be sitting there now, instead of in the hot noonday sun. "I remember."

"I've tried before to kick the habit. It never worked. Maybe it won't work this time. I found a monastery where they try to cure addicts. It was a hell of a treatment, the worst two weeks of my life, but so far, it's worked."

"Maybe this time it's because you want it to."

"Maybe. I want to be with Brett and Billy. I don't want to be a hindrance to them, maybe get them hurt or killed. I have to make it this time, Rachel."

"You can do it." She laid her hand on his arm. His skin was tight and dry, the bones too prominent. There were dark shadows under his green eyes and deep lines of pain and stress bracketing his mouth. "I know it can't be easy for you."

"I'm trying my damnedest to stay clean this time but it's hard. Jesus, it's hard." His hands were shaking. He shoved them into the pockets of his pants. "There's no place to go but inside my own head. I've spent fifteen years trying not to remember what's locked up inside me. Now I haven't got anyplace to get away from the memories."

"I know, Lonnie. I don't have any place to hide from myself anymore, either." They didn't look at each other, but he reached out and folded his hands over hers.

"I miss my dreams. I don't know how long I can last without trying to get them back."

"Lonnie..." A jeep appeared out of the forest and drove up alongside the truck. Rachel had been so absorbed in the conversation, she hadn't been aware of its approach.

"It's the colonel and Billy."

Rachel shaded her eyes. It was Brett and Billy in the jeep, both armed and dressed in the same camouflage-patterned fatigues and soft-brimmed hats as the others.

Lonnie stood up, then reached out a hand to help her do the same. "We might as well let him know you're here, right off. The turnoff for the road they're drivin' is about three hundred yards ahead of where you came in. I doubt they saw your truck."

"I wish I'd known about that road. It would have saved me a long, hot hike."

"If the colonel don't want you to find somethin' around here, you won't, and neither will your brothers."

BRETT PICKED UP the M16 from the front seat of the jeep and slung the strap over his shoulder, as he watched his men loading the last of the gold bars into the truck.

Billy gave a long, low whistle. "Well, if that don't beat all." Brett swung around to see Rachel walking across the clearing toward them. "Guess I owe Lonnie a buck." She was wearing brown slacks and a long-sleeved white shirt. Her hair was shoved up under a Tigers' baseball cap. She smiled at Billy but wouldn't meet Brett's gaze, focusing instead on a point somewhere near his left shoulder.

"You shouldn't be here." He didn't think it would be this hard to see her and not touch her, reach out and take her in his arms.

"Last night Billy said . . ." She did look at him then and their eyes locked and held.

"Everything's changed since last night. Something's spooked Khen Sa."

"I know." Rachel lifted her hand and laid it on his arm, briefly, a fleeting caress that shook him to the foundation of his soul. "I came to warn you. Get out of here, go someplace where they can't find you. The authorities know about you and Khen Sa. They're looking for you."

"How do you know that, Rachel?" He could see in her eyes how hard it was for her to say the words, to warn him, when she believed what he was doing was wrong in the eyes of man and God.

"My brother told me." She closed her eyes, as though fighting back tears, but when she opened them again, the blue-gray depths were clear, though shadowed by sorrow. "I took Father Dolph's truck and came here to warn you."

"Billy." He didn't look away from her.

"Right here, Colonel."

"Better take the jeep and check out the padre's truck. If Simon McKendrick is anywhere near as thorough as I suspect he is, it might be carrying a homing device."

"That's impossible." Rachel came to her brother's defense in the space of a heartbeat. "How would he know I'd steal Father Dolph's truck and come to warn you?"

"Because he thinks like I do. How many vehicles are there at the camp, not counting bikes and scooters?"

Rachel looked puzzled. "Three or four, I don't know. Four, I guess. The pickup. A jeep and two flatbed trucks. I couldn't drive the trucks. And there was Simon's rental car. I . . . I didn't think I could get the keys out of his pants pocket without waking him up." She raised her chin defiantly. "I didn't have any trouble getting the keys to Father Dolph's pickup out of his office, though."

"I bet you didn't." He didn't smile at her but he wanted to. She looked pleased and contrite all at the same time and it was an engaging combination. "Your brother wouldn't have any trouble figuring that out, either. He probably planted homing devices on the pickup and jeep, just on principle."

Her face paled. "Then I've only made it easier for him to find you by coming here."

"Maybe, maybe not. It makes no difference, Rachel. We're pulling out in an hour, anyway."

"Brett." She clutched his arm with frantic fingers. "Don't do this, please. Keep the gold. There must be hundreds of thousands of dollars here. Isn't that enough for you? Do you have to deal in death and misery, as well?"

"You don't know what you're saying."

Rachel's gaze swung in Lonnie's direction. "Do you want others to live through the same hell heroin has put you through?"

"No. That's why..."

"Can it, Lonnie. We don't have time for long-winded speeches." Brett clenched his jaw so tight, he could feel a muscle jump in his cheek. He didn't have time for this, time for her, for them, now. This deal was too important to let anything interfere, no matter what it cost him personally. There were too many lives at stake.

"I'll go with you, Brett. Anywhere you want, if you'll only walk away from this." His heart slammed against his chest. If he had ever harbored any doubts about how much she loved him, they burned to ashes at the sound of her words. She was offering herself, freely, completely, and she was turning her back on everything she thought was right and honorable in the world.

"Rachel..." He'd kept his own counsel for so long, he didn't know where to start.

"Tell her, Tiger," Billy said gruffly, "so she can tell Ahnle. If something goes wrong, I don't want the woman I love to think I was nothin' but a filthy, rotten drug dealer." Brett twisted his head. His eyes locked and held with his friend's. "It ain't much to ask, man."

"What is he talking about?" There was a note of panic in Rachel's voice he'd never heard before. He swung his head back to find her staring at him as though he were a stranger. "What is he trying to say?"

"We aren't dealing for Khen Sa's heroin for ourselves, Rachel," Lonnie said quietly, proudly. "We're working for the king, himself. Brett told me two days ago."

"The gold belongs to the Thai government." Brett covered her hand with his. Her skin was as cold as ice.

"The government? I don't understand." She not only looked confused, she looked terrified. "Billy?" She turned to him. "Please, explain."

"We aren't the bad guys, Rachel. We've been workin' with the Thais and Uncle Sam to bring this deal off."

"I didn't know." She closed her eyes as though to block out the sight of his face, or to contain some inward pain of her own. "Micah was right all along.

You should have told me.'' There was a desperate little catch in her voice.

"No one is supposed to know," Brett said, and there was no way he could disguise the grimness in his voice. "There've been too damned many leaks already."

"Then please, Brett, don't go." She looked at Billy, at Lonnie. Her eyes were enormous in her pale face, their color the blue-gray of thunderclouds before a storm.

"We have to go through with it, Rachel. There's no backing out now."

"Even if it gets you all killed?"

"Yes."

She laughed then, a funny, choked little cry that froze his blood. She pressed her fingers to her lips. Her voice dropped to a ragged whisper. "Then you are a knight in shining armor, after all. And I'm still nothing but a whore."

She turned and ran toward the temple.

"Rachel, wait." Understanding blazed through him. Suddenly he knew what sort of nightmares from the past still haunted her.

"Go after her, man," Billy hissed. "She's hurtin' bad. She needs you."

"So does this mission." His men, his duty came first. The habit was too deeply ingrained to be shunted aside without a struggle.

"I know that." Billy slapped his hand on Brett's shoulder, made him look at him. "But if this deal goes sour, don't come up to me outside the pearly gates and tell me you wish to hell you'd have told her you loved her one last time."

So Billy felt it, too, that awareness at the base of his brain, in his gut, that told him something was wrong.

"How long will it take you to check out the padre's truck?"

"Give me thirty minutes." Billy grinned.

Brett made his decision. "Give Lonnie the word on your way out of the clearing. Come after me when you get back."

He'd set his own timetable, made his own deadline. He had thirty minutes to be with Rachel. It wasn't much, but it might have to be enough to last them both for a lifetime.

RACHEL SLID INTO A HEAP at the base of the well and pulled her knees up under her chin, wrapping her arms around her legs to help keep the misery trapped inside. It had all come rushing back to confront her in the time it took to draw a breath, in the time it took for her to realize that Brett was the man Micah had always insisted he was—brave, loyal, true to himself. And she was the worst kind of liar, because she lied about herself and to herself.

She felt soiled and shamed and betrayed. Her carefully filtered memories could no longer block out the reality of the past. She remembered it all, the hands, the faces, the bodies, as she was passed among them, one after another....

"Rachel!" Brett's voice came from far away. She didn't look up when his shadow blocked the light; her mind had turned too far inward. "Rachel?" He pulled her to her feet, wrapped his arms around her, but she couldn't feel his warmth and stayed rigid in his arms. He shook her, hard enough that her teeth rattled in her head. She felt his insistence, the strength of his will and knew he wouldn't leave her to the past.

"Brett, let me go," she begged. "Please, let me go."

"No."

He pulled her tighter into his arms. She felt the rough cotton of his shirt as he pressed her face against his chest. She could smell the jungle dust on his clothes, the dampness of his skin, the faint clinging odor of pipe tobacco, and she wanted to stay there, safe and loved, forever. *Except that he wouldn't love her anymore, not after he knew the truth.*

"Tell me, Rachel. Don't keep it inside any longer."

"I can't." She shuddered and struggled once more to be free. The sanctuary of his embrace was too tempting; it weakened her resolve. She needed to be alone where she could control the horror, shut it away, seal it off again in that hidden corner of her mind, so that she could go on as if nothing had happened and only she would know about the aching numbness in the center of her soul.

"Yes, you can." He leaned against the base of the wall, pulled her more firmly into the saddle of his hips and tipped her chin up so that she was forced to meet his eyes. "Whatever you did in that camp, you did it to survive."

She looked at him and her tears blurred the rugged, beloved outline of his face. Watching him was her penance. She had to see his love for her die when she told him the truth. "I sold myself to the camp commanders, each one of them, in turn. And over the course of four years, there were quite a few." She heard the brittle harshness of her voice and barely recognized it as her own. She waited for his censure, his withdrawal, but it didn't come. He only held her tear-filled gaze and was silent. "When we were hungry enough, or cold enough, I even accommodated the guards so that I could get us another bowl of rice or an extra blanket." She struggled against closing her eyes to keep from seeing the disgust he must surely feel for her. She couldn't do it; she dropped her lashes and felt the tears fighting to break free.

"Who do you mean by 'we', Rachel?" His question and quiet, matter-of-fact tone caught her off guard. Her eyes flew open.

"Father Pieter... and the others."

"What others?" She could have withstood his interrogations if he'd ranted and raved, but his calm, soothing voice, the gentle stroking of his hand on the back of her neck, were her undoing. She turned her cheek into his palm and let him gentle her, as though she were a frightened kitten.

"The other women and children. There were sixteen of us, all Vietnamese, except for Father Pieter and me. They kept us separated from the men's side of the camp. I... I never knew if there were any other Americans or Europeans being held there."

"You felt responsible for all of them, didn't you? You bartered yourself to keep them all alive."

"I was the camp whore." It was an ugly word. It was an ugly truth.

"Were the other women raped?"

"Yes." She was crying now and couldn't seem to stop. "You don't have to try to point out the error of my reasoning. I know what happened to me wasn't any different than what happened to them. My brain knows that," she said helplessly, "but my heart says differently." Dry, choking sobs rose in her throat and she swallowed hard to push them back. "After a while I quit fighting. When they sent for me I went. Willingly."

"No. You did what you had to do to survive. That's all. That's what we all did over here. Lonnie. Me. Billy. All of us."

Rachel shuddered. The past was too close; nausea boiled up inside her. "I kept on going until I realized, finally, that I was pregnant. They left me alone after that. I think it was an embarrassment to them. No one wanted to be held responsible if any of the brass from Hanoi showed up. They moved Father Pieter and me apart from the rest. The guard started taking long walks away from our compound, leaving us alone. Then one day we just walked away into the jungle."

"Jesus Christ." His fingers bit into the flesh of her arms. "You've kept this to yourself all this time?"

"I didn't want anyone to know. It was so long ago. The officials in Washington believed me when I said the camp commander raped me and the baby belonged to him. My family believed me because they love me. When I begged them not to talk about it anymore, they did as I asked. They think I'm noble and brave and good because I survived and I'm going on with my life, as if it matters...." She laughed and shook her head. "How wrong they are."

"You were a victim, Rachel," he said between clenched teeth. "A prisoner of war. You had no choice. Nothing that happened to you, nothing you did was your fault." She shook her head, letting the scalding, shameful tears free at last. "Rachel." There was a note of desperation, of pleading, in his voice she couldn't resist. "Look at me! Listen to what I'm saying. I love you, Rachel. What do I have to do to make you believe me?"

"Don't say that." She lifted her hand and covered his mouth with her fingers. "Don't. Not now. All these months I've lied to everyone, lied to myself, most of all. I passed judgment on all of you. I thought I was better. I thought I was wrong to love you. Not because of me, but because of what I believed you to be, a common criminal. I was so damned smug, so damned self-deceiving. I'm not worth your love."

"Yes, you are." Brett grabbed her arms, shook her so hard that her hat fell off and her hair tumbled around her shoulders. Her head dropped back and she was forced to look at him, be caught up in the limitless depths of his blue eyes once more. "I love you. God, Rachel, there's no time." He pulled her close, set his mouth on hers and kissed her as though he'd never let her go.

Rachel tasted the salt of her tears on his lips, let his tongue enter her mouth, let him set the pace of a joining that was as close as they could come to another more intimate joining of hearts and bodies. She felt a slow burning heat start to melt the ice inside her, push back the stark, cold terror in her soul.

"I promised you new memories, Rachel. Let them start now. Let go of the past." His hands tangled in her hair; he held her face still. He kissed her again, a kiss that went on and on, as if he could never get enough of her. *As if this kiss must last forever.* Fear clutched at her.

"I love you." She whispered the words over and over again as his lips skimmed her cheeks, her eyelids, the bridge of her nose. "I love you. Stay with me."

He groaned, then lowered his mouth to hers once more, and she kissed him back with a desperation born of knowing she might never see him again. *How could she find her way out of the darkness of her soul without his strength to guide her, without him beside her to help her accept and banish the past?*

"Stay with me."

"I can't. God, how I want to, but I can't." He held her pressed so tightly against him she couldn't breathe. "I want to make love to you. Prove to you how beautiful you are to me, inside and out."

"We need time, Brett." She cradled his face between her hands. She could feel the hard line of his jaw beneath her fingertips, the tension in his neck and shoulders, as she let her hands slide down to rest above the strong, heavy beat of his heart. "But we don't have time, do we?"

"I set these plans in motion long before I met you. Khen Sa can't be allowed to get his heroin to market. We can't let him ruin any more lives."

"Like Lonnie," she said very softly.

"And countless others. We can bring Khen Sa to his knees if we get the heroin without giving up the gold. He's never brought his entire crop into one location before this. He's always been too wily for that."

"Until you offered him more gold than he could refuse."

"And now I have to make sure he ends up with no gold and no heroin."

"Brett?" She rested her head against his chest, still shaken and weak in the knees but comforted by the beat of his heart beneath her cheek.

"What, love?" He stroked her shoulder, let his hard, strong palm rest against the softness of her throat.

"Brett, I'm scared." She couldn't stop herself from voicing her fears. "I have a feel—"

"Colonel."

Rachel lifted her head, turned within the protective circle of Brett's arm, toward the sound of Billy's voice. He was standing in the archway leading into the sheltered courtyard. Rachel rubbed her hand across her cheeks to wipe away the tears.

"What did you find?"

Billy crossed the small courtyard in three swift strides. He held out his hand. "This." A small gray box rested on his palm. A tiny red light blinked steadily on its surface.

"Activated." Brett frowned, letting his hands slide down her arms to her wrists. "Your brothers are looking for you."

"Can you tell how long it will be before they find this place?" Rachel asked.

"No. And we can't stick around to find out."

Brett let go of her wrists. *He was leaving her.* Just like that, going away, possibly to his death, and she would never know his touch again.

"I'm going with you," she announced, bending down to retrieve her hat. She pushed her hair up under it and set it firmly on her head. She avoided looking directly at Brett or Billy. "I'll leave that thing on the temple steps with a note for Simon and Micah, telling them I'm safe with you.''

"You won't be safe with me." Brett's voice was no longer that of a lover, of the man who had pulled her back from the edge of despair only minutes ago. "You're staying right here and greeting your brothers in person. That's an order." He was a soldier, a leader, and he expected to be obeyed.

"I'm not being left behind."

"I'm not taking you with me and have to worry about your safety, as well as my men's.''

"I can take care of myself." She refused to be cowed by the blazing anger in his voice.

"You're not coming with us. For God's sake, Rachel, act like the intelligent woman you are and don't fight me on this. Sit here in the sun and wait for your brothers to come and get you." For one heart-stopping moment she saw his love and fear for her mirrored in his expression. Then a mask dropped into place and he was once more the soldier of fortune, the hardened warrior she neither knew nor understood.

She opened her mouth to refuse.

"And if you don't, I'll lock you into my cell, so help me God."

Anger flared inside her. For a moment it burned away her fear for him. "You wouldn't dare."

"Try me." He reached around her, picked up his rifle and stalked away.

"Brett!" She started after him.

Billy grabbed her by the wrist and held her back. "Listen to him, Rachel. We can't take you along. You'll be safe here, even if you have to stay the night."

"Don't leave me behind, Billy, please." She couldn't plead with Brett. Her pride held no such power over her where Billy was concerned.

"I can't disobey the colonel's orders." He gave her hand a squeeze. "Take care of Ahnle and Domha for me." He reached around his neck, removed a chain that held a worn set of dog tags and a small key. "Give this to Ahnle if anything happens to me. My lawyer has orders to turn over the contents of the safety deposit box to whoever presents the key. There's enough money there to get her to the States, or wherever she wants to go. You can get the lawyer's name and address at the Lemongrass."

"Billy." She refused to cry. "You've got to come back. All of you."

"Sure we do." He, too, spun on his heel and was gone.

Rachel stared at the gray box and its blinking light in her hand for a long moment. Her thoughts were too confused and chaotic to sort into rational order. All she knew was that she couldn't stay behind while Brett risked his life. Somehow, she had to find her way back to Khen Sa's camp. She started walking, then began to run.

She would follow them in Father Dolph's pickup. It would be easy to trail the heavily loaded truck in the soft earth of the forest road. She kept running, through the temple, trying not to cry, to give in to her fears. *If she could be with him, near him, she could keep him safe.*

Rachel burst into the sunlight that fell full on the temple steps in a blinding glare, making her blink and raise her arm to shield her eyes. The clearing was deserted. There was nothing to show that it had held two dozen men and their vehicles just moments before. In the distance, the sound of the jeep's engine faded away, as if it were being swallowed alive by the jungle.

They were gone.

"Brett!" She slumped against the thick stone doorway. "Come back! Don't leave me."

Her cries echoed back to her, ricocheting off the walls of the ruined temple and the living wall of gray-green jungle beyond. She took a few wobbly steps into the sunlight and sank to her knees, dry-eyed and trembling. Her hand was curled around the homing device, although she was no longer aware of it. Terror flooded over her, black and suffocating, stronger than ever before.

Alone.

She was still there, a small, huddled figure in the fading twilight, when Micah and Simon walked into the clearing three hours later.

CHAPTER FIFTEEN

RACHEL THOUGHT THE NIGHT would never end.

It seemed as if they'd driven forever through the moonless jungle, over roads deserted of all other traffic, passing through sleeping towns and villages as they sped northward, but the hours they spent waiting for the Thai army helicopter at the airport in Chiang Rai were longer still. She almost lost her nerve again, waiting, felt her hope slipping away, but Simon and Micah were there for her; she wasn't alone and so had been able to make it through the night.

Now it was daylight and they were on their way, at last, to rendezvous with the crack team of Thai Rangers and DEA observers at the point where Brett and his men would head down into Khen Sa's valley on their own. She had no idea what strings Simon had pulled to get them on the helicopter. She didn't care. All she knew was that she refused to be left behind again, alone, waiting for fate to decide her future, as she'd been forced to do so often in her life.

Rachel leaned back against the hard bench seat of the aircraft but the vibrations made her head ache. She sat up and rested her hands on her knees, closed her eyes, tried not to think of anything at all.

"Are you okay?" Simon hollered above the roar of the engine.

"I'm fine." She'd repeated the assurance several times since her brothers had found her huddled on the temple steps. She still wasn't certain they believed her, but what she said was true. She was all right, at least for the moment.

"Hang on. We'll be there soon." Simon settled back against the uncomfortable bench and watched the mountainous terrain speed by below them. His dark brows were drawn together in a frown. He hadn't wanted her to come along. He'd told her it was for her own safety that she stay behind in Chiang Rai. But in her heart Rachel knew it was because he thought Brett's mission was doomed to failure and he didn't want her there to see him die.

One of the Thai military attachés riding with them addressed a question to Simon that Rachel couldn't hear above the roar of the rotors directly overhead. *Too many others were aware of what was going on.* Rachel's heartbeat skidded in fear. The presence of two American DEA observers and two Thai attachés in the helicopter with them told her that more plainly than any words. She narrowed her eyes against the rush of wind from the open hatch and tried to think of something else—anything else but the danger Brett and the others were facing.

She studied Micah's intent face as he, too, watched the heavily forested hills and sharp stone ridges pass beneath them. During the war how many missions had he flown in his small, light spotter plane, over just such country? How many times had he faced death in the jungle from mechanical failure and gunfire from the ground? How many men had he sent to the deaths in the skies over Laos when he'd commanded the

Ravens at the end of the war? Would he help her talk Brett out of this suicidal mission if she got the chance?

Rachel closed her eyes wearily.

"It won't be long now."

She opened her eyes to find Micah watching her as closely as Simon had done. The lines of his face were taut with strain, but his eyes were clear and filled with excitement. Rachel had the answer to her last question then. Micah would not try to dissuade Brett from delivering the gold to Khen Sa. He would honor his friend's commitment to his cause, even if he knew he was sending him to his death.

"I know." She gave him a lopsided smile. "You and Brett Jackson are very much alike, aren't you?"

"What makes you say that?"

"I wanted you to talk him out of going." It seemed incredible that they should be carrying on such a personal, intense conversation in voices so loud they were almost shouting. But time was too short to wait until they landed to voice her concerns.

"I can't do that, Rachel."

"I know that, too. Men of honor are very hard to deal with." *Or to love.*

"You have to trust him, Rachel. There's no one better at what he does than Tiger. If he thinks he can get the heroin and the gold out from under Khen Sa's nose, then he can."

She'd stuck the ball cap in the waistband of her slacks when they boarded the helicopter. Now she pulled it out and traced the embroidered white *D* on the crown with her fingers. "You think he'll make it, don't you?" She felt a small stirring of new hope, strengthening hope.

"I pray he does." Micah settled back against the seat.

"What are you two discussing over here?" Simon asked, leaning close. The DEA men were watching with interest. Rachel shot Micah a pleading look.

"Rachel's tired," he yelled back. "It was a long night."

"You should have tried to get some sleep in the car." *Poor Simon*. Rachel couldn't help but smile. *He was still trying to take care of them both*.

"I did try." Her smile turned impish. She stuck the cap on her head and pulled it down tight to keep the wind from blowing it off. "You still drive like a bat out of hell, just like you always did."

"I'm an excellent driver."

"Yeah, sure." Micah gave a snort and settled back in his seat. The shadowy memories of war and death that hovered around them retreated for the moment. She loved her brothers so. She had been right to fight so hard to stay alive all those years so that they could be together again, as a family.

The helicopter banked to the left abruptly and started to descend. "We're here," one of the DEA men hollered, the one who had been staring at her a few minutes earlier. She hadn't caught his name back at Chiang Rai. She still didn't know what it was and she didn't care. She clutched the strap hanging above her head for balance and looked out the hatch. They were dropping alongside another, heavily armed helicopter, its blades rotating idly, its crew aboard, as if ready to take off at a moment's notice.

There was no road leading in to the site, but a faint track snaked through the trees, toward a break in the ridge-line. Rachel caught a glimpse of laden ponies, picking their way along the steep path, before the trees shut off her view. Her heart jerked painfully in her chest.

They were gone. She was too late to say goodbye.

HE'D KNOWN FROM THE beginning that the operation might end in a violent confrontation with Khen Sa, but he had believed the risk was worthwhile. Singleton and Major Phounjam, who was in charge of the Thai troops, agreed with him, although the king, devout Buddhist that he was, wanted as little bloodshed as possible. Brett, himself, never had any doubts—until Rachel showed up. Walking away from her again had been close to impossible. And it made him question what he was doing.

Maybe he should pull back; turn the ponies over to Khen Sa, take the heroin and run. No one would blame him. A good poker player knew when to cut his losses and toss in the cards. This felt like one of those times. Then he thought of the guns and ammunition Khen Sa could buy, probably had already ordered from the Vietnamese or the Chinese, and he knew he had to recover the gold.

Just over two hours later, Brett dismounted inside the periphery of Khen Sa's camp, took his bearings and walked to the head of the pack train, where Billy was arguing with one of the warlord's lieutenants.

"What's wrong?" Brett demanded in English.

"Damned idiot wants us to march these ponies right out into the middle of the village square to unload them. Says it's more *convenient*." He grunted dismissively. "My mama didn't raise no fool. We'd be sittin' ducks out there." As always, when he was under pressure, Billy's Georgia accent grew stronger. He ordered Khen Sa's henchman away with a curt command.

Brett waited until the man was gone. "Don't move the ponies or the gold until I've talked to Khen Sa. Keep Naga and six or eight of the others with you and the gold. Leave Chan in charge of the rest. I don't want anybody developing an itchy trigger finger and getting us all blown to kingdom come."

"Exactly what I intend to do." Billy grinned, but it never reached his eyes. "Speakin' of trigger fingers, did you see that guy's weapon?"

"Chinese," Brett said shortly, "and brand-new. Probably used the quarter-million we gave him as a down payment."

"Your hunch was right. It appears to me the general's gonna be in a hell of a fix if he don't come up with the rest of what he owes."

"Be careful."

"Don't worry. I have no intention of meetin' my Maker on a fine day like this." The words were lightly spoken, but his expression was cold and completely focused, alert to every sound and movement that might mean danger or betrayal.

"What do you want me to do, Colonel?" Lonnie asked, coming up behind Brett. His thumb was hooked into his belt loop, just in front of the revolver strapped to his waist.

"Stay with me." There was no way Brett could be sure how the younger man would react if they came under fire. Lonnie had been so traumatized by the war, by combat, that he'd never recovered. His body was so damaged by his addiction that he was an unknown quantity in a firefight. Brett couldn't trust him on his own, and he couldn't leave him behind.

"This place gives me the creeps. It's too ordinary-looking, you know? I'd have figured Khen Sa would have doubled his soldiers for a deal like this."

"He has," Brett said. "He's just keeping them under wraps, and that's what bothers me. Any good commander would have beefed up his forces for an operation like this on general principles. But only a man bent on a double cross would keep them hidden from view."

"In other words, watch your ass, buddy," Billy said, giving Lonnie a punch on the shoulder.

"I already feel like my eyeballs are going round in circles from trying to do just that. Here comes the general," Lonnie said through stiff lips. His eyes were bloodshot and his skin jaundiced. His hands were shaking, but he'd been clean for three weeks and felt in control.

"Stick with me," Brett told him once more. "Billy, if anything goes wrong, get those ponies the hell out of here. If Khen Sa does pull a double cross and tries to keep the heroin, he'll make his move on you first."

"Don't worry. He ain't gonna get the gold."

Billy knew it was a fight to the death. A man like Khen Sa couldn't be stopped unless he was destroyed. Brett could count on Billy. There wasn't a better man Brett could have at his back. "Don't try to be a goddamned hero." What he meant but didn't say was "Don't get yourself killed."

"I ain't no hero."

"Colonel." Lonnie's gaze flickered past Billy's shoulder. Brett turned to face Khen Sa. He had no idea if the Thai Ranger captain assigned to keep him in sight was observing their conversation from his vantage point on the ridge above camp. If he wasn't, they

were in worse trouble than before. The other patrols
would only move in on his signal. Visual contact was
their only means of communication. They couldn't
afford to take the chance of bringing any kind of radio transmitters into the village. Khen Sa was no fool.
He was watching Brett just as closely as Brett was
watching him.

"Take it easy, buddy," Lonnie called over his
shoulder to Billy as he followed Brett to where Khen
Sa was standing.

"Watch your backside," Billy reminded him once
more, and only Brett recognized the emotion in his
voice.

"Mr. Jackson," Khen Sa said with a thin smile and
a bow so slight it was an insult. "It is very good to see
you again."

"We've brought the gold," Brett said, ignoring the
greeting and the smile. His scalp prickled with the
awareness that he was being watched. By the Thai
captain, he hoped, as well as by Khen Sa's soldiers,
some of whom were lounging in the doorways of various huts, their weapons close at hand.

"Bring the ponies forward. We will take the gold
from their packs and load what you have purchased."

Brett shook his head. "I make a gift to you of the
ponies. We have brought others for the heroin."

Khen Sa's face grew hard. "You do not trust me?"

Brett remained silent.

The other man's hand moved toward the revolver at
his waist, then relaxed. He smiled again. "Of course,
we will be happy to accept the gift of your ponies." He
motioned toward the big barn-like structure that
housed the opium refinery and the heroin. "You will

want to make sure you are getting what you pay for. If you will follow me..."

Two of the warlord's bodyguards joined them, flanking their leader. All three of the men kept their distance from Lonnie and Brett. The feeling of being watched grew stronger. Brett felt sweat trickle down his spine. He took off his hat and tucked it into the waistband of his pants, the prearranged signal for the Thai captain to be ready for whatever happened next.

Brett stopped some distance from the open side of the building. Inside, it was dark and shadowed in contrast to the tropical brightness of the day. "Bring out the heroin and I will have the ponies brought forward."

"You are a hard man to bargain with."

Khen Sa raised his hand and all hell broke loose.

Brett had no idea if the warlord intended to call his men to bring out the bags of heroin, or if he intended to do away with him, then and there, but the Thai captain, from his vantage point on the ridge, had no such doubts. He opened fire and shots rang out from the other patrols of Rangers, as well. They were answered almost immediately from within the camp. One of the ponies screamed in pain and Brett hoped Billy got his men to safety before Khen Sa's soldiers started picking them off one by one.

He took off at a crouching run, trusting Lonnie to keep close behind him. The only cover they had any hope of reaching was the opium barn itself. Behind him, he could hear Khen Sa yelling orders and staccato bursts of automatic weapons fire, neighing horses and Billy, shouting, as he deployed the men. Brett kept running. Billy and the others were on their own, but if Billy got the gold to safety, Brett knew his friend would be back to help him fight his way out of the spot he was in.

A spray of bullets erupted from the doorway of a nearby hut. Brett hit the ground in a rolling dive that landed him behind the dubious safety of a stack of packing cases, stenciled in Chinese characters. A moment later, Lonnie dropped down beside him with a grunt.

"You okay, buddy?" Brett asked, not taking his eyes from the men surrounding them on three sides.

"I'm okay," Lonnie replied.

"Our best bet is still the opium barn." The bullets were coming closer. Khen Sa's men were zeroing in on their location. "It's the only defensible building in the whole damn camp."

"It's a cinch we can't stay here."

Brett took aim and fired at the dark rectangle of the doorway where the last shots had come from. He watched with grim satisfaction as one of their attackers pitched face forward onto the dusty street and was still.

"Good shot."

"Get ready to move."

"I'm right behind you."

"Go!"

Brett took off at a half-crouching run, Lonnie on his heels. Bullets shredded the air around them. Brett felt the sting of wood splinters as the packing crate barricade disintegrated under a barrage of automatic weapon fire. Lonnie grunted in pain and stumbled to his knees. Brett reached out a hand and hooked it under his elbow, half dragging, half carrying him the last three yards to the barn.

Brett pulled Lonnie behind a waist-high wall of neatly stacked, hand-stitched cotton bags of processed heroin, each one resembling a five-pound bag of flour and each and every one worth almost a million dollars on the street. He took a moment to scan the shadowy building. It appeared to be deserted. He dragged deep calming breaths of air into his lungs. Khen Sa must be very sure he could deal with them if he'd left the area unguarded.

Or perhaps, the men guarding the heroin had been called off to deal with Billy and the two dozen armed men they'd brought with them? In any event, for the moment, they were safe. There were no windows behind them and no way anyone could sneak up on them from the open side of the building. He figured they had about two minutes to decide their plan of attack.

Brett glanced over at Lonnie and saw the spreading, dark red stain on his shirt.

"Jesus Christ, you're hit! How bad?" he asked gruffly, refusing to recognize his own pain at seeing his friend's injury.

"Bad." Lonnie's face was white and pinched, his breathing labored. "Real bad."

"Hang on, buddy. We'll get you out of here as soon as we can."

He pulled his handkerchief out of his pocket, folded it into a pad and shoved it inside Lonnie's shirt. It was the best he could do. "Billy will work his way here as soon as he gets through with Khen Sa."

"Must be puttin' up a hell of a fight. Ain't no one shootin' at us." Lonnie tried to smile but couldn't. His face was a mask of shock and pain.

"Sure he is, but we might still have to make a run for it, buddy."

Lonnie shook his head. "I can't."

"You have to, Corporal." Brett considered their chances if he tried to carry Lonnie out of the building. They would be sitting ducks and they both knew it.

"I ain't gonna make it, Tiger. I've seen a lot of guys buy it. I remember how they said it feels. I'm numb. I don't hurt at all. That's one of the signs." His eyes flickered shut.

Brett slammed another clip of ammunition into his rifle. "I'm not leaving here without you, Corporal."

"Is that an order, sir?" Lonnie looked faintly amused. A small trickle of blood appeared at the corner of his mouth. He lifted his hand, slowly, to wipe it away.

"It is." There was noise and movement outside the building. The sounds of gunfire from Billy's position had died away while Brett tended to Lonnie's wound.

"If Billy made it, they'll be comin' after us." Lonnie pushed himself higher against the bags of heroin. Almost on the words, shots rang out, embedding themselves in the bags of white powder, in the roof and the dirt floor.

"Just hang on." Brett fired back, heard one of their attackers scream in pain and then fall silent.

"If Billy...didn't make it," Lonnie said, his breathing labored, "I don't want them to get this stuff back, too."

"They won't."

"Let's make sure. My life hasn't amounted to much for the last fifteen years. But it looks like I've got one more chance to be a hero." The effort to speak was draining his strength.

"What do you have in mind, Corporal Smalley?" Brett slid down behind the bags and placed the last clip of ammunition he had with him in the gun.

"I'd like to go out with a bang." Lonnie's smile was a death's head grimace. "There's chemicals...in here...and gasoline for the generator. This place should go up like a Fourth of July rocket and all this China White with it." He stopped talking, as a sudden spasm of choking stole his breath.

Brett fired a random burst and slid over to support Lonnie's shoulders until the choking ceased. "If this building goes up, so do we." He watched the younger man closely, the pain in his chest threatening to take control. He fought it back. *Not now, later, he would mourn.*

"Not you, Colonel. Just me. Let me do it. Let me go out a winner."

CHAPTER SIXTEEN

THE RADIO RECEIVER INSIDE the major's tent crackled into life once more. Rachel clenched her fists around the bowl of cold, sticky rice a soldier had shoved into her hands a few minutes ago. She hadn't eaten any of it. She couldn't, because it would surely stick in her throat and choke her. Still, she didn't throw it away—as long as she was holding it, she could resist the temptation to clamp her hands over her ears to keep from hearing what was said.

It was all going so horribly wrong.

The major hadn't left the tent since the first reports of fighting began to come in, half an hour before. Simon and Micah and the two DEA observers had been allowed inside to study maps of the area around the village and to be made familiar with the positions of the major's men.

Because she was a woman, Rachel had been asked, politely, to remain outside. It made no difference at all to the Thai officers, that she had been inside Khen Sa's camp. Rachel finally quit arguing with them. Throwing a temper tantrum wouldn't help Brett and the others. Instead, she'd sat down on a packing crate of field rations just outside the tent and stayed there, listening to the rapid-fire exchanges in Thai, as they were relayed back and forth between the command center and the embattled patrols.

She still couldn't be certain what had happened. All she knew was that the Thai captain in charge of the main patrol had believed Khen Sa intended to attack before the heroin could be transferred and he'd opened fire on the camp. She didn't even know if Brett and the others were still alive.

Micah came out of the tent. His khaki shirt was open halfway down his chest and stained with sweat. He pulled his hat out of his belt where he'd shoved it and put it on. Rachel set the bowl of uneaten rice aside and stood up. She adjusted the brim of her hat to shield her eyes from the tropical brightness of the sun.

"Micah?" Had something happened she didn't know about? Had they sent her brother to tell her the man she loved was dead?

"It's hard to tell what's going on, Sis," he said, shaking his head. "I don't know more than two dozen words in Thai."

"I've been listening." Rachel crossed her arms beneath her breasts and tried to stop the trembling that seemed to have affected every muscle in her body. "It sounds very bad, Micah."

"Simon told me Billy got the ponies carrying the gold out of the camp. Sounds like they took some heavy casualties doing it, though."

"I know." She bit her lip. "What about Brett?" She couldn't trust herself to translate the sometimes-garbled transmissions and rapid, colloquial Thai with any accuracy.

"He's still pinned down in the refinery building."

"Lonnie's with him?"

"You heard that?"

She nodded, tears filling her eyes. She dashed them fiercely away. "I hoped I had translated it incorrectly."

"They're alive, Rachel. That's all I can tell you. The patrol leader says they're still returning fire, but he doesn't know if they're wounded, or how long they can hold out without help."

"And that's the one thing we can't give them—our help." She lifted her hand to her mouth to keep from crying out. "It's not fair, Micah. We had so little time together. There are so many things I don't know about him, so many things I want to ask him, tell him." She turned away so he couldn't see her cry. "Why is it always so hard to wait?"

Micah reached out to comfort her but never got the chance. At that moment, the idly turning rotors of the gunship helicopter located beside the tent began to revolve in earnest.

Rachel whirled to face her brother. "Micah, what does it mean?"

"I don't know," he admitted, "probably just a precaution." But his face was tense and he had trouble meeting her frightened gaze.

"It means the soldiers there can't handle Khen Sa's men alone, doesn't it?"

"That's possible." Her brother was hedging. She could hear it in his voice.

"Or it means that they've already lost the battle and they're going in to destroy the heroin so that Khen Sa can't sell it again."

"Rachel, you're jumping to conclusions."

"I'm not, Micah. Something terrible has happened. I know it." She grabbed his hands, held on so tightly he winced. "I feel it. Here, in my heart."

Journey with Harlequin into the past and discover stories of cowboys and captains, pirates and princes in the romantic tradition of Harlequin.

Printed in Canada

"I'll find out," he yelled over the screaming whine of the departing gunship. "I'll find out, I promise."

He started back into the tent but stopped when he saw Simon and the two DEA men coming out.

"Simon." She was beside him in a heartbeat. "What happened?"

He didn't answer her for a moment. The two DEA men kept on walking, fast, toward the helicopter they'd arrived in. "Simon. Tell me what's happening." As she watched, terrified, a Thai medical corpsman went rushing by, carrying a field surgery kit. "Tell me," she all but screamed, as the small helicopter's engine roared to life.

"We don't know yet. There's still a lot of shooting going on. They're sending the gunship in to mop up. As soon as the Rangers can get down into the village, they will."

One of the DEA men, already in the helicopter, signaled him to hurry.

"Micah, come on," Simon yelled.

"Where are you going?" Rachel screamed.

"To Khen Sa's camp." Simon started to say something more, but Rachel was already running toward the aircraft.

"I'm not staying here," she threw over her shoulder. "I'm going with you. I have to know if he's still alive."

"WE CAN'T WAIT ANY LONGER to see if Billy got the ponies out," Brett said grimly. "We've got to blow this place now."

"Can you get to the gasoline?" Lonnie's head rolled back and forth against the bags of heroin.

"I'm going to try." Brett estimated the distance to the back of the building where the small barrels of fuel were stored. He just might make it if he kept low and moved fast. "If we dump them and let the gas soak into these bags, you're right. This place should go up like the Fourth of July." He fired one last burst to discourage any more kamikaze attacks by Khen Sa's men while they talked. "If I make it. I'll be back for you, buddy."

Lonnie reached out and grabbed his sleeve. He shook his head. "Just hand over your dad's lighter."

"Goddamn it, no!" *No more dying, no more of his men losing their lives to a war they couldn't win.* Twenty years of fighting was too long, too damned long.

Lonnie looked him straight in the eye. "I'm already dead, Colonel," he said with simple dignity. "Give me the lighter and get the hell out of here."

Brett reached into his shirt pocket and handed over the worn silver lighter. He flipped the lid and flicked the wheel; a small blue flame leaped to life. He reached out, placed it in Lonnie's hand and folded his cold fingers around it.

"Maybe now you can quit smokin' for good."

"You bet." Brett squeezed his thigh. The muscles were stiff and lifeless. "Give me a minute."

"That's about what I've got left." Lonnie looked down at the flame in his hand. "Don't try bein' a hero and come back for me, Colonel. I'm already halfway home." He smiled then, and for a moment he was the cocky young medic Brett had first met all those years before, in another war, another lifetime.

"You don't have to do this," Brett whispered gruffly.

"Yes, I do."

Brett laid his hand on his shoulder.

"No time for long goodbyes," Lonnie gasped. "Get out of here, Colonel."

Brett turned his back on his friend and crawled toward the barrels of gasoline. Behind him, he heard shouts and knew Khen Sa's men had decided to rush the building.

"Come on, jackasses," he said between his teeth. "You're going to get one hell of a warm welcome." He pulled the barrels over on their sides, one by one. The first was empty, the second only half-full, but the other two were filled to the brim. He forced the lids off with the wooden butt of his rifle and watched the explosive liquid rush across the floor to be soaked up, greedily, by the dry white powder in its cotton sacks. One small rivulet meandered along some hidden pathway of its own, pooled at the corner of the stack of heroin stacks and then disappeared behind it.

Brett started running at a half crouch along the back wall of the building.

It was going to be very close.

The explosion caught him just three steps from the door.

THE BUILDING THAT HELD Khen Sa's opium refinery burned furiously as the helicopter circled very high above the village. One or two trees close by also burned, but for the most part, the fire was confined to the building. The heavy jungle undergrowth, this soon after the rainy season, was simply too wet to ignite.

Rachel strained her eyes to see what was going on below them. The smoke was thick and pungent, billowing straight up into the sky until it was caught and ripped to shreds by the rotating blades of the big gunship that continued to circle and strafe any areas of the village that were still returning fire.

"How long before we can land?" she shouted to Micah, who was sitting closest. He shrugged. If any shadowy demons of his wartime experiences were troubling him, they didn't show. The only expression Rachel could discern on his dark, rugged face was worry over his friend's safety, and concern for her.

"The gunship says we can land after they make another pass." The DEA man, Jurras, whose name Rachel had finally learned, relayed the message via earphones from the copter pilot. "The last of Khen Sa's men abandoned their position just after we got here."

"Probably covering the general's retreat." Simon leaned closer so that both Micah and Rachel could hear.

"He's going to have a hell of a time explaining today to his Chinese and Vietnamese friends."

"Playing both ends against the middle is damned risky business in this part of the world." Micah made a grab for the seat, as the helicopter banked sharply and began to descend.

"Heavy casualties," Jurras relayed. "They want the medics on the ground, pronto."

Rachel closed her eyes against a rush of dread that threatened to pull her under into total darkness. *She would not believe he was dead until she had no other choice.* When she opened them again, she saw both her brothers watching her, and the love and compassion in their eyes was almost her undoing.

Don't pity me, she wanted to scream out above the churning beat of the rotors, *don't pity me.* Instead, she said, "I'm all right." She pulled her hat down more firmly on her head. "I'm all right. Simon, you're closest. Let the medics know I'm a nurse and that I speak Thai. They might need my help." He nodded and she turned her head to look out at the ground, approaching at a dizzying speed, so that she didn't have to be brave for their sakes a moment longer.

"I'm all right," she repeated to herself. *But, dear God, please don't let him die, don't let me be alone again.*

As soon as she jumped out of the helicopter and looked around, Rachel knew her prayer might not be answered. There were wounded and dying men everywhere. Her only consolation was that she recognized none of them. After a quick discussion with the Thai medics, they split up into three teams and began evaluating the injuries. In less than fifteen minutes, two of the most seriously wounded Thai Rangers and three of Brett's men were placed in the helicopter and airlifted to the hospital in Chiang Mai.

She worked steadily alongside the medics for over an hour, keeping her fears at bay by simply refusing to consider them. The gunship made three more passes over the clearing and then settled to the ground. The distracting beat of its rotors faded away, normal jungle sounds began to return, and if she tried very hard not to listen, she couldn't hear the crackle of flames from the burning building, or smell the smoke.

Her back ached and the sun beat down on her head. She straightened from helping one of Brett's men pull his shirt down over the heavy padding of dressing on a wound in his shoulder and winced.

"Once a combat nurse, always a combat nurse." She whirled around to find Billy Todd grinning at her from a dirt-streaked, ashen face. He hobbled closer, leaning on a teak staff, supported on the other side by Micah's strong right arm. "I figured you'd get here, somehow."

"How bad is it?" she asked, indicating the wound in the fleshy part of his thigh, a few inches above the knee. She pulled off her rubber gloves and grabbed a new pair from the surgical field kit the medics had supplied.

"Didn't hit nothin' vital." He'd torn a strip from his shirt sleeve and tied it around the wound. Rachel picked up a pair of bandage scissors to cut the cloth and found her hands were shaking. She bit her lip and willed herself calm.

"I'll be the judge of that. Has the bleeding stopped?"

"Yeah."

"Good." She knelt beside him, slit his pant leg from above his boot to his hip and surveyed the wound. "T&T," she said, satisfied now that she'd seen for herself what Billy said was true.

"What the hell does that mean?" Micah asked, as he watched her irrigate the wound with an antiseptic solution. His expression was grim. Rachel smiled up at him, reassuring, as she worked.

"T&T means through and through. There's an entrance and exit wound. It's clean. Billy's right—being a combat nurse is something you don't forget." She finished the dressing and peeled off the gloves. "You need to check in at the hospital, too, get this looked at by a surgeon."

"Doctors and hospitals can wait."

"I can give you something for the pain." The fear was back, stronger than ever. She busied herself with vials and syringes. As long as she kept working, she could keep the fear at bay, keep from thinking about Brett. She touched the small glass bottles of morphine. They represented what was bright and good about the poppy, the standard by which all pain medication was measured.

"No. I have to get the gold back to the command base before dark. Khen Sa's men are scattered all over these hills. It won't take them long to regroup. The gunship can only fly cover for us until sunset."

Rachel looked at him and saw the agony and loss in his eyes. She closed her own against the sharpness of the pain in her heart and knew, suddenly, why tortured souls like Lonnie's sought oblivion with dangerous drugs such as heroin.

"Where's Brett and Lonnie?" Rachel finally blurted out.

She heard footsteps behind her and turned her head to see Simon coming toward them. No one said anything. No one was going to make it easy for her.

"Where are they?" she repeated. The three men looked at each other, waiting for one to speak. "Billy!" Rachel couldn't stand the silence. She tried to take a deep breath and almost choked on the acrid smell of smoke in the air.

"I never saw them after the shootin' started." His hand clenched around the teak staff and he pulled himself to his feet. "They were headed for the opium barn."

"Simon?" He'd been with the Thai captain directing the operation, interrogating two of Khen Sa's soldiers who had been captured by Brett's men.

"We can't be certain, Rachel. The two we got are just boys, fourteen, fifteen at the oldest and scared to death. They speak very little Thai."

"For God's sake, will you tell me what you know?" She bit down on the inside of her lip so hard she tasted blood.

"They saw two men go into the barn. One of them was wounded."

"Brett?" She would not cry. Not now, not yet.

Simon shook his head. "It was Lonnie. They were positive. They'd never seen a man with red hair before."

"Go on." She was so stiff she couldn't move.

"Khen Sa ordered them to rush the opium barn when he learned Billy had managed to get away with the gold. Three men tried and died for their trouble. The general was furious. He ordered an all-out assault, but the barn blew up before they could make their move." She was starting to shake. Micah took her in his arms, held her tight. She melted against him, then felt her heart and soul harden as an icy shell formed inside her.

"Then the explosion? It wasn't an accident?"

"I don't think so." Simon found it hard to meet her eyes.

The tears came then, hot and stinging, but they could do nothing to melt the icy carapace around her heart. She was alive. She would survive. But she was alone again, this time, forever.

"Is he dead?"

Simon was silent. He looked away, then slowly back at her. "No one could have made it out of that inferno alive."

CHAPTER SEVENTEEN

IT HAD BEEN WINDY ALL DAY, but as the sun dropped low in the western sky, the wind relaxed into a playful breeze and a team of kite fighters, in the park across the road from Brett's house, attempted to launch a *chula*. The enormous kite was over six feet long and the team was having trouble getting it aloft. Several *pakpao* kite fighters already had their small, one-man kites in the air, and good-natured insults flew back and forth between the combatants and were audible to the watchers in the garden.

"The red and yellow one is very pretty," Ahnle said, as she finished giving Domha his bottle. "I like it best."

"The breeze is too fitful to launch the *chula*," Billy said, taking the baby from his mother as the youngster fussed to be set free.

"I thought so, too," Rachel agreed, "but there it goes."

The big dragon kite caught the breeze and spiraled high into the air. Immediately, one of the small kites charged, zigzagging toward the big kite, trying to dodge past it and get to the other end of the field. The *chula* was slow and hard to maneuver, but its team was skilled. With a smooth change of direction, they cut across the small kite's path, snarling its string and sending it crashing to the ground.

"I hoped the little kite would make it," Ahnle sighed.

"He never had a chance," Billy said. "He's too slow." He pointed his finger at another of the kites. "I'll put my money on that purple and gold one there. He's a runner, like a good scrambling quarterback. Watch. He's gettin' ready to make his run."

Rachel looked up, shielding her eyes from the metallic brightness of the sunset sky. The purple and gold kite climbed high and fast, its owner running swiftly downfield toward the *chula's* handlers. He pulled the purple diamond down sharply, let it slip under the big kite's string, then let it fly high and swift once more.

"Ha," Billy gloated, "told you so."

"Beautiful," Rachel said, and meant it.

"We'll have to get the boy a kite when he's older. If he's going to be livin' in Bangkok, he'll have to know how to 'fight' a kite." He smiled at the little boy bouncing happily on his good knee. "Won't we, buddy?" Domha laughed, in perfect agreement with Billy's plans for his future.

"Billy, stop! You bounce him too hard," Ahnle protested, only half-seriously.

"He likes it."

"He will spit up," Domha's mother predicted, "and that is most unpleasant."

Billy looked perplexed. He shot a glance at Rachel, who shrugged, hiding a smile. "He did just finish his bottle," she reminded him.

"Whoa, fella." Billy slowed the pace of their game.

Domha laughed and gurgled, urging his friend to resume their play. Billy shook his head. "Your mama thinks you'll barf if we keep it up."

"Barf? What new word is this?" Ahnle looked to Rachel for guidance.

"It's American slang for spitting up," she explained.

"Barf?" Ahnle repeated the word, a slight frown between her brows. "What a strange word. American is a difficult language, much more troublesome than English. Sometimes I do not understand it at all."

She frowned harder when both Billy and Rachel laughed at her puzzlement.

"What joke, now, do you share at my expense?" she asked good-naturedly.

"Nothing." Rachel's thoughts erased the smile from her face. *How amazing the human spirit was.* She could enjoy this gentle joke at Ahnle's expense, smile and laugh aloud, while inside her, a cold, hard lump of misery had taken the place of her heart.

"Whatever word you call it, I don't want him doin' it on my clean shirt."

Billy sat the youngster down and watched him take a few uncertain steps toward his mother.

"I can't get over how fast he's learnin'. Two weeks ago he took his first step. Now he's walkin' all over. In another two weeks he'll be runnin' everywhere he wants to go." He spoke with a father's pride and the absolute certainty that Domha was the most remarkable baby ever born on the earth.

"He does learn much quickly." Ahnle reached down to gather the child into her arms and smiled at the man she loved.

Rachel turned her head away, looking out over the twilight-shaded garden, pretending to watch the *chula* soaring victoriously, after vanquishing another of its small foes. She blinked back fresh tears before the others could see. It worried them all to see her cry. She tried not to, but the tears came too easily and too often these days.

"Billy," Ahnle said in a prompting tone of voice. Rachel was only half listening to their conversation. She was lost in her own thoughts, fighting the cold, aching sense of loss that was stronger at some times than at others, but that was always with her.

Two weeks. Brett had been gone—dead—for two weeks.

It may as well have been two lifetimes. She had not thought it would be so hard to go on without him.

"Rachel?" Billy's voice was rough but gentle. "It's time to leave for the Lemongrass."

She shook her head. "You go on without me. I'm not hungry, really. Nog's wife made fruit salad and left it in the refrigerator. That's all I want."

"You need more," Ahnle said, sounding a great deal like Rachel's mother. "Come with us."

"I'll be fine here." She tried another smile, knew it looked as strained as she felt and let it slip away. "Take Micah and Simon with you. They both love the food. They won't turn down the invitation."

"It is not good to be alone so much." From the corner of her eye, Rachel saw Ahnle lift her hand to Billy in a pleading gesture.

"Let her be, Ahnle," he said softly.

Coming close to death had changed something in Billy. He no longer seemed afraid to show his growing love for Ahnle and her son. Rachel was going to miss them when she went back to Camp Six. There was no doubt in her mind, at all, that Ahnle would remain here, in the city, with him.

"Go. I'll be fine." Rachel repeated the phrase that was her stock answer to any query about her health or state of mind.

"We won't be late," Ahnle promised.

"Stay as long as you like. Is Nog's wife sitting for Domha?"

"No," Billy answered. "He's coming with us. We're showin' him off tonight." He stood up, slowly, favoring his injured leg. Ahnle stood, also, and handed him her son, then tucked herself close to his side to lend him support. He'd given up using a cane several days before, but his injured leg was still stiff.

"Rachel, are you sure?"

"Let her be, woman," Billy ordered with mock gruffness. He smiled down at Rachel. "How about a nightcap when we get back?"

"I'd like that." She leaned back against the bench and narrowed her eyes. She craved solitude, but when she was alone, she felt the fear and loneliness beating dark wings against her soul. She fought the urge to break into tears again. She'd cried and cried the first days after they'd returned from the hills and it had done no good. Crying couldn't change what had happened. Lonnie was dead. Brett was dead. And she was alone, as she'd been for so many years.

The sunset faded to mauve and rose; the short, tropical twilight crept across the garden, silvering the light. In the park only one small fighter remained to challenge the dragon kite. She hoped he made it. As she watched, the little kite made its last run. Its handler held it in tight, let it soar quickly to the left as the big kite feinted to the right, then pulled it back, sending it plummeting dangerously low to the ground before it darted beneath the dragon kite's string and raced on down the park to victory.

"He made it," Rachel said half-aloud to herself. "I'll make it, too, Brett. I'm a survivor—you taught me that about myself, but I'm so alone."

The kite fliers gathered up their fighters and with much banter and trading of insults, they dispersed into the gathering night. Silence descended around her. The air was heavy with the scent of night jasmine and honeysuckle. Crickets began to sing in the undergrowth, a raucous chorus that soon overpowered the silence.

Rachel felt cut off, sealed within herself, and she was afraid. "You promised me memories, Brett," she said in the same soft whisper. She needed to hear the sound of a human voice, even if it was her own. "You didn't tell me I would have to remember them alone."

"I DON'T THINK IT'S A GOOD idea for Rachel to be so much by herself," Micah said. He stood at the screened opening that replaced one wall of the room Brett had used as his study, looking out over the garden at the park beyond. "I think we ought to make one last stab at getting her to come home with us."

"Be my guest. I don't think it will do any good."

There were times, Micah realized, when he could happily wring his brother's neck. This evening was one of them. He turned around. Simon was sitting behind Brett's desk, an antique mahogany table of remarkable craftsmanship and great beauty. His fingers were laced behind his head. He looked tired and strained. But there was something else, an air of suppressed excitement that hadn't been there before.

"Doesn't it bother you that Rachel's decided to stay in Thailand and go back to Camp Six?" Micah asked, frustrated by his brother's incomprehensibly cheerful mood.

"She's a grown woman. She knows her own mind."

"Ahnle and Billy have been trying to get her to stay here with them. At least until they've settled... Tiger's estate."

Even now, it was hard to believe his friend was dead. But there was no denying the fact that two bodies, burned beyond recognition, had been found in the ruins of the opium barn. An old-fashioned silver cigarette lighter had been found with one of them. Billy had identified the lighter as Brett's. When Micah heard that, he had to accept the reality; his friend was gone.

"I think it's time we get back to the States ourselves." Simon's observation interrupted his unhappy thoughts. "I'm scheduled for debriefing in less than a week. And we'll need to find a buyer for the pearls before then."

"I'll leave that up to you."

Billy had produced the black velvet jeweler's box yesterday. Brett, he said, had intended to give them to Rachel. She, in turn, passed them on. The satisfaction of knowing that Colonel Ky had been brought to justice, thanks to Brett and Billy, and was likely to end his days in a Russian military prison for trying to smuggle heroin into the Soviet Union, was payment enough for Micah. The pearls were merely icing on the cake. Although he had to admit he'd be glad to use the money they'd bring to pay off the mortgage on his house. Thinking of his home made him think of the woman he loved.

"Maybe Carrie..." His wife had brought him back from the dark wastes of sorrow and regret. She and Rachel were genuinely fond of each other. Perhaps she could help persuade his sister to come home.

"Carrie needs you with her. In Michigan. Not halfway around the world. Especially now that you know for sure there's a new McKendrick on the way."

Micah's black mood lightened abruptly. He couldn't help but smile. A fax had arrived at the embassy three days earlier, addressed to him, in care of Simon. It was a copy of a bill from Micah's family doctor for a routine pregnancy test performed on Carrie Granger McKendrick. The results were positive; the balance due. It was like Carrie to let him know such earthshaking news in such a lighthearted manner.

"Rachel needs me here, she needs all of us."

Once more Simon changed the subject. "I think you might want to read these dispatches I brought back with me." He indicated the pile of papers lying beside the pearls.

"I'm not interested in that stuff." It was growing darker. A car pulled into the driveway. Micah thought it might be Nog, returning from market, but then saw the old man drift into the garden like an arthritic shadow and begin to light the stone lanterns that bordered the walkways. The garden looked peaceful and serene; his thoughts were not.

"Okay," Simon continued, undeterred, "I'll read them to you."

Micah turned to face his brother once more. "All right, you read them to me." His tone was not encouraging. The only light in the room came from a lamp by Simon's left elbow. Light from beneath its shade poured across the desktop, but his brother's face remained in shadow. Micah couldn't read his expression, only sense his excitement.

"It says that a secret witness's testimony before a grand jury in New York has led to the indictment of the Shan warlord, Khen Sa, on ten counts of attempting to smuggle heroin into the United States."

"He'll probably never come to trial. It wasn't worth the loss of Tiger's life, and Lonnie Smalley's, just to make it official."

"It might just be the encouragement someone needs to turn him in. Khen Sa made a lot of enemies when that heroin went up in smoke. Powerful, vengeful enemies. You still think it was all for nothing?"

"Men were killed, including my friend. Our sister's heart is broken and you sit there spouting the party line. That's not like you. What the hell's up?"

"Take it easy, big brother." Simon didn't sound offended. He sounded happy. "Things aren't always the way they seem."

"What the hell is that supposed to mean? Death is always the way it seems. It's the goddamn end of everything." Micah took an angry step away from the window.

"Not necessarily," a familiar male voice said.

"Tiger?" Micah appeared rooted to the floor for a long minute, then strode across the room to grab his friend by the arm. He held on tight. "It's really you, man?"

"It's me. Rumors of my death were slightly exaggerated."

"Simon," Micah whirled on his brother. "You son of a bitch, how long have you known?"

"Only since this morning, so don't jump down my throat." Simon rose from behind Brett's desk to shake his hand. "For what it's worth, I had no idea State was pulling this stunt. I guess once you walked down out of those hills and they realized they had a real, live eyewitness on their hands, they just couldn't resist the cloak-and-dagger stuff."

Brett's expression was grim. The left side of his face was still bruised and slightly swollen. He looked dangerous and very angry. "I never knew. They didn't want me making phone calls but they swore all my messages went through. It wasn't until we got back to Bangkok yesterday that Alf Singleton told me everyone thought I was dead."

"When Alf told me what was going on, I made a bet with myself that you'd be out of the palace in twelve hours or less." Simon looked at his watch. "That was eleven hours and seventeen minutes ago. Congratulations. Sometimes those audiences with His Majesty go on for days."

"Not when the guest of honor goes AWOL." Brett grinned but it did nothing to lighten the tension in his eyes, the stiffness in his back and shoulders.

"Will someone tell me what's going on?" Micah growled. "For two weeks we've thought you were dead."

"I damn near was." Brett flicked a glance at his left arm, resting in a sling, and the cane he had hooked over his wrist. "Where's Billy?"

"At the Lemongrass with Ahnle and the baby. He'll be madder than hell that he missed your return from the dead."

"And Rachel?"

"In the garden," Simon answered.

"Does she know yet?"

"No. I didn't tell her."

"I still haven't got this figured out." Micah released Brett's hand abruptly when he saw him wince. "Do you mean the State Department has had you under wraps since the raid and never told anyone?"

"It was for my own safety, they said."

"What happened?"

Brett took a deep breath. It wasn't hard to see his patience was stretched to the breaking point. But Micah wouldn't let up till he had an answer.

"Plain dumb luck is what happened. The explosion blew me out through the wall and halfway up the hill. I was out cold till after dark. I don't know how Khen Sa's soldiers missed finding me. When I stumbled in to the base camp the next day, the only men there were DEA and CIA. It's the kind of setup they like, and I was too out of it to object, until it was too late. I'd never have gone along with testifying to the grand jury if I'd known they'd told all of you I was dead. Look, it's a long story. Simon'll tell you what's been going on. I've got to see Rachel."

"Christ, I feel like Alice after she fell through the rabbit hole." Micah raked his fingers through his hair. "You'll fill me in later?"

"Much later." A twist of a smile lifted the corner of his mouth. He limped out of the room, leaving an astonished Micah staring at the empty doorway.

"I think we ought to be moving to a hotel." Simon crossed to the bar and poured a whiskey, neat. "Give Brett and Rachel some privacy. What do you think?" He held the glass out to Micah, who downed it in a swallow, then gestured for a refill.

"I think this means that Rachel won't be coming home with us for sure," Micah said, and broke into a grin.

"I'd say that's a safe bet." Simon grinned, too. He looked around at the beautifully furnished, comfortable room, the tropical garden coming to life in the moonlight. "I could get used to spending a few weeks here every year. Say, sometime around the middle of January, or so?" One dark eyebrow lifted a fraction of an inch.

Micah got the message. "Great place for a winter holiday. I wonder if anyone bothered to tell old Tiger just what kind of globe-trotting family he's marrying into?" He laughed and slapped his brother on the back.

"If he has any sense, he'll marry her tomorrow, before Mom gets wind of it and starts planning a wedding from seven thousand miles away."

The possibility of just such an eventuality wiped the grin from Micah's face.

"God, I never thought of that." He held out his empty glass. "Pour me another drink."

Simon laughed and obliged. Micah lifted his whiskey in a toast.

"To the McKendricks."

"One and all."

SHE WAS SITTING ON A BENCH near the spirit grotto pool, her arms curled around her legs, her chin resting on her knees. She was wearing a white blouse and a full white skirt. She shimmered like moonbeams in the shadows cast by the lantern light.

"Rachel," he said very softly. He didn't want to frighten her, yet he had no idea how to avoid doing so.

"Brett?" She didn't turn around. He leaned forward slightly to see her face. Her eyes were squeezed shut. There were tears on her cheeks. She'd been crying. For herself? For him? She was still crying. His heart began to beat with a slow, heavy urgency in his chest.

"Yes, it's me."

"I . . . I thought I heard you talking a few moments ago. It frightened me. Are you a ghost?" Her voice broke on the last word and it came out in a breathy whisper.

"No. I'm not a ghost."

"Then I'm dreaming."

"Your eyes *are* closed," he pointed out.

"But I'm awake."

He took a step forward, held out his hand. "Touch me."

She shook her head, still not looking at him. "I can't," she whispered a little desperately. "I couldn't bear it if you're a figment of my imagination. If I reach out and touch you and you evaporate like smoke in the wind, I couldn't stand the disappointment. I'm trying to be brave, for the others, for myself, but it's so hard."

"I'm real, Rachel, alive and whole," he smiled ruefully. "Almost."

Her eyes flew open. She whirled around on the bench.

"Now do you believe me? No self-respecting ghost wears his arm in a sling."

She stood up in a swirl of white cotton and pressed herself against him. "Oh, God, you are hurt. How badly? Tell me."

"I'm fine," he murmured against her hair, his eyes tight shut against the unfamiliar sting of tears. "I'm fine."

"Where have you been? Who's been taking care of you? Why didn't you let me know you were alive?"

The last was a cry from the very depths of her soul.

"Believe me, Rachel. I would have told you, but I didn't know they'd lied to you. I'm sorry, angel, so sorry."

She was crying so hard he thought she would come apart in his arms. He pulled her close, held her as tightly as he dared. He didn't want to talk, to relate the miracle that had kept him from being blown to kingdom come with Khen Sa's heroin; he didn't want to explain the machinations of diplomats and spies and military hotshots that had kept him incommunicado since he'd walked out of the jungle in a daze. He only wanted to feel her in his arms, touch her, hold her, love her.

"Shhh, don't cry." He kissed her tearstained cheeks, her eyelids, her lips, over and over again, as if to reassure himself, as well as her, that he was truly among the living.

"I wanted to die, myself, when they told me you and Lonnie were dead." She looked into his eyes in wonder. "What happened, Brett? How did you escape? The fire, the smoke..." Her voice trailed off. She wrapped her arms around him so tightly his bruised and battered ribs protested, but he didn't make a sound. The pain was more than countered by the pleasure of holding her in his arms once more.

"Who told you about the fire?" he asked, half-drunk with happiness, high on the scent of her hair and skin, the honey of her lips, the feel of her breasts pressed tight against him.

She moved a little away from him so that she could see his face, touch the bruises, the jagged new scar at his temple. "No one told me about it. I was there."

"Oh, God." He pulled her close. "I told you to stay put, remember? I would have given anything to spare you that."

"They told me they identified your body." Her voice broke. "I stayed at Khen Sa's camp as long as they would let me." He felt her take a deep breath against his chest. "Billy said it was you... and Lonnie...."

"Lonnie is dead, Rachel. The other body must have belonged to one of Khen Sa's men."

"But the cigarette lighter?"

"Lonnie had it in his hand." She shuddered and he felt new tears wet the front of his shirt. He stroked her hair, soothing her. "He'd been shot, Rachel. He was dying. But he blew up the heroin. He saved my life, and Billy's and the others. At the end, when it counted most, he was the man he was meant to be."

"I'm glad. He was trying so hard to stay straight this time. He wanted to turn his life around."

"Maybe he would have made it all the way back this time."

"I'd like to believe that." She lifted her hands to cradle his face between her fingers. "Oh, Brett, I never believed in miracles, not until now, today. Father Dolph is right, they do happen, once in a great while, if you pray hard enough and your need is great enough." Rachel let her hands slide down over his chest. She reached up on tiptoe to kiss him, softly, sweetly, a butterfly caress, over in a heartbeat. "Promise me you'll never leave me again."

"I promise." His kiss sealed his pledge. It was a long time before his mouth left hers, before his breathing slowed enough for speech, before time began to move forward again. "You'll have to promise me something in return."

"Anything." She smiled through her tears. Diamond bright, they sparkled on her lashes, made her eyes dark reflecting pools in the moonlight. Brett felt his heart jerk to a stop, then slam against his chest in slow, heavy strokes.

"Marry me, as soon as possible."

"Brett..."

"I love you. I wasn't free to tell you that before. I am now."

"I love you, more than anything else in life." She closed her eyes for the space of a heartbeat. "Almost more than life itself..." He felt her hesitancy.

"The past is truly over and gone, Rachel," he said, reading her thoughts.

She smiled and there was only a hint of old sadness left to darken her eyes. "I know that. That's what I wanted to say. I've learned so much these past three years, Brett. Simon taught me to face my fears head-on. Micah has shown me that you can let go of the past and move on with your life. And you. You've given me the most precious gift of all. You've taught me to love again, freely, completely. Even—" her voice faltered a moment, then went on "—even when I thought I'd lost you forever, I didn't give in to darkness. You taught me how to reach my inner strength. You helped me banish the terror of remembering, forever. I will be very proud and happy to be your wife."

"It's not going to be easy for a while. We might have to leave Thailand for a few months, maybe spend some time traveling, let things settle down. The restaurant will be fine with Billy and Ponchoo running it. Would you like to go someplace quiet and secluded for a start?"

"Or we could go back to the States. It's been a long time since you've been home, hasn't it, Brett?"

"A long time."

"I don't care where we go, as long as I'm with you. Haven't I proven that these last months, chasing you back and forth through the jungle?"

"Funny, I was under the impression I was chasing you."

She smiled with a hint of mischief. "Perhaps you were, part of the time." Her hands slipped over his chest, caressing him lightly, arousing, tantalizing. "I want you, wherever we are, wherever we go." She reached up on tiptoe to kiss him again. This time there was no hesitancy, no holding back, only hunger and need and desire that threatened to flame out of control.

"I suppose we should go inside. The others will want to see you, too." She sighed and again he had no trouble reading her thoughts.

"I don't think we'll have to worry about spending a lot of time with the others tonight." He turned her slightly to face the house. It was dark. "We're alone."

"Truly?" She whirled back to him. "I want you, Brett. I want to hold you close. I want you with me." She took a breath, let it out on a sigh. "I want you inside me, loving me so that I can truly believe you're here with me and not just a wonderful dream."

"I want you, too, love." He wanted her in his bed. He ached to make love to her, fill her, satisfy her, complete her and himself, but he held back. "Rachel. There's one more thing you have to know. You can't go back to Camp Six. At least, not until Khen Sa's no longer a threat. It's just too dangerous."

"I understand."

"You'll have to wait until it's safe."

"I can wait. I've learned something about patience, I think." She tugged on his hand, started walking. Just outside his bedroom, she paused. "There are other places here that I can be of use."

"More of them than you can count, I'm afraid."

"I'll find them, if you'll help me."

"You are a most remarkable woman, Rachel Phillips."

"You are a most remarkable man, Brett Jackson. There's one other thing I think you should know."

"What's that?" he asked, as she looped her arms round his neck for a long, drugging kiss that left them both breathless and on fire.

"I've been using your bedroom. I . . . I felt closer to you there. Do you mind?"

"Not a bit. Come inside, love."

"Why?" she asked, holding back, teasing just a little.

He smiled down at her. "I promised you new memories to replace the old ones. This is where we begin." He stepped away from her, over the threshold. "Come with me, Rachel. Turn your back on yesterday, reach with me toward tomorrow." He held out his hand.

She rested her fingers on his palm. He folded his hand over hers. She stepped toward him. "New memories," she said, and smiled, "for tomorrow and all the days to come."

COMING IN 1991 FROM
HARLEQUIN SUPERROMANCE:

Harlequin romances are now available in stores at these convenient times each month.

Harlequin Presents
Harlequin American Romance
Harlequin Historical
Harlequin Intrigue

These series will be in stores on the 4th of every month.

Harlequin Romance
Harlequin Temptation
Harlequin Superromance
Harlequin Regency Romance

New titles for these series will be in stores on the 16th of every month.

We hope this new schedule is convenient for you. With only two trips each month to your local bookseller, you will always be sure not to miss any of your favorite authors!

Happy reading!

Please note there may be slight variations in on-sale dates in your area due to differences in shipping and handling.

HDATES

HARLEQUIN'S "BIG WIN"
SWEEPSTAKES RULES & REGULATIONS
NO PURCHASE NECESSARY TO ENTER OR RECEIVE A PRIZE

1. To enter and join the Reader Service, scratch off the metallic strips on all your BIG WIN tickets #1-#6. This will reveal the values for each sweepstakes entry number, the number of free book(s) you will receive and your free bonus gift as part of our Reader Service. If you do not wish to take advantage of our Reader Service but wish to enter the Sweepstakes only, scratch off the metallic strips on your BIG WIN tickets #1-#4. Return your entire sheet of tickets intact. Incomplete and/or inaccurate entries are ineligible for that section or sections of prizes. Not responsible for mutilated or unreadable entries or inadvertent printing errors. Mechanically reproduced entries are null and void.

2. Whether you take advantage of this offer or not, your Sweepstakes numbers will be compared against the list of winning numbers generated at random by the computer. In the event that all prizes are not claimed by March 31, 1992, a random drawing will be held from all qualified entries received from March 30, 1990 to March 31, 1992, to award all unclaimed prizes. All cash prizes (Grand to Sixth), will be mailed to the winners and are payable by check in U.S. funds. Seventh prize will be shipped to winners via third-class mail. These prizes are in addition to any free, surprise or mystery gifts that might be offered. Versions of this sweepstakes with different prizes of approximate equal value may appear at retail outlets or in other mailings by Torstar Corp. and its affiliates.

3. The following prizes are awarded in this sweepstakes: ★ Grand Prize (1) $1,000,000; First Prize (1) $25,000; Second Prize (1) $10,000; Third Prize (5) $5,000; Fourth Prize (10) $1,000; Fifth Prize (100) $250; Sixth Prize (2,500) $10; ★ ★ Seventh Prize (6,000) $12.95 ARV.

   ★ This presentation offers a Grand Prize of a $1,000,000 annuity. Winner will receive $33,333.33 a year for 30 years without interest totalling $1,000,000.

   ★ ★ Seventh Prize: A fully illustrated hardcover book published by Torstar Corp. Approximate retail value of the book is $12.95.

   Entrants may cancel the Reader Service at anytime without cost or obligation to buy (see details in center insert card).

4. This Sweepstakes is being conducted under the supervision of an independent judging organization. By entering this Sweepstakes, each entrant accepts and agrees to be bound by these rules and the decisions of the judges, which shall be final and binding. Odds of winning in the random drawing are dependent upon the total number of entries received. Taxes, if any, are the sole responsibility of the winners. Prizes are nontransferable. All entries must be received at the address printed on the reply card and must be postmarked no later than 12:00 MIDNIGHT on March 31, 1992. The drawing for all unclaimed sweepstakes prizes will take place May 30, 1992, at 12:00 NOON, at the offices of Marden-Kane, Inc., Lake Success, New York.

5. This offer is open to residents of the U.S., the United Kingdom, France and Canada, 18 years or older, except employees and their immediate family members of Torstar Corp., its affiliates, subsidiaries, and all other agencies and persons connected with the use, marketing or conduct of this sweepstakes. All Federal, State, Provincial and local laws apply. Void wherever prohibited or restricted by law. Any litigation within the Province of Quebec respecting the conduct and awarding of a prize in this publicity contest must be submitted to the Régie des loteries et courses du Québec.

6. Winners will be notified by mail and may be required to execute an affidavit of eligibility and release, which must be returned within 14 days after notification or an alternative winner will be selected. Canadian winners will be required to correctly answer an arithmetical skill-testing question administered by mail, which must be returned within a limited time. Winners consent to the use of their names, photographs and/or likenesses for advertising and publicity in conjunction with this and similar promotions without additional compensation. For a list of major winners, send a stamped, self-addressed envelope to: WINNERS LIST, c/o Harlequin Reader Service, 3010 Walden Ave., P.O. Box 1396, Buffalo, NY 14269-1396. Winners Lists will be fulfilled after the May 30, 1992 drawing date.

If Sweepstakes entry form is missing, please print your name and address on a 3" ×5" piece of plain paper and send to:

In the U.S.
Harlequin's "BIG WIN" Sweepstakes
3010 Walden Ave.
P.O. Box 1867
Buffalo, NY 14269-1867

In Canada
Harlequin's "BIG WIN" Sweepstakes
P.O. Box 609
Fort Erie, Ontario
L2A 5X3

Offer limited to one per household.
© 1991 Harlequin Enterprises Limited   Printed in the U.S.A.

LTY-H191R

Take 4 bestselling love stories FREE

Plus get a FREE surprise gift!